RELEASED

A HORROR SHORT STORY
ANTHOLOGY

Edited by
S.Faxon & Theresa Halvorsen

NBBP

No Bad Books Press, LLC

Copyright © 2021

All rights reserved. No part of this publication may be reproduced, distributed or transmitted in any form or by any means, without the prior permission of the publisher, except in the case of brief quotations embodied in critical reviews and certain other non-commercial uses permitted by copyright law. For permissions request, write to the publisher addressed "Attention: Permissions Coordinator," at the address below:

No Bad Books Press, LLC 302 Washington St. Ste 731, San Diego, CA 02103
Publisher's Note: This is a work of fiction. Names, characters, places, and incidents are a product of the author's imagination. Locales and public names are sometimes used for atmospheric purposes. Any resemblance to actual people, living or dead, or to businesses, companies, events, institutions, or locales is completely coincidental.

Ordering Information:
Quantity discounts are available. For details, contact the Sales Department at
nobbpress@gmail.com
No Bad Books Press, LLC
Dive Into Different Worlds With Us

Cover Design by S. Faxon
Editing By Theresa Halvorsen, S. Faxon
Proof Read by Stephanie Reali
Layout and Interior Design by S. Faxon
ISBN
978-1-955431-02-6
Library of Congress Control Number:
2021919077
www.nobadbookspress.com

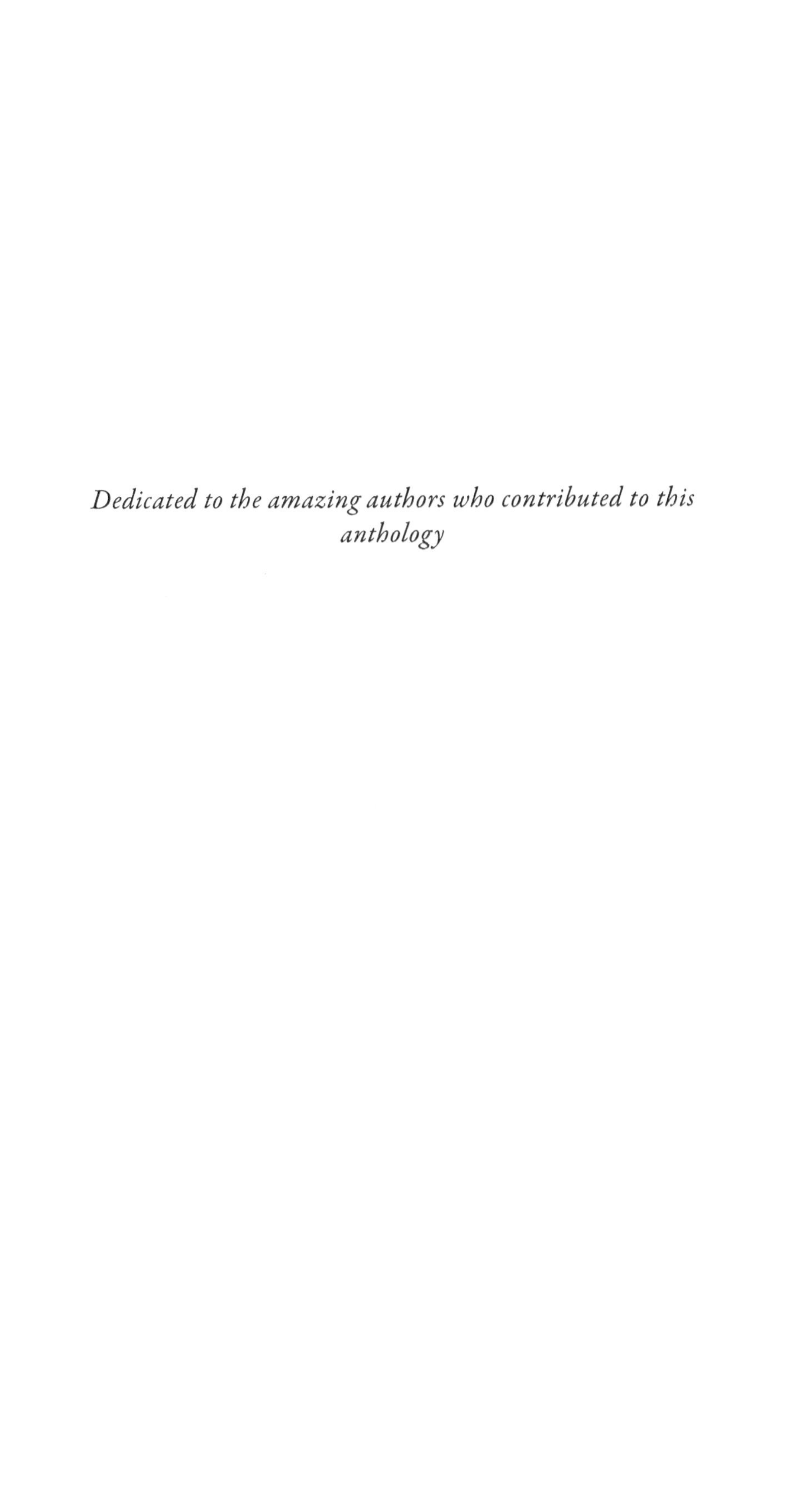

Dedicated to the amazing authors who contributed to this anthology

RELEASED

Contents

A Note from the Editors

There's nothing worse than that moment when you realize something has escaped, whether it's a beloved pet, a child you lost in Disneyworld (true story!), or that weird thing with the lights you collected in a mason jar. Theresa and Sarah (S. Faxon) wanted to explore this concept while supporting the writing community we're grateful to be a part of.

Originally, when we sent out the call for submissions, we expected a blend of genres, from fantasy to science fiction and everything in between. Instead, we got the wonderful collection of horror and dark fiction you have before you.

Released is No Bad Books first anthology and we're equal parts thrilled and terrified by these stories. We hope you enjoy them as much as we did and that they give you the same heebeejeebees we had as we read them.

This book would not have been possible without the knowledge and wisdom we gained from the Independent Book Publishers Association, the Horror Writing Association, and the support from the authors who contributed to this book. We are forever grateful to them and are so excited to welcome them into the No Bad Books Press family. A huge shout-out to Stephanie for assisting with the final proofreadings too!

Sarah would like to thank her friend Jenny for the inspiration for the story she created and her incredible romantic partner, Salvatore, who is the biggest supporter of her dreams. She'd also like to thank her parents and sisters who are her biggest fans!

Theresa would like to thank her family and in particular, Brad for always supporting her dreams.

Pour the beverage of your choice, consider turning the lights on, and enjoy *Released*!

Liberation
by
Kevin David Anderson

To most people it was just an ordinary Thursday, but to Caroline, today was the day she decided to rid herself of the spiders living in her brain. Even though they pulled only a single spider from that woman in Brazil, there had to be more than one in her own brain, living just under the skullcap like lizards burrowed beneath the floorboards.

It had to be more than one. She had so much passion and determination when she was young, it would take several brain-dwelling parasites to eat it all. The spiders lived off of the brain impulses of her desire, feeding on her resolve to do the things she really wanted to do. "That's what the spiders live on," Caroline had said to her roommate exactly one week ago.

From her favorite chair in their small living room, Wendy shook her head. "Please tell me you're joking, Caroline."

Stepping toward Wendy, Caroline's intensity grew.

"It's all right here." She held out the medical journal, dated July 1986, and pointed to a picture of a woman lying unconscious in an archaic-looking operating room. Then she slid her finger across to the opposite page to a murky photo of something hideously pale, swollen. The photograph was slightly out of focus, like all the images ever captured of Bigfoot and the Loch Ness Monster, but a multi-legged form was discernable.

It had the characteristics of a spider but looked more like some underwater creature—a mutated octopus or alien squid. The arachnid's legs were thick, like tentacles, splayed out on a porcelain table. Pools of blood spotted the off-white surface, and a pair of forceps lay next to the spider, providing a sense of scale. The creature's creamy white frame looked to be about four inches in length. The image reminded Caroline of salamanders discovered deep in subterranean caves. Living their whole lives in darkness, the creatures appeared pasty, sickly.

Leaning in, Wendy traced a finger along the picture's caption. "It says it didn't have any eyes."

"It doesn't need them," Caroline said, grinning. "It lives in darkness, feeling its way around." Just like the salamanders.

Wendy stood up. "This doesn't prove anything, Caroline. You don't have spiders living in your brain, for God's sake." She put a hand on her hip, sighing deeply. "Okay, let's be logical about this for a second. That woman, whoever the hell she is, lives in Brazil. And I'll admit there is all kinds of freaky shit living in the rainforest that we don't know about yet, but spiders that eat your determination, turning women into breeder cows? Come on! And even if there were, how did they get to Seattle? I don't remember you vacationing in Brazil recently, or ever."

Caroline had anticipated this question, because it had occurred to her as well. She had never been out of the state of Washington in her life, let alone south of the equator. She had always wanted to travel. Paris, Rome, Vienna. But when it came down to it, her resolve to make the arrangements seemed to evaporate. Damn spiders!

Caroline slapped the journal closed. "I didn't need to go to Brazil. The spiders were brought to me."

Wendy raised a brow. "What?"

"The rainforest has been harvested and exported for our consumption since the fifties."

"What are you talking about?"

"Where do you think most of our medicines come from? Our birth control, Prozac, Valium? Hell, even our makeup, moisturizers, eyeliner, lipstick. You name it. It all comes from the rainforest. Women have been inundated with this stuff for more than fifty years."

"Jeez, you've given this a lot of thought."

"Is it so hard to believe that these parasites could have hitched a ride in our birth control pills or some hair product packaged by men for women?"

Wendy sighed and held out a hand. "Look, I know you've gone through some rough shit. That asshole husband of yours getting custody of your kids—God, I don't know how I could live with that. But it doesn't mean there's anything wrong with you." Wendy stepped forward, her green eyes empathetic. "You've got your life on track now. In a few months, we'll both pass our exams and be certified RNs. It's gonna be—"

"I don't even want to be a nurse," Caroline snapped. "That's what I'm talking about. It was my husband's decision. He made all the arrangements. Where we would live. When we would have kids. What kind of career I should have. Why I needed to get a second job to pay for his education. Who he would fuck behind my back."

Caroline pictured the unwanted events in her life. "Through everything, I never raised an objection. Didn't complain, not once. My existence is like a movie I'm watching. I didn't want to have kids. I don't think I even wanted to get married. All my life I've wanted to do things. But I've never done them. Not one."

When Caroline looked up again, she noticed Wendy had backed away.

"Don't you see?" Caroline gestured to herself. "It's not just me. Why do you think women are second-class citizens? Why do we accept lower pay for the same job done by a man?" Caroline pointed at Wendy. "Why did you sleep with all those guys when you said you really didn't want to?"

Wendy's eyes flashed with anger. "There are no spiders living in our brains, goddamn it. I can't believe I'm even having this conversation."

"That's what they want you to believe."

"The spiders?"

Caroline nodded. "And men."

Wendy quieted for a moment, seeming deep in thought. She blinked and then looked at Caroline. "I've put up with all your craziness, but this... I can't be here right now." She hurried toward the front door of their small high-rise apartment. "Being your friend is just too hard. I'm gonna... I'm gonna just go."

Caroline rushed after her, catching the door as Wendy opened it. "You don't really want to go. It's the spid—"

"Let go of the fucking door," Wendy said, harsh words soaked in fear. Caroline felt like she'd been doused with a bucket of cold water. She let go of the door.

Wendy moved through the opening, and without looking back said, "Get some help, Caroline. Seriously."

Caroline slammed the door.

That was a week ago, and Caroline hadn't seen her since. Two days later Wendy returned to the apartment to get her belongings while Caroline was on duty at the hospital. She must have been in a hurry because she left a couple of things. Knick-knacks mostly, some cookware. Even the note she wrote seemed rushed, echoing her final words to Caroline.

Get some help. Please.

Placing the stainless steel bit of the cranial drill on the bathroom counter, Caroline surveyed the instruments of her liberation. Scalpel, forceps, sutures, and gauze, laid out according to size on the countertop. After a moment's pause, it suddenly struck her funny that the countertop resembled the chalky porcelain table in the medical journal photo of the Brazilian brain spider.

She almost laughed but stopped herself—the sutures above her hipbone were still very tender. She had performed a preliminary procedure on herself earlier in the morning, extracting the few ounces of fat she'd need later to plug the hole.

She picked up the forceps and turned them over in her hand. If she used too much pressure, she might tear the legs off, allowing the spider to scurry to the safety and darkness of her gray matter. Need a soft touch. Her surgical instructor had said the same thing moments before the first brain surgery she had assisted with. The patient, some man, died on the table, but not before Caroline got an excellent crash course in poking around the human brain.

She set the forceps next to the Tupperware container holding her body fat. She pinned back her auburn hair, exposing the pale patch of scalp she had shaved clean, just an inch above her ear. It glistened with a single bead of sweat in the soft glow of the bathroom light. She tapped the shaved area with her finger.

Numb.

She had only injected herself with a third of the recommended dose of anesthetic for such a procedure—one requiring the patient to remain conscious. A full dose might have made it difficult to stand or keep a clear head. In any case, her partial dose meant there would be some pain. How much?

Putting her hands on the counter, she stared at her small frame in the mirror. She wore only underwear and an Alanis Morissette concert T-shirt. She hadn't actually gone to the concert. She'd wanted to, but didn't.

The bathroom window behind her was reflected in the mirror. Its curtain was open and the Seattle skyline bled through. The Space Needle was as erect as ever, jutting up from a pubic-layer of fog, reminding her who really ran the world.

She wanted privacy, so she turned and drew the curtain. Liberation was often a lone pursuit.

Days before, she had begun picturing how she would do this. Do it quickly. Do it fast. Don't think about it. Thinking might let the spiders know you're coming.

She picked up the scalpel and touched it to her numb flesh. She had planned to cut a fast X-shaped incision but, when she pulled the blade back, the wound looked more like a bleeding cross.

She dabbed with the gauze until the flow of blood subsided, then wiped away the sweat on her brow. Using the scalpel, she cut deeper and then peeled back the folds of flesh, exposing her skull. Not much, just enough to touch the drill bit to bone.

No pain yet.

She lifted the drill and inserted the bit in the breach on her scalp. When the stainless steel point touched her skull, she felt the contact all the way down her spine. The sensation reverberated through her limbs, tapering off like ripples on a liquid surface.

She breathed fast, forcing the air in and out. Her heart raced. She pressed her lips together and gritted her teeth.

Very soon now, she told herself. *Liberation.*

The sound of the drill coming to life startled her, but not enough to lose focus. She gently pushed the drill inward, keeping her hand steady. Thin bands of smoke laced with ground bone fragments drifted up from the point of contact. *Perfectly normal,* she told herself. *Doing fine.*

The drill went deeper, and she kept a close watch on the depth, trying to avoid completely piercing the meninges—the three layers of membranes protecting the brain. She was amazed at the lack of pain, but as the familiar burning smell reached her nostrils, a blinding white light exploded in her skull.

Agony pulsed like a camera flash going off in her brain. Each flash caused her knees to buckle a little more. She closed her eyes and screamed, reaching for the mirror. *Open your eyes, goddamn it, open your eyes. Fight through this.*

She opened one eye and then the other. The drill bit wasn't moving. Her finger had come off the button. *Damn it.* But as she pushed the bit forward, she realized nothing solid was pushing back. She had broken through. She backed the drill out and unfolded the surgical mirror that was rigged to the medicine cabinet.

A clear yellow-tinted liquid was dripping from the hole. *Oh, shit. Cerebrospinal fluid.* She had broken through the middle meningeal layer—the arachnoid. Images from her textbooks depicted this area as a cobweb of thread-like strands attaching to the innermost region. It was where the spiders lived. But the appearance of cerebrospinal fluid meant she had gone below this into the subarachnoid layer. There was only a finite amount of this precious fluid protecting her brain. Losing a little was okay; most people did throughout their lifetime. But losing a lot was deadly.

She tilted her head to keep the fluid from spilling out. She picked up a penlight, clicked it on, then aimed the beam into her exposed brain. The fluid seemed to be stabilizing. *Thank God.*

Her pain had tapered off, except in regions completely foreign to where all the action was. The muscles around her ribs ached enormously and pulsing pains anchored themselves in the soles of her feet.

She took a deep breath and switched the penlight on and off, aiming the flickering beam into the hole in her skull. Up until this point, her plan contained elements of familiar territory. As a surgical RN, she had assisted many similar procedures on dozens of patients. But the next part of her plan was sheer guesswork.

She hoped that the brain spiders had evolved like other creatures that inhabited the dark. Bottom-dwelling enigmas living in the deepest ocean trenches shared a fascination with the eyeless subterranean salamanders. Although none needed light to survive, they would be drawn to it by an instinctual curiosity. Even the creatures without eyes turned toward the light, like a blind man sensing the exact moment someone else enters the room.

Caroline's thumb ached as she continued to flick the light on and off. Rotating the penlight in her hand, she tried using her index finger to press the button but found it difficult to aim the light. Then it occurred to Caroline that she could leave the light on and wave it back and forth over the hole. From the spider's point of view, it would look the same. Why didn't these things occur to her sooner? Maybe the spiders feed on common sense as well. That would explain a lot.

Minutes went by. She started to feel dizzy. *I can't do this much longer.* "Come out, come out, wherever you are."

Suddenly, there was movement. Subtle at first. Probing. Just an ivory tip. Then, a white needle-like leg emerged.

Caroline stopped moving the penlight and held her breath.

The thin pasty leg explored the lit area like a blind person's cane. Then it abruptly stopped. Motionless. As if it was suddenly aware of being watched.

Caroline reached down for the forceps. Her hand fell on the empty counter. She wanted to look down at the countertop for the instrument but was afraid to take her eyes off the tiny leg's reflection in the mirror. If she looked away, it might disappear. She locked her gaze on the arachnid, willing it to stay.

She felt along the counter as the spider's leg investigated the jagged edges of freshly cut bone. Another leg appeared. Then another.

Caroline's fingers grazed the forceps' handle. *Thank God.* She lifted them and opened the needle-nosed end. She eased the instrument forward, watching her movements in the surgical mirror.

Three legs, almost an inch long, protruded from her skull. Each one seemed determined to explore a different area of her scalp.

The open forceps hovered over the thickest point of two legs, and Caroline swallowed hard. She felt six years old again, playing that silly game, Operation. The similarities were uncanny. Use your tweezers to remove the ghost-white plastic bones without touching the metal edge. A steady hand wins the game, but graze the edge and you lose your turn.

More was at stake than losing a turn. If the spider broke free or she tore its legs off, she would lose her one chance to regain her will. Her life.

She clamped the forceps around the spidery appendages and, using a touch so soft and accurate she could have picked up a grain of rice, she began to pull.

The spider didn't come at first. Several other legs appeared, and it looked like they were searching for a way to anchor themselves. Then it began to slip. It slid quickly through the hole like a newborn calf being born. Caroline flicked it into the sink, unclamping the forceps. She glanced down at it, but there was new movement in the mirror.

A second spider had found its way to the hole, its legs probing at the light. *How many,* she wondered. *How many?*

Ten minutes later she had her answer. There were three in all. The third seemed to climb through the hole of its own volition, needing very little encouragement from the forceps. Maybe the spiders sought a kind of liberation of their own.

She repaired the meninges and packed the hole in her skull with her own body fat. This should have been surprisingly painful, but it wasn't. She knew that the body's pain receptors could turn themselves off in extreme conditions, but she didn't think that's what was happening. As she sutured her scalp, she glanced at her body in the mirror. She remembered it being so small before, dwarfed in the ceiling-to-countertop glass. But now it looked as if the mirror could barely contain her frame. She felt different. She *was* different.

Liberated.

The last suture tied, she clipped the excess stitching away. As she laid the scissors down, exhaustion hit her. She bent forward, bracing herself on the counter. Her head hung over the sink, hair dangling above the porcelain. She drew slow, deep breaths and took her first opportunity to examine the parasites. She blinked a few times, not immediately registering what was wrong.

Gone.

The sink was empty.

She smiled as she pictured the watery arachnids scurrying down the drain, traversing the miles of plumbing under the city. *Liberation, my friends. Liberation.*

The air in the bathroom smelled foul, so she staggered to the window. She wanted to draw the curtain open, but she ended up pulling it off the rod. Pressing her forehead to the glass, she looked down at the women scurrying on the streets that spun out like a web from downtown. *So many women,* she told herself. *There are more of us than there are men.* She felt troubled watching the women rushing to jobs they didn't want, raising families they didn't want, hell, even wearing shoes they didn't want.

There're so many of us. So many women needing liberation. I'm gonna need a lot more drill bits.

There was a tapping at the bathroom door. "Hey, Caroline. It's me, Wendy. I know I should have called before coming over like this."

Caroline pushed away from the window.

"Especially after how I left and all. I'm sorry about that. Anyway, I just wanted to come by and pick up my pots and pans. I met this guy and he wants me to cook my Italian casserole for him tonight. I know, I know, I hate to cook, but I really like this guy."

Caroline moved over to the counter.

Wendy rapped on the door again. "Are you in there?"

Caroline grinned at her tall and free-willed image in the mirror. She picked up the drill.

Time to start the liberation.

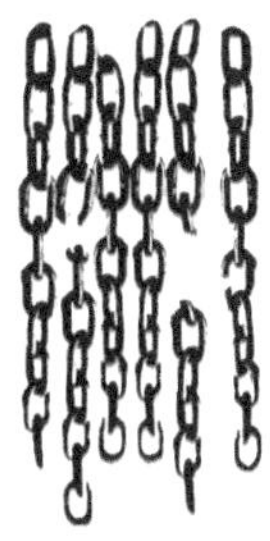

TERRIFIED LAMBS
by
NICOLE M. WOLVERTON

THE BOOTH WAS stuffed full of ceramic and plastic figurines. A whole row of tanned Josephs gazed in every direction, an expression and pose for every occasion. Behind that, a line of virginal Marys supplicated in twenty different ways.

On another shelf, a woman in a long pink robe was frozen mid-pomegranate picking, the tree a twisting, anemic specimen. Next to her was a stocky shepherd who stood before a little white lamb, belly up, tied by its back hooves to a bush—the lamb's terror-crazed face bore wide eyes as it watched the shiny silver knife in the shepherd's fist slice up and down, up and down.

"Is that...battery operated?" Olive gasped. The shepherd's arm swung in a continuous, deadly arc. "That's so screwed up. What kind of crazy person wants a permanent slaughter scene in their Nativity?"

Ravi, standing next to her, shrugged. "Why not? How is it any different from having the crucifixion mounted in every Catholic church? Jesus dying on a cross, hands and feet nailed, is fairly horrifying."

"For starters, I've never seen an animatronic crucifixion scene, with figures pounding nails through Jesus' hands and feet every second of the day."

"Fair enough."

Olive stared at the knife as it descended again and again. She could almost hear the terrified lamb's screams, imagine the intestines splashing out and the blood running down the hillside. "It's weirdly mesmerizing."

The one noise that wasn't imaginary, audible even over the chatter of the crowds at the Christmas market in Plaza Mayor, was the wheezing mechanical click and whoosh on the knife's down-swing, followed by a metal-squeezed groan, like the grinding of rusty clock cogs. Olive's skin popped up with gooseflesh, and this time not from the cold Madrid air. She jammed her hands in the pockets of her jeans.

"I think I'm going to buy it." The words were out before Olive realized she'd even said them aloud. "I need a souvenir, right? I'm probably not going to find anything more unique than that." She dug around in her purse for euros and handed them over to the vendor, her eyes focused on the slashing arm and the shiny miniature knife.

***

Olive named the figure with the knife Buffalo Bill. His lamb was named Clarice. Bill and Clarice were given a place of honor in Olive's tiny one-bedroom apartment in South Philly when she arrived home from Madrid. They were forever killing and being killed on a long black shelf that hung just above Olive's green couch.

The figurine crowded beside the snow globe that had come from her and Ravi's trip to Paris and the plaster cast of a sculpture from Vigeland Park in Oslo, Norway. Ravi's souvenirs were never that kitschy. He collected paintings from local artists—real art that was framed and hung on a wall. He was so much more refined than Olive. Maybe that was why he'd never expressed a romantic interest in her. She was always just his bestie.

Or maybe it was because she was tall and skinny, pale and weak. The girls he went out with were capable-looking, strong. None lasted very long, though. A month, maybe three. He got bored and moved on to the next.

The last one—her name had been Greta—actually showed up at Olive's apartment after Ravi blew her off, begging Olive to intervene on her behalf. That was in early December, before Olive and Ravi had flown off to Madrid.

"Can't you say something to him?" she'd asked.

"Like what? It's not like he listens to me," Olive said through the door, cracked open wide enough to see that Greta's long blonde hair had been pinned up in a dramatic top knot. Her mascara was smeared, lips trembling, soft as wings. It was the only weak-looking thing about her, those lips. *She* probably didn't collect weird figurines.

"Are you kidding? You're his best friend."

"So? I can't make him love you."

Behind the door, Olive had texted Ravi: *Greta wants you to take her back—she's here and she won't leave me alone.*

The reply came moments later: *Just shut the door. I'll give you her ticket to Madrid.*

Olive rolled her eyes. This was the way it always worked. He'd plan some trip with a woman, then decide she wasn't the one, and Olive would take her place on the vacation. She didn't mind, not really. The travel was a nice bonus, even if Ravi was preoccupied with his bad taste in women.

And this time, in Madrid, Bill and Clarice had come home with Olive. It was a singular pleasure to walk in her apartment door and see Bill killing Clarice over and over again and think about that day in the plaza—especially now that it was Christmas week. Ravi had already met a new girl, days after they'd landed back in the States. Some leggy girl who worked out like crazy in a gym around the corner from his apartment, so he probably wouldn't be around much. But Olive had the wheezing mechanical click and grinding groan of the shepherd figurine to keep her company. She ate dinner to its soundtrack. And when she went to bed, she paused by the shelf above her couch.

"Good night, Bill. Good night, Clarice."

***

Teaching second-graders was hard work. The constant smiling.

Counting by even and odd numbers over and over again. Faking enthusiasm for the same stories every year. Winter recess was meant to be savored—away from the usual passel of seven-year-olds. Olive could do whatever she wanted. That morning, when she woke up—a day before Christmas—she lingered in bed and listened to the distant sound of Bill killing Clarice in the living room.

As Olive weighed whether to spend all day reading or leave the apartment for a pedicure, her phone rang. Her mother's photo popped up on the display. Speaking to her mom was *not* on Olive's agenda for the day, but she picked up the phone, feeling virtuous.

"Good morning, sweet pea," her mother trilled into her ear. "I left you a little something on the front mat of your apartment. Why don't you go get it before it gets cold or before one of your neighbors gets curious?"

"I thought you and Sam were going to Aruba for Christmas," Olive said.

"Sam got called away for work. Some kind of emergency with the oversight board. Are you heading toward the door?" Her mother was an over-excited chihuahua of a woman. Olive could picture her, trembling and yipping, convulsively sipping coffee in the sunshine yellow kitchen of Olive's childhood home. Even at seven in the morning, her mother would be perfectly coiffed and made up, as though expecting fancy company any moment. "I don't hear you moving."

"Okay, okay." Olive slid out of bed and shoved her feet into the blood-red slippers Ravi had bought her last Christmas. She suspected they'd been meant for his girlfriend du jour. "I'm up. How long is Sam going to be gone?"

"Oh, you know how it goes with him. He'll get all caught up in whatever is happening, and I won't see him until January. I've half a mind to go on a cruise by myself. Unless maybe you want to come along. My treat. What do you say? The two of us on the loose in the Caribbean? It'll be fun."

Buffalo Bill was mid-stroke when Olive emerged into the living room, and Clarice looked appropriately stricken. Olive grinned.

"I don't think so, Mom. Those ships are floating petri dishes, and I'm bombarded by germs enough in the classroom." She twisted the deadbolt and cracked open the front door. "Besides—"

"Sweet pea!" her mother squealed from the hallway and barreled into the apartment, knocking Olive back several steps. A rush of glacial air came with her. When had it gotten so cold in the building?

Olive slammed the door shut and wrapped her arms around her flannel pajama-clad chest. "Mom, what are you doing here?"

"Like I said, Sam's out of town—so why should you and I both spend Christmas alone?" She tossed a small suitcase onto the couch and unbuttoned her camel dress coat. "I'll spend a few nights, we'll do brunch, catch up. It'll be like old times." The coat landed on the suitcase, and her mother grasped Olive's biceps. "Your stepfather being away this year turned out to be such a gift. How often do I get to spend quality time with my sugar booger?"

"What if your sugar booger has plans, Mom?" Olive delivered the line with a joking tone and a smile, although she meant every word.

"Oh, you!" Her mother dove in for a wet kiss on the cheek and then released her. "Why don't you go get a shower, and I'll tidy up this place a bit. I'll stow my bag in your bedroom. It'll be like we're gal pal roommates." She whirled and collected her suitcase and coat...and then froze. "What is *that*?" She pointed to Bill and Clarice.

"Oh, I picked it up in Madrid when I was there with Ravi a few weeks ago. It's supposed to go in a Nativity village. Ravi says it's a big thing in Spain—people have these giant Nativity scenes. There are plots and subplots. You should see the kind of figurines you can buy for them. The shepherd is kind of funny, right?"

"It's positively creepy is what it is." Her mother's hands twitched toward Bill and then retreated. "And that noise. How can you stand it? I'm—" She reached out again, this time seizing the figurine by the base. Bill continued to slice at Clarice, determined, until she pried out the batteries. "I'm afraid that'll drive me nuts." She slid the batteries into the pocket of her pink cardigan and smiled broadly. "That's better."

She placed the figurine, Bill's knifing hand arrested in mid-swing, back onto the shelf. If not for Bill's singular focus on killing Clarice, Olive was sure he'd be glaring at her mother with pure hatred. The silence in the apartment was unbearable, even more so when her mom insisted on filling it with chatter about what the neighbors were doing and her bridge club and the ladies at the hair salon. But Olive pasted a smile to her face and nodded at appropriate intervals like a good daughter should. And when her mother insisted on dressing up and heading to lunch at a stuffy steak restaurant, Olive went along with that, too.

"How's Ravi?" her mother asked when they were seated.

"Good. He got a promotion just before we went away."

"Now that's a good man. Why haven't the two of you ever gotten together?"

Olive sighed. "How many times do I have to tell you? He's not my type, and I'm not his."

Her mother snorted. "I've seen Ravi's type. You know, if you worked out and made an effort with your hair, you *could* be his type."

"Mom, come on. I'm fine just the way I am."

"Of course you are, sweet pea." Her mother reached over to pat Olive's shoulder. "I just don't want you to end up alone. It's not as though you have men beating down your door to date you."

"I like my life the way it is." Olive put a prim expression of contentment on her face and twisted her napkin under the table.

By dinnertime, Olive's cheeks hurt from forcing her face into friendly contortions, and she understood Bill's dogged need to do away with Clarice just a little better. She had texted Ravi a few times—when her mother visited the ladies' room, when her mother ran into a friend while shopping for knick-knacks—but there'd been no reply. Unsurprising but still annoying. She'd spent the afternoon saying nice things about him, gritting her teeth every time her mother made a passive-aggressive crack...

The least Ravi could do was text her back.

On the bright side, her mother had consented to supper back at Olive's apartment. Olive didn't have the energy for another meal out. She barely had enough energy to eat pizza with her mother without snapping, but she managed—even when her mother kicked her out of her own bedroom for the night.

Olive made a cocoon for herself on the couch below the shelf where Bill once again unceasingly sliced into Clarice. The sound of unending murder, restored with a fresh set of batteries, lulled her to sleep and filled her dreams.

***

Olive awoke on Christmas Day thinking of Madrid—the way Gran Vila had been decorated with lights, the giant metal trees covered in glowing designs in La Puerta del Sol, and the rows of small red chalets in Plaza Mayor, filled to the brim with Nativity village figurines. She unfolded herself from her makeshift bed and groaned, rubbing at her back. She was a grown woman. It was undignified to have to sleep on her own couch while her mother slept like a princess. Olive was a good daughter, but perhaps that had its limits.

She heated up water in the electric kettle and glared at her still-shut bedroom door. While the tea brewed, she made toast and barely poached eggs. She grumbled around forkfuls of breakfast, swearing at her mother, at her aching muscles. Still, the bedroom door stayed shut.

Olive huffed.

She folded the blankets, piled them on top of her extra pillows, paced the living room to the tempo set by Bill's swinging arm. She plopped into her armchair and typed out a text message to Ravi: *Mom's driving me nuts—sleeping late on Christmas Day. Probably resting up so she can torture me again today with more mother-daughter time. Anyway, Happy ho-ho-ho.*

Still, the bedroom door stayed shut. She rolled her eyes and flicked on the television and flipped around until she found a movie marathon.

Halfway through the film, the front buzzer rang. Probably her neighbor—the woman who always dropped off a tin of holiday cookies that Olive would never eat. The thought was nice, but eating random cookies was a sure ticket to the hospital or maybe even the morgue. You just never knew about a stranger's intentions. Olive straightened her clothes and pushed her hair back before pasting on a fake smile and opening the door.

Ravi stood on the other side. He smiled when he saw her. "Merry Christmas! Thought you might be able to use some buffer between you and your mom."

Olive pulled him inside and laughed. "Joke's on you. She's still sound asleep. I've been banging around out here for over an hour. Who knows, maybe she took a tranquilizer last night."

Ravi shucked off his coat and threw it on a chair. "No wonder. The murderiest little shepherd is really loud. I would have needed something to conk me out, too." He nudged the figurine with his finger. "What's on the agenda—" He peered closer at Bill. "Was this guy's knife always covered in blood? I didn't notice before."

Neither had Olive. She shrugged. "What are you even doing here? I thought you'd be wrapped in a blissful haze with your latest girlfriend right about now."

"She talks too much." Ravi wrinkled his nose.

"So you came here? To hang out with my mother? She who talks too much *and* throws in insults for kicks?"

He laughed. "Trust me. It's better than listening to someone wax poetic about the finer points of Scooby Doo and then baby talk you to death about wedding china." He paused. "Hold on—I'll get her out of bed." He banged on the door and hollered, "Eleanor Daley, get up right this instant. I've come to accompany my two favorite ladies to breakfast. Or church. Or both. Dealer's choice."

The door clicked open under Ravi's fist.

He grinned at Olive and pushed it open. "It's about time, young la—" He took a quick step back and slammed the bedroom door shut before turning to Olive, his face knotted. His phone was in his hand a second later, and he was thumbing the keyboard while dragging Olive toward the front door.

"What are you do—"

"911? Yeah, you need to send…I don't know, send everybody." He pushed Olive into the hallway. "There's blood everywhere, and I think my friend's mother is dead. She looks dead."

Ravi squeezed Olive's hand and gave the dispatcher the address while her stomach went hollow. What was he saying?

"No, we're outside the apartment," he continued. "I thought maybe whoever did it might still be in there…right. No, we'll stay right here."

"*What* is happening?" Olive asked when Ravi put the phone in his pocket. She clutched at his sleeve, and he put his arm around her and led her farther down the hall.

"Something terrible." His face was the color of curdled milk. "She was lying there, all bloody, and her eyes." He swallowed convulsively. "Maybe this isn't something you should be hearing."

"She's…dead?" Olive shivered. The words in her mouth didn't make sense.

"She has to be. There's no way—"

Olive wriggled out from under his arm and made for her front door. "What if she's not? What if she needs help?"

He caught her around the waist and hauled her back. "There's nothing you can do for her. She was…she looked…Olive, she's been…disemboweled, I think. And you don't know who might still be in your apartment. What if he was planning to hurt you too, and I interrupted him?"

"What if she's still alive?" She fought against Ravi's arms. There was nothing in her head but what she could imagine—her mother, guts hanging out of her, hurt and scared.

"She's not." He pushed her against the wall gently. "She's not okay."

Within minutes, several police burst down the hallway, and then a moment after that came an ambulance crew. None of them came out, though, with or without her mother. Olive's neighbors peeked around the corners, and people from other floors began arriving, gawking at Olive, still in what she wore to bed, still too shocked to cry. Ravi, talking to the police. The police, asking questions she couldn't answer—questions she couldn't even understand. And finally, Ravi guiding her down the hall and out of the building, helping her into the car, and driving her to his place. The girlfriend du jour pouted, and Ravi told her to get out.

When the apartment was quiet, Ravi held Olive's hand. "I grabbed a few things from your living room...just to make you feel at home." He placed the shepherd figurine and pushed the batteries into place. The knife swung, and Clarice screamed. Ravi paled. "Maybe that wasn't the best idea." He reached for Bill.

"No, no," Olive pushed his fingers away. "Leave it."

Ravi nodded. "Okay. Do you want to rest? Do you need anything else?"

Olive shook her head and cuddled into the couch. He stood and laid a blanket over her, then her coat. She drifted off almost immediately. She dreamed of blood and the mechanical sound of a slashing knife, high-pitched screams that weren't Clarice's. The feel of a knife in her hand, swinging and slashing, was as vivid as though she herself stood upon a pedestal in someone's sprawling Nativity scene.

In her dream, she laughed a metal-squeezed groan and stabbed the lamb again and again until Ravi's screams filled her head.

The Night Of Missing Children
by
Joe Baumann

After Lewis closed and locked the door, Calum hugged him from behind. Both resisted the urge to throw it open and call to Thomas to come back, and they stood there long enough that the motion-detecting porch light shut off. Thomas, the darkness outside seemed to say, had truly gone.

"Come," Calum said finally, his voice soft as he peeled himself from Lewis. "Let's have a drink."

They kept pricey, dusty bottles of dark liquor atop the hutch in the dining room, which was home mostly to cannisters of coins, ticket stubs, receipts that they tossed down at the end of each workday, emptying their pockets of stray dollar bills, the occasional facial tissue, cherry lozenges when the dry weather made their throats crack. They knew Thomas pilfered the dough sometimes but, as far as they could tell, he hadn't taken up smoking or other hard drugs and, if he drank beer with his friends, he did so safely.

At least, so far. Who knew what would happen tonight.

Calum pulled down a bottle of Blanton's Original while Lewis opened one of the cabinets and extracted a pair of rocks glasses. They didn't raise a toast because neither could think of a thing to be happy about. All they found themselves able to do was hope that Thomas came back in the morning.

For a long time, they wouldn't have expected otherwise, but then their neighbors, Lynn and Donovan, were shocked when their daughter Cindy didn't return three years ago. Sometimes they could hear Lynn's sobbing through an open window while they ate brunch on their back deck. Once, Thomas sat with wide eyes, his mouth full of French toast, unable to chew. Syrup started leaking from between his lips before Calum cleared his throat, which seemed to snap him out of it. He looked from Lewis to Calum, swallowed, his tongue licking at the corners of his mouth, and said, "Why wouldn't she come back?"

His voice was thin and cracking, not out of fear, Lewis thought, but thanks to the ravages of adolescence. It seemed like Thomas had shot up six inches that summer and had whirled through the kitchen on an hourly basis, staring into the pantry while he shoved chips and cookies and granola bars and Pop-Tarts in his mouth. He peeled slices of cheese from their deli bag, folding them up and noshing them in single bites. He heated Hot Pockets up three at a time. He was still skinny, and he had the body of a cross-country runner even though he hated exercise—unless he was on a tennis court or in a sand volleyball pit. He never stayed out late. Even when his best friends turned sixteen before him and could drive him wherever he might want to go, he always returned before midnight, as though to do otherwise would turn him into a pumpkin or a mouse.

"But that's the thing," Calum had said, when Lewis pointed out their son's good behavior. "It's always the good ones you have to worry about."

They sat down on the living room sofa and turned on the television, all blue light and noise, and soon enough Calum leaned forward, plucked up the remote, and turned it off. They both finished their first drink fast, and Calum, standing, said, "Fuck it. I'll just bring the bottle."

They stretched out, Lewis nestled between the couch cushions and Calum's body, which was warm and rigid. He had to snake an arm past Calum's head to pick up his glass; if he held it in his hand, he'd drink too fast. But then he wondered if there was such a thing on a night like this. He decided, quickly, that there wasn't and gulped down the bourbon, his eyes tearing at the sear as he tried to stop himself from coughing.

"Sexy," Calum said, managing somehow to pour Lewis another drink without having to sit up and without spilling anything on the floor or himself or Lewis' outstretched arm.

The room was full of sour silence. Normally, Lewis and Calum could sit in this contented emptiness for hours, so long that Thomas tended to come marching out of his bedroom, frowning, wanting to know if something was wrong. Had someone had a stroke? Were they both dead? Were they high? Had they passed out? What's wrong with you two? The last, usually, he said with a laugh, high and celestial and sweet.

Lewis was tempted to talk about his missing night, but he knew he shouldn't. That would mean he expected Calum to talk about his own, and one of the understood rules was that the things one did on that night were private. If you wanted to share what you did, fine. But you never asked another person.

Not that Lewis had many secrets. While his classmates were busy with drugs, booze, and probably gobs of awkward sex, maybe some graffiti and petty theft—though, in general, by the time his missing night had come around, the only destructive kind of behavior that was generally accepted was the self-destructive sort—Lewis had simply wandered. He had caught sight of a gaggle of girls he knew and followed them for a bit, thinking he might finally speak with the cheerleader he harbored a crush on. But then those girls had met up with half a dozen football players, including the quarterback, on whom Lewis also had a crush. He had peeled away before anyone noticed him and spent most of the night sitting by himself on one of the swings at a nearby park. He was back at his front door before dawn, and he had slipped inside, careful not to wake his parents, whom he knew were relieved and thrilled to find him already munching on a bowl of sugary cereal when they appeared in the kitchen seeking coffee and eggs.

He let Calum fill his drink again. Lewis knew that he'd have trouble when he finally tried to stand up; already his vision was spangly at the edges, his tongue feeling loose. Rather than say anything, he pecked at the back of Calum's neck. The skin was smooth and tight, and he felt an urge to lick it.

"Oh," Calum said. His neck vibrated as he spoke. "Okay."

Their mouths were both sticky with booze, Calum's breath woody and tart and a bit smoky. Their bodies were tangly and twice they nearly fell off the couch. When Lewis started to unbuckle Calum's belt, Calum said, "Maybe not here."

"But who's going to see?" Lewis said.

Calum looked up at the ceiling, eyes rolling around until they settled back on Lewis's face. He smiled, laughed, and shoved his hands down Lewis's underwear, his fingers cold. Lewis let out a small gasp.

"Whoops," Calum said.

***

Their relief was brief but necessary. Lewis pressed his ear to Calum's chest and said, "Your heartbeat's slower than mine."

Calum grabbed Lewis's wrist, fingers pressed on the delicate inner side. "I'd say they're similar."

"You don't need to lie," Lewis said. "I know I'm nervous."

"So am I."

They pulled on their clothing and made sandwiches. Lewis kept glancing out the kitchen window, wondering if he was seeing bodies moving through the dark of their neighborhood. Calum spread mustard on wheat bread and then stacked strips of deli turkey and roast beef. He found day-old bacon for crunch, then laid down slices of cheese.

"If you had to guess," Lewis said, "What do you think he's doing right now?"

"You know we shouldn't think about it. Eat."

"Just hypothetically."

"You'll stress yourself out," Calum said. He bit into his sandwich. Lewis watched him chew.

"I think I'll stress out more if I think but don't speak."

Calum swallowed and blinked at him. "Then speak."

But Lewis found himself suddenly unable to. When he tried to envision the trouble Thomas might be getting into, all he could see was himself, sixteen and alone, legs whisking through the air as he swayed forward and back on that swing, the rusted chain groaning under his weight. He'd spent hours staring up at the night sky, full of plump clouds moving fast and hard, bright stars jangling and slaloming as he swung. His neck had gone sore, his hands twitchy and cramped from gripping the chains.

He let out a sigh. "I guess I have no idea what he's doing."

Calum seemed satisfied by this answer. He nodded and took a bite of his sandwich, then gestured toward Lewis. "Eat."

"I don't know if I'm hungry."

"You're always hungry," Calum said. "Don't be one of those weirdos in movies who suddenly lose their appetite."

Calum was right, of course. Lewis was starving. He bit into his sandwich, relishing the vinegar sting of the mustard and the salt of the bacon. He nodded. Calum nodded back. The refrigerator hummed and, for a moment, he thought everything would be okay.

***

Lewis knew that they should just go to bed. They were drunk, they were sleepy from sex, they were bloated with sandwich meat and bread. But Calum, after finishing his last bite, threw himself back down on the couch and poured another round. Then he stared at Lewis, his eyes puffy underneath, like he hadn't slept in days, which was entirely possible. Until today, Lewis hadn't let himself think too much about Thomas' missing night, and he'd managed to while the nights away in dreamless sleep, the kind that slips by in bare blinks, hours erased as if they never happened. He knew Calum wasn't having that kind of luck because he was always yawning and groaning in the morning, slurping down too much coffee.

Lewis sat down next to him.

"Now what?" Lewis said.

Calum shrugged and sipped. Lewis let the bourbon hit his lips, but he didn't drink.

"Don't pretend," Calum said. "If you don't want to drink, don't."

"How could you tell?"

"I can always tell."

Lewis let that sit fat in the air.

"I was a loser," he said.

"Was?"

Lewis socked Calum lightly in the shoulder, which elicited a smile.

"On my night. I didn't do anything interesting."

"Neither did I." Calum's face was a map of shadows, one eye and cheekbone hidden in the gloom of night, the other lit up by the side-table lamp.

"I find that hard to believe."

"Believe it or not."

Calum grew up in a house not dissimilar to their current one, though much nicer and larger, a two-story with bright columns like bleached teeth, a decorative second-story balcony inaccessible from the inside, a kidney-shaped pool in the back yard with expensive lawn chairs and topiary. Lewis tried to imagine Calum wandering his neighborhood all by himself, refusing to get in trouble. Rich kids were supposed to have easy access to drugs, a cavalier attitude about sex. Wouldn't he hop in someone's car, go careening off at high speed to some party, snort cocaine or pop E while drinking needlessly expensive keg beer before finding someone to bed down with? Lewis couldn't picture Calum alone, shuffling down a sidewalk, finding his way to a park bench or a curb, leaning back and staring up at the night sky. But he liked the idea that they'd both spent their nights doing nothing at all.

"You weren't a loser in high school," Lewis said.

"No," Calum said. "But I was lonely."

Lewis set his hand over Calum's and nodded. This, at least, he understood.

***

The bottle was half empty, but Calum had done most of the drinking; he was passed out on the couch, letting out wet, rhythmic breaths with the steady cadence of a grandfather clock. Lewis extricated himself from Calum's prone form and returned the bottle to its place among its peers. He rinsed their rocks glasses, peering into the living room as he turned on the faucet. Calum didn't stir. Lewis poured himself some water and drank two helpings, swishing the second through his teeth because his mouth had gone dry.

Outside was deeply dark. Lewis checked the pulsing green of the microwave's digital clock: nearly two. Returning his attention to the window, he leaned over the sink to peer through the glass, which stubbornly reflected a wavering, puffy version of his face. He stared for a long time before accepting he would see nothing of interest.

Lewis knew he should go to bed; his alarm was set for five-thirty so he could get to the junior high school where he tried to get students interested in anatomy and physiology and the body's systems, regularly failing miserably. He should pull Calum up, help him stumble down the hall and into their bedroom, where he would have to remove Calum's socks and jeans and peel off his shirt, his limbs noodly, his body loose and goofy from too much alcohol. Lewis knew that Calum would groan and beg for extra sleep in the morning, and that Lewis would thus be left to greet Thomas on his own. Or worse, to face Thomas' absence on his own.

Instead, he decided to sneak outside. Checking once more that Calum was KO'ed on the sofa—his breathing was still regular and wet, and, if nothing else, louder and soggier than before—Lewis unlocked the front door, the metal click a booming noise like a bomb had just exploded. He sucked in a breath and turned the knob, expecting a rush of clamorous sound. But all that swooped in was the late-night breeze, cool and moist, and the tiniest sounds of bugs.

He pulled the door shut behind him. The porch light snapped on, and Lewis felt like a cat burglar invading his own property. He glanced back through the side light; he couldn't see Calum, but there were enough lamps on inside still that the additional outdoor glow shouldn't be enough to wake him. Lewis tried to steady himself. As he sat down on the lip of the porch—a simple concrete slab, ten feet long and half as wide, the only decoration a quartet of simple columns holding up the roof awning—he realized he was trembling. He set his hands down on the concrete and leaned back to listen to the darkness.

Their house was situated deep in a labyrinthine subdivision of two-story homes, a branching maze of culs-de-sac and four-way stops; the only way to stumble upon their property was purposefully, the streets with tree-themed names curling and looping and shooting off one another a dozen times. Mulberry Trail was hidden several left and right turns from the main thoroughfare, and Lewis couldn't imagine, as he sat with his eyes closed, that any of the children out in the night would find their way to his street. He could picture Thomas, an itinerary already constructed in his head—perhaps pre-planned with his friends—of where to go, what to do, his route out of the tumble of their suburban enclave sharpened and sure.

Lewis stood. He decided, despite the hour, to take a walk. He knew the streets by instinct after six years in the neighborhood, and there was no worry of getting lost, even if he chose to march down a street that led further into the maze of manicured lawns and two-car garages. When they first moved in, ten-year-old Thomas wanted to explore, so Lewis and Calum and their son had spent many weekend afternoons wandering. At each intersection, Thomas would blurt out "Left!" or "Right!" or "Forward!" and they would follow his instruction. Not once did Thomas grow frightened or express any concerns over being lost, even when Lewis felt the tiniest bite of nerve that he had no idea where they were. He wrestled with himself on these trips, a part of him desperate to map their route, another part equally hopeful that they would end up completely lost, forced to maneuver their way through a totally foreign landscape. But no matter how random their turns were, they always made their way back home eventually.

***

He walked for a long time, his bare feet blistered and stinging against the sidewalk. More than once, he stepped on stray pebbles and twigs, but he bit down on his lip to not shriek out. He kept moving, the streets that were familiar in the daytime suddenly obscure and foreign in the dark, picture windows and columns and mailboxes and driveways and landscaping all warped by darkness and shadow and the heaviness of night.

As if pulled by an indistinct magnetism, he eventually found himself back on his street. On the lowest, longest horizon, the first signs of daylight were breaking through, Easter egg colors just beginning to gleam at the lowest edges of the black. Lewis passed houses he'd been inside before, during block parties or barbecues or the Super Bowl. People had come knocking after he and Calum and Thomas pulled up in their car, followed by the moving truck that disgorged their couches and Calum's heaping boxes of books. They brought wine and pies, and then later, when Lewis's mother died, they brought casseroles, leaving them on the porch, ringing the bell and scurrying away, their condolences squashed at the bottom of stationery that explained how long to reheat the dishes in the oven. He knew his neighbors' names, waved hello when he left for work in the morning, and saw them dragging out their trash cans or recycling bins or bending down to pick up the newspaper.

A voice calling out his name broke the silence. Lewis juddered and looked around, his eyes suddenly unaccustomed to the dark. He heard his name a second time and was finally able to locate the source: his next-door neighbor, Lynn. She was sitting on her front porch wearing a plush terry-cloth robe. He squinted through the dark and made out that she was holding a coffee mug with both hands. She looked snug and comfortable, like she was in a Folgers commercial and the sun was about to blink over her shoulder as she sighed away all her worries.

"You shouldn't be out," she said.

"Neither should you," he said.

"Come. Sit."

Lynn was going gray at the roots and wrinkled at the eyes. He saw her bounding through the neighborhood sometimes in Lycra, working up a swelter that stained her clothes. Burning off all her sorrow, he thought sometimes.

"School night," she said. "Won't you be tired in the morning?"

"Everyone will be tired in the morning."

"That'd make a good song title."

"What about you?"

Lynn sipped her coffee. "I always stay up this late."

"Always?" Lewis said.

The darkness was lifting fast. Lewis tried to remember the last time he'd watched a sunrise. Yes, his job teaching thirteen-year-olds the basics of physical and biological science required he wake up early, but he spent the transitory hours between dark and light showering, brushing his hair, making Thomas breakfast, filling his satchel with graded papers, maneuvering through traffic en route to the junior high school. He never got to savor the morphing of night into day.

"Ever since Cindy," Lynn said. "Every time I hear a noise at night, I'm convinced it's her, coming back. Donovan sleeps in the guest room now because of it."

Lewis couldn't quite make out her face—the porch light was off, and the fast-arriving day wasn't quite solid enough to give her features shape. Her lips were still indistinct smudges in the dark, but he could hear how far away she was, and he could imagine how her eyes were unfocused, thrust back in time and gazing off into space.

"But if you mean out here, like this? Well," Lynn sipped her coffee, "Every missing night. And every Wednesday. Just in case. Hers was a Wednesday."

"Right."

"You're worried about Thomas."

It wasn't a question.

Lynn pulled in a breath through her nostrils. It sounded difficult, like she was congested by spring allergies. "He'll come back. Most of them do. Cindy was an exception."

"But you never can know, can you?"

"No, I guess you can't."

"I'm sorry."

"For what?"

"That she left and didn't come back."

Lynn sighed and, through the dark, one of her hands reached out and fell onto Lewis's shoulder. Her fingers squeezed at the muscle as though she was digging, trying to reach into him and stroke the knob of bone. Despite the discomfort, Lewis didn't lean away or tell her to stop. He let her probe for a long moment before her hand stopped, fingers shaped in a claw around his arm.

"I know she'll be back someday."

"How can you know?"

She shrugged, and he felt the motion down through her fingers. "I have to. If I don't, then what else is there?"

"Why do you think we do it?" Lewis said. "The missing night. Why have it at all?"

Lynn was silent for a long moment. "I think we all need to get things out of our system eventually. Why not when we're sixteen?"

"You think there's enough built up by then?"

She shrugged.

"What did you do?" Lewis asked it before he could stop himself, and he wanted to pull the words back in. Instead of berating him, Lynn just laughed.

"Things," she said. "Things both worth talking about and not worth it at all." When Lewis said nothing, she stood, releasing his arm. "I should get inside." She let out a yawn and stretched. Real light was starting to seep through the darkness, leaking between the houses on the other side of the street in mealy, low bands.

"I'm sure you'll see Thomas soon," she said and then, before Lewis could say anything in response, turned and walked into her house, shutting the door carefully behind her.

Lewis stood. An early-rising songbird trilled. Far in the distance, on the edges of the neighborhood, he could hear the first noises of cars, of workers heading off to work or coming home. He wondered when he would see the first child slouching back. Lewis looked down both ends of the street and saw no one. Finally, he started the walk toward his own house.

Morning light winked off the windows. Lewis realized he hadn't taken his phone with him, and he felt a squeeze of guilt that he'd left Calum drunk and dazed, alone. Lewis hurried to open the door, but it was locked. He didn't remember locking it, and, like his phone, he was without his keys. His stomach flopped like he'd been dropped from a high height. He banged on the door.

Lewis stood for what felt like an eternity, waiting. More light popped through the trees. He heard a garage door rumble open a few houses down. Lewis kept listening for the sound of Thomas approaching. He turned away from the locked door, craning to look down the street, but his vision was blocked by the dogwoods in his and Lynn's yard, their bright white-purple blossoms in full burst. In the pale, earliest light, they almost glowed.

Then the sound of the lock turning. The door opening. Lewis hoped it would be Thomas, that he had somehow miraculously beaten Lewis home. He would gather his son up and thank him for coming back, wouldn't ask any questions about where he'd been or what he'd done. Lewis would simply be grateful for everything inside, the life waiting for him, the things he would tell himself would always and forever be enough.

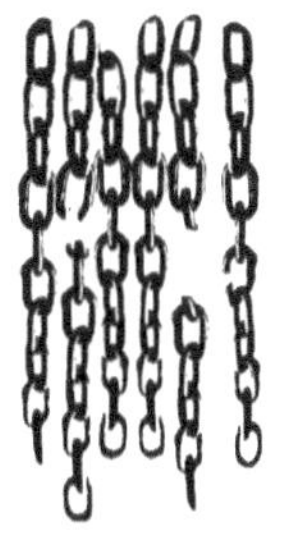

We See You
by
Evan Baughfman

Hairy black spider legs protruded from the woman's face. Inside her skull, a massive arachnid forced its appendages through her cheeks. The wriggling limbs resembled morbid piercings from a tattoo parlor for the damned.

The big spider sat atop her tongue and poked its head out of her screaming mouth, like a turtle emerging from its shell. The woman's eyes were bulging white orbs, rolled backwards, mercifully incapable of seeing the nightmare living in her head.

She clutched her throat as she choked on the overgrown tarantula. Her nightgown was blanketed in thick webbing, and her wrists were bound together by spider-silk manacles.

"Wow," said Julia, watching from the comfort of her car. "Gross."

It was certainly one of the creepiest Halloween decorations Julia had ever seen, and it was also, by far, the best lawn ornament in the neighborhood that year. Whoever had designed it was a maniac. And extremely talented. The animatronic statue was finely detailed and realistic.

There was no way anyone but the bravest trick-or-treaters would step foot near the thing.

Julia rolled down her tinted window to snap a quick photo of the spider-infested woman. A couple walking their Yorkie moved through the shot, so Julia paused. The dog yipped at her.

Julia lifted—and hid beneath—her sweatshirt's hood. "Hi," she said to the couple. "How are you?"

They didn't reply, continuing their evening stroll and pulling their barking terrier along the sidewalk on a purple leash.

Julia repositioned her phone for the photo. Its flash briefly lit up the night. She then examined the picture, noticing just how plain and nondescript the house behind the decoration seemed to be. It was a beige one-story box. If it weren't for Spiderface, one would never even know the homeowners had any Halloween spirit at all.

Tomorrow, the suburban streets would be packed with costumed children and parents. But tonight was Julia's opportunity to enjoy the holiday. She wasn't a fan of other people. Kids, especially. They frequently stared and pointed at her.

"Why's she look that way, Mommy?" they often asked.

"She's sick, honey," mothers often said.

Whenever Julia heard parents oversimplifying her condition, she wanted to scream a life lesson. "Be careful, kids, because some men are fucking psychos! I'm not sick, okay? When I was ten, my mom's ex-boyfriend got piss-ass drunk, and he tried burning down our house with us still in it! I couldn't get out in time!"

But Julia never clarified things. An outburst would only make people more frightened of her. Nobody really cared to know her truth anyway. They didn't want to spend any more time with her than they absolutely had to.

It was why, when she worked at fast-food restaurants, she was never positioned at the cash register or drive-thru. She was always hidden in the back, with the grease.

With the fire.

Eventually, she found a better job, and now she did telemarketing from home. People still avoided her—and were occasionally cruel— but at least Julia knew their insolence had nothing to do with her scars and uneven skin grafts.

Before every major holiday, Julia drove through nice neighborhoods to see how wealthy folks dressed up their properties. On her block, people didn't decorate much. During October, porch pumpkins either were stolen or ended up smashed on the ground.

Whenever she entered safer streets, Julia imagined a different life for herself. One without bars on her apartment windows. One where she could celebrate the seasons like normal people did.

She'd recently enrolled in virtual college courses. Would she someday be able to afford a manicured yard and three-car garage of her own? Would her future neighbors embrace her despite her differences?

Julia finally said goodbye to Spiderface and continued her search for other sinister scenery. She came across a couple of Styrofoam cemeteries and an inflatable ghoul, but nothing compared to that tortured, cobwebbed woman.

Julia couldn't quite shake the ghastly image from her mind. It would be a truly awful way to die, as a host to some eight-legged parasite.

And there had been Julia, gawking at the poor lady while she suffered. Why did Julia do that, when she knew exactly what it felt like to have people gape at her in horror?

And what was the woman's name? Nancy? Elizabeth? Katherine? Thinking of her as "Spiderface" was a bit rude, wasn't it? Demeaning. Julia still ached from the stings of teenage schoolmates calling her "Burnice" and "Burnadette" back in the day.

Julia shook her head. It was pretty ridiculous that she found it easier to connect to a decoration than to another living human being.

In a cul-de-sac, she noticed a house adorned with neon lights. They formed the shape of a vampire bat. Julia idled her car, rolled down her window again, and got her phone's camera ready.

She immediately noticed that the photograph she'd taken of Spiderface now only displayed grass and a home's bland exterior. The woman was missing from the frame.

The hell...? Where had she gone?

Had she ever been there in the first place?

Worried she might be going insane, Julia drove back to the house.

Indeed, the statue was absent.

Had Julia somehow mistaken the decoration's location?

Even if that were the case, why would she have taken a picture of an empty lawn?

She peered back at her phone. The photo still showed a scene without Spiderface.

A shadow enveloped Julia.

Spiderface stood at the driver's side window.

Her cobweb-shackled hands reached forward.

"*Friend*," the arachnid in her head hissed. "*We were looking for you.*"

Julia screamed. She pressed hard on the gas pedal, tires squealing against asphalt.

Quickly, Spiderface grew smaller and smaller in the rear-view mirror.

Was it a trick of some kind? A person wearing an elaborate costume? A twisted figment of Julia's imagination? Or an impossible entity? What was it?

What? What? *What*?

Julia wasn't sticking around to find out.

Her heart beat at lightspeed. She ignored a stop sign and hung a sharp right, eager to hit the freeway as fast as she could.

She raced past a police cruiser moving in the opposite direction. "Shit!"

Julia slowed the car's pace, but it was already too late. The officer U-turned and signaled for her to pull over with his red and blue lights.

They met beside a small park.

High beams blinded Julia from behind as the officer approached her vehicle.

When he reached her door, he said, "License and registration, please."

Julia already had both items in her hands. She passed them over.

"Lower your hoodie for me."

Julia complied.

The officer asked, "Know how fast you were going?"

"Too fast."

"Speed limit's 25 around here. Safe to say that you were doing a lot more than that."

"Sorry."

"You been drinking at all tonight, ma'am?"

"No."

"Coming from a Halloween party, perhaps?"

Julia shook her head. She hadn't been invited anywhere in years. And if she were ever invited out, she'd decline the offer. The last place she wanted to be was anywhere loose-lipped boozehounds had the opportunity to ask her uncomfortable questions.

"No party, huh? Then what's with the...?" The officer studied her driver's license. "Oh."

That's right, she wanted to say. *It's not a mask. Not make-up. It's how I look every fucking day.*

The officer said, "Sit tight. I'll be back in a moment." He returned to his car. As she waited, Julia looked for Spiderface. But nothing slunk in the shadows.

The officer approached once more. He said, "What're you doing out here tonight? You're a little far from home."

"Looking at people's Halloween decorations. Taking photos."

"Funny you mention that. See, we just got a couple of calls in, saying someone suspicious is driving around, taking videos of different properties. The car fits the description of your vehicle."

"Oh. Well, that's a misunderstanding. I was taking pictures, is all."

"Been a few burglaries around here lately. Know anything about that?"

"No, sorry. Look, I can show you the pictures, if you want..."

"That won't be necessary at the moment." He studied her car. "Tinted windows, huh? Don't see many of those anymore..."

Julia nearly blurted, "Well, I'm trying to hide these good looks, dumbass!"

"Can you have your passenger roll down their window, too, please?"

Passenger? What pass—

The rear-view mirror revealed Spiderface lounging in the back seat.

In.

The.

Back.

Seat.

Fuck! How?!

Because it was a monster! A spirit!

Not a person! Not Julia's imagination!

Something dangerous!

"God!" Julia cried. "No!" She unbuckled her seatbelt and began to open her door.

"Stop!" The officer reached for his holster. "Stay where you are!"

"*Yes, friend*," said the mouth-spider. "*Stay with us.*"

"That woman in the back…she…she wants to hurt me!"

"*Oh, friend. Why spread lies?*"

Julia screeched at the officer, "Let me out! Please!"

"Hold on." The officer was visibly confused. "Why are you saying this now? Nothing seemed wrong before."

"I can tell you everything! Just let me out!"

"I don't…" The officer hesitated. "Stay in the car. Don't move."

"*Friend, we promise not to bite.*"

"Fuck this!"

"Ma'am, please, just—"

Julia threw open her door. She leapt into the street.

Apparently, the officer felt threatened. He Tased Julia with fifty thousand volts to the chest. She slammed face-first onto the road. Her muscles spasmed. Her skin felt like it was on fire.

On.

Fucking.

Fire!

The officer knelt beside her. He cuffed her hands behind her back.

He yelled at the figure in Julia's back seat. "You, remain where you are! Stay still!"

He retracted the Taser darts and lifted Julia up by her armpits. He dragged her to some itchy grass and laid her down in it.

Then he used a radio to call for backup. He had his gun pointed at Julia's car.

He ordered Spiderface, "Open the door, and step out, slowly."

Regaining her faculties, Julia managed to get herself into a sitting position. She watched as the back door creaked open.

The officer nodded. "Good. Now come out, hands up."

Nothing exited the vehicle.

"Out, now!" the officer boomed. "Hands above your head!"

Spiderface still refused to budge.

"I said—"

A strand of spider-silk whipped out of the back seat, catching the officer in the throat. It yanked him off his feet and into the car.

The door slammed shut behind him.

Inside, the man screamed. Muffled gunshots rang. The night fell silent except for sirens looming in the distance.

Julia forced herself to her feet. She knew that she'd be blamed for whatever fucking mess had just been made in her car.

She had to get out of there. And think.

Tears obscuring her vision, Julia stumbled into the park.

She tried moving carefully down a hill but lost her footing anyway. Since her hands were cuffed behind her, she had no way to brace for impact. Momentarily dazed, she groaned in the grass.

"*Friend,*" a voice carried on the wind. "*Where are you?*"

Julia bit her tongue and struggled to stand.

"*Aren't you lonely?*"

Julia was back on her feet. She ran.

Up ahead was a playground. Somewhere to hide, to collect her thoughts! She ran even faster.

Was Spiderface closing in? Probably. Julia was too terrified to look over her shoulder and see.

In less than a minute, she reached the swings. To her left was a tall spiral slide. At its top, a point of entry was covered with a canopy. A suitable spot for temporary shelter.

Julia trudged through sand and climbed the structure's plastic stairs.

"Oh," Julia said. "Hey."

Somebody was already hunkered down at the top of the slide. It was a man with long hair and a bearded, gaunt face. In the moonlight, his wide eyes seemed to glow. Beside the man was a bulging backpack.

"The fuck're you?" he growled.

"I'm...Sorry, I'll go."

"Get the fuck away from me!" He moved toward her.

Julia saw the knife in the man's hand and backed across a tiny bridge.

"The fuck're you?" he repeated. "Ugly-ass fucking...fucking demon! Can't come for me! I didn't do nothing wrong! Nothing! Can't come for me!"

Okay, so the guy was on drugs. And from his addle-brained perspective, Julia was some kind of monster materializing from the darkness.

"Shit. Sorry, I'm leaving, alright? I'm going."

"Gonna kill you!" the man threatened. "Wanna die? Huh? Wanna get fucking killed?"

Spiderface appeared below. She sprang upward, as if lifted by an invisible trampoline, tackling the man at the bridge.

He landed on his knife, the blade entering his ribcage. He wailed as a hungry spider chewed on his throat.

Julia didn't hesitate to jump off the playground structure. She hit soft sand.

Three hundred meters away, a pair of police cars had arrived on scene. Should she go to them? Or would they, too, mistake her for a menace surfacing from the shadows?

Julia had no desire to get Tased again. Or to suddenly become riddled with bullets. So she zeroed in on a row of nearby homes. If she could reach one of them, explain to the inhabitants that she was in trouble, and get them to call the police over for assistance, it might be a safer course of action.

"*Don't go,*" said Spiderface. "*Friend, we're lonely, too.*"

The first house was lifeless. No lights on inside. Not even an illuminated porch.

The second house was a two-story beast. A downstairs room shined bright.

Julia reached the front door. Next to it was one of those video-camera security bells. Before she even rang the thing, a woman's voice spat from a speaker, "Yes? What do you want?"

"Thank God! Help me, please! Someone's out here, trying to—"

"Not interested, freak. Take that nonsense elsewhere."

"Wait, what? Someone's after me! You have to help—"

"Look, we know it's Mischief Night. Devil's Night. Whatever you want to call it."

"I'm not...not trying to trick you! Prank you! Call the police! Please!"

"Find somebody else to fall for your crap."

And that was it. End of conversation.

Julia kicked the door. "Help! Call 9-1-1! Help me!"

But the voice never returned.

Another one replied, "*We hear you, friend.*"

Julia didn't dare look back. She raced across the lawn to the next property. As soon as she did, the sprinklers turned on.

A man in plaid pajama bottoms stood on the other side of his yard. He growled, "Get your ass out of here."

He'd purposefully set the sprinklers on her, hadn't he?

"I can't. I need—"

"You need to stop, is what you need. And you need to go back to wherever it is you came from. We don't condone your kind of shit around here."

"Please, just listen!" Julia stepped toward the man but slipped and fell in wet grass. Water blasted tears from her face.

"No, you listen. A lot of us on this block—including me—believe in our Second Amendment rights. Do you understand what that means?"

Couldn't he see her handcuffs? That she wasn't a danger to him?

"Just call the pol—"

"I don't need the police. That's what I'm trying to tell you. Now, you've got five seconds to get your stupid ass off my lawn before I do what actually needs doing."

"Please, don't—"

"Five...Four...Three..."

Soaked head to toe, Julia made it to the sidewalk, hesitant to try another house. Still, she moved on.

Pajama Pants yelled after her, "That's right! Go on back home! Get!"

Fine. Yes. Excellent idea.

She wanted to get as far away from that blowhard as she could. Once she put a few addresses between the two of them, she tried another strategy.

Julia screamed for help. At the top of her lungs, from the safety of the sidewalk, she begged for somebody—anybody—to call 9-1-1.

No matter how loud Julia got, no one peeked through a window to see what she needed. Nobody came to her aid.

Not even when spider-silk wrapped around Julia's ankles and dragged her into a yard barricaded by towering hedges.

The overgrown tarantula sat atop Spiderface's head as its host mindlessly pulled Julia closer to them. Closer.

Julia loudly protested. The tarantula's spinneret fired webbing across her lips, silencing her, and effectively burying her hope alive.

The spider explained, *"We need a friend. So do you."*

Julia shook her head. No, she didn't.

No.

She.

Did.

Not!

"Together, we'll bring joy. Laughter. Smiles."

The hell was it babbling on about?

What joy?

What laughter?

What smiles?

"We'll be appreciated, friend. No longer feared. Loved."

Julia mumbled for the arachnid to shut the fuck up and just let her go.

Let.

Her.

Leave!

"They'll notice you, friend. The same as we do."

Julia was now close enough to see Spiderface's white eyes shifting in their sockets. They were squirming. Something was inside them, prepared to break free.

"We see you, friend."

Oh, shit.

Oh, no.

Those weren't eyes at all. They were—

Twin eggs split open in Spiderface's skull. A sea of spiders swarmed over the woman's nightgown and then blanketed the lawn on their brief journey to Julia's flailing body.

"We see you."

The spiders surged over Julia and went to work.

***

Twenty-four hours later, in front of a boring, beige single-story home, Julia, wrapped like a mummy in webbing, lay at Spiderface's feet. Together, they entertained a never-ending crowd of candy-seeking families.

"Isn't this great, friend?" the giant spider asked Julia. *"You aren't alone anymore, and people light up whenever they look your way."*

Tons of visitors posed for photos with the disturbing Halloween decorations.

Alive and aware, Julia, mouth still muzzled by spider-silk, tried pleading for help with her eyes. A few folks met her gaze, but none believed what they were witnessing.

At one point, some teenager stared at Julia and said, "Damn, look! This chick's face is all jacked up!"

His friend laughed. "An allergic reaction to spider bites!"

"Creepy as fuck!"

They took their picture and left.

Thousands of people saw Julia screaming that night.

But, also, they did not.

Unleashed
by
Chris Bannor

Hudson felt pressure against the back of his mind and eyed the guards around him. As far as he knew, none of them felt the same. This wasn't the first prisoner's soul he'd carried in his head, though, so what was different this time?

There were rumors about stewards who had gone crazy because of the soul in the back of their skull. Always a guy who knew a guy who knew a guy. Hudson had heard a hundred stories in his three years with Soul Security. He never believed them. Not until one of his friends had lost a bond. Not until now, when he could hear it echoing in his skull.

Him. I'm not an it. I'm a him. And my name is Legend.

Hudson refused to have an argument with his own head. No matter how many souls currently lived there.

"Hey Hudson, are you heading up?" Alicia asked.

"Yeah. They figured if he hasn't escaped by now, the bond took. His body stabilized in stasis, so no reason for me to have to stay in the Cage any longer."

"Beers?"

"Tomorrow night?" he asked. "My only plan for the night involves me and my big, comfortable bed at home."

"Maybe try finding someone to share it," Alicia teased. "You spend too much time alone."

"Yeah, I'll get right on that."

She spread her hands wide and smiled. "You know my girlfriend and I would always welcome you."

He threw a towel at her, which she caught deftly. "Your girlfriend could kick both our asses. And I don't date coworkers," he answered.

"Who said anything about dating?"

She left the locker room before he could answer. Today, it was a relief. He was exhausted. The doctors said the bond was established. All the extra tests he'd asked them to run had come back clear. But something wasn't right. According to the records, Prisoner Legend Patrick's body was stable, and his mind was firmly held in the Dax-notch at the back of Hudson's brain.

And they always tell you the truth about everything, right?

"Shut up," he muttered under his breath. He grabbed his jacket and emergency bag and left the locker room. The staff level was above the rest of the prison, but he still had to take the elevator up another two floors to sign out. He stood at the elevator banks and waited his turn.

Fuck. What time of day is it? Will I see the sun again?

Hudson ignored the voice. It was the only way to stay sane. Some prisoners were too dangerous to leave in a cell, and some were in too much danger. Some just had enough money that they could ride out their prison sentence as a passenger.

Hudson never had to worry about that. He was born with a strong notch. He was perfect for high-security work, and he was paired with the most difficult cases because of it.

He'd never had this level of interference from a prisoner, though. It was troubling, even if it was just a voice in the back of his head.

How long before you crack? Before you tire of my questions and start answering? I've got nothing better to do. They stuck me in your head without my consent, and I am sure as hell not going silently into that good bullshit.

Hudson rubbed his forehead and was grateful when the elevator doors opened.

He proceeded to the security gate and dropped his belongings into the bucket as he passed through. The alarm went off, and he already had his hand on the necklace that he was required to wear around his neck. Currently, it had Legend Patrick's soul scan recorded on it. The guard took the data recorder and plugged it in, reviewing it against the soul in his head. After a moment, they handed it to him, and he put it back around his neck.

"New one?" the guard asked.

Hudson smiled. "Can you tell?"

"The scan is still settling. Nothing to worry about. You look tired. Get some sleep. You've earned a good night's rest."

He laughed as he grabbed his things and left the building. The sun was still out, and he let the rays fall on his bare arms. He hated extended stays in the Cage.

Tell me about it.

***

"How are you feeling, Hudson?"

His weekly psych-check was daily now.

"Annoyed," he blurted. "The contract is very specific about this. When there is a problematic prisoner, we have a right to turn it down. They stuck him in my head without asking, though, and now I'm forced to come in daily to pass your test."

"You're paid very well to come in every day."

"They've reminded me. I had a right to say no, though. Why is everyone forgetting that?"

"You've never said no, no matter the prisoner. Does this one bother you?"

"I can hear him."

"Do you speak to him?"

"No," he lied. It was a small lie, but one he felt deeply. He was doing his best. "But I hear him." He rubbed his hands together and looked back at the day's therapist. He hadn't caught her name on the way in.

"Did you read the prisoner's file?"

"I never do. It doesn't matter what they did. My job is to keep their souls alive and safe from harm or from harming anyone else. I'm not the judge or jury."

"It might help you deal with him."

"I have the file. If I need that sort of reinforcement, I'll look at it. But I've never had to before. I know the routes I need to take if he becomes an issue."

"Have a good day then, Steward. And know that you are doing your people a great service."

Oh yes. What a service. Keep a soul in the back of your head while the body rots and you pretend to be doing a good deed.

***

He knew he was in a dream, but the surroundings were unfamiliar. The ocean was a pale rose-gold that Earth had never seen, the sky a brilliant red. Pale sand slid under his feet. The two suns of Mangasha were setting. He'd seen it in pictures, but he'd never visited.

"So you aren't going to tell the psych-officer about this?"

Hudson stared out across the waters, but he felt Legend behind him. The first time it happened, he'd thought it was just a dream. He knew better now, but those first few nights he'd made mistakes.

"Dr. Simpson would have a lot to say about this," Legend said, as he moved close enough to touch.

Hudson tried to ignore him, as he'd done every night since he realized Legend was the one that brought him to this strange world. He failed again.

"Doctor who?"

"You don't even remember their names anymore. The psych-officer from last week? The one you lied to."

Hudson couldn't defend himself, either. It wasn't his first lie to a psych-officer, but it had been blatant.

"This doesn't affect the bond," he snapped. "Whatever trick you think you're playing, my hold on you is steady."

"I'm not trying to weaken your hold. I just want you to know about the person you're imprisoning. I'm stuck in your head all day long. Can't we share a little space?"

"This isn't a pleasure cruise," Hudson said, as he turned to look at Legend. Legend smirked, and Hudson regretted his turn of phrase, but he didn't address it. "You incited violence and rebellion on Mangasha. This is prison."

"Is that what they told you?"

"I saw your file."

Legend's brow furrowed, and he tilted his head slightly. "You told the psych-officer you never look at them."

"I did this time," he admitted. "You've broken the bond of six different stewards. One of them was a friend of mine."

"I don't pick the stewards. And I had nothing to do with the strength of the bond. I wasn't trying to hurt them. I just wanted to be heard."

"You got into their heads. You shouldn't be able to do that!"

"And here we are."

"Is this what you did to them?"

Legend shook his head. "No, there was never anything personal with them. I never saw them like I see you. Hudson, I'm not who you think I am."

"Right. I'm sure it was all just a misunderstanding."

"No. I was a political protester. They started the violence and blamed me. They silenced everyone that opposed the government's sanction of the Wassak people. The Wassak had a right to rule themselves, but the government went in and stripped them of that. Of everything."

"Stop. I'm not a judge, and this isn't a court of law. You had your chance at trial," Hudson said as he turned away.

Legend grabbed his arm and pulled him back around. "Do you really think my trial was fair? That the judges who sat on it didn't have pockets lined with the money stolen from my people?" He shook his head. "You'd think someone who spends his time in the criminal justice system would know better than that."

Legend frowned and looked Hudson over before he stepped back. "I always thought if I could just reach one person and tell them, someone would understand. I tried with the others, but none of them would listen to my words." Legend's voice grew quiet in disappointment. "You can't set me free, but I thought maybe you were the one that would see the truth."

Legend disappeared, and Mangasha dissolved around him.

Hudson woke in the dark of his bedroom. He could feel the soul at the back of his head stirring, but there was no pressure and no voice.

Hudson took a deep breath and tried to still his mind. He should never have let Legend get to him. He should never have lied to the psych-officer. He should never have been given a political prisoner.

***

"I was informed you've been looking into the history of Mangasha."

Busted.

Hudson stretched his neck to the right until it popped. He wasn't sleeping well. He had asked the doctor to give him something to knock him out, but Legend could interrupt his sleep patterns, even with the drugs.

"I saw a vid of the beaches, and I was thinking it might be a good vacation spot."

"Looking into the protests three years ago?"

Dr. Simpson had called him in. It was never good when a psych-officer took an interest in you.

"You know who I am," Hudson said. She nodded. "It looked nice, but I'm not going to walk into an unstable country. Hell, if there is a hint of unrest in a village I want to drive through, I call it off. There's a reason I haven't taken a real vacation since..."

"You aren't your father," Simpson said.

"Not that anyone cares." He let out a deep breath as he looked down at his hands. "I'm not supposed to work with political prisoners for a reason."

"There were...unusual circumstances that required a very specific host for this prisoner."

He sat up straighter at that. He had assumed there was some sort of mix-up. "This guy's psychic index is high enough he could get a job as one of us. That's why you paired him with me. I was the only one that could keep hold of him."

She nodded but didn't say anything else.

"Is he strong enough to break the bond?" That was the biggest concern with any prisoner. Usually, a prisoner with strong mental capabilities was isolated from the population so they couldn't harm anyone. If the prisoner could break the bond, they could destroy the steward's mind and take over their body. It had happened in the early days before they understood enough.

She still didn't say anything.

His jaw opened, but he couldn't think of anything to say.

I'm not that person! I would never hurt you.

For the first time, Hudson didn't care about the regulations or his own self-imposed rules.

But you could, he challenged.

He could sense Legend's hesitation.

I don't know.

"We didn't have a choice. You're right. The others weren't strong enough." Simpson interrupted his inner conversation.

"Then why not isolate him like you do the others? Soul Security could have turned his case down and left it to the regular prisons."

"They didn't believe isolation would contain him."

"You thought it wasn't safe enough to put him in isolation because, even at a distance, he could coerce people, but you thought it was safe to put him in someone's head?"

"We thought with your history—with your father—he wouldn't be able to corrupt you."

Hudson? What history? Who was your father?

He stormed from the room and left the building.

This was no emergency placement. No accident. A chill ran down his spine as he looked back at the building. The men who ran Soul Security did it on purpose. The idea terrified him, and brought up one question he needed to answer. *Why?*

***

"Hey, Hudson, what are you doing up here? You aren't scheduled for a removal, are you?"

Hudson didn't know his name, but the tech had helped in a few of Hudson's procedures. "Psych sent me up. They said the prisoner's body was unstable and they needed to synch?"

"I don't have any orders. Let me see what I can find out."

"Sure. Can I sneak back and borrow a slab? It's been a hell of a day. And if you're chasing paperwork, it might take a while."

The tech nodded as he started punching keys. "Have a good nap. I'll let you know when we're ready for you. Which psych-officer was it?"

His name is Andrew. He was part of our bond procedure.

"I have no idea, Andrew. The psych-officers aren't like you. They just want to watch my head explode."

Andrew laughed. "They aren't all that bad."

"*You* take a nap on one of their couches." Hudson headed past the desk and toward the doors.

"No thanks. And Hudson, you can grab a slab up here anytime." Hudson gave him a friendly wave, then ducked through the door. He rushed through the waiting room and towards the storage rooms.

What are you doing, Hudson?

They shouldn't have given you to me, Legend. Hudson passed three doorways before he found the right one. He pushed it open and walked up to the front desk.

"You don't have an appointment," the man behind the monitoring desk said.

"Andrew said I could grab a few Z's on an empty slab. You look pretty tired yourself. Why don't you take a nap too?"

Hudson hadn't always known he was a high-level psychic but, once he did, he stopped the tricks he'd been playing. Not until he found Soul Security had he found a way to wield his abilities peacefully.

He never let psychic tests measure his true abilities either. It scared him too much. It reminded him of his father.

He doubted himself at that moment as he watched the guard yawn, then put his head down and fall asleep at his station. He doubted himself as he slipped into the guard's thoughts and found the codes he needed. He didn't doubt his purpose, though.

Hudson found Legend's bed and sent it to an open slab. He watched as the automated system brought forward the stasis bed.

He ran toward it and checked the data. Most of it was nonsense to him, but there were a few key things every guard in the prison needed to know in case of an emergency. He typed the guard's code into the bed and watched as it began to light up. He took a moment, then, to look at the face through the glass.

Hudson, what the hell are you doing?

None of this was an accident. He'd been careful of the questions he asked, and who he asked, but it all came back to this: *They want you dead. Your followers haven't given up, and your government wants to discredit you and turn the people against you. They're going to use me to do it.*

The bed beeped, and its lights turned red to warn anyone close by that it was in revival mode.

Why would they do that? What could you do that would—

Nothing! I would never do anything to hurt people, but it doesn't matter. They're going to make sure I can't. And if the men behind Soul Security tell everyone my real name, no one will blame them for my death.

Who are you?

My father is Hank Walkson.

The silence at the back of his head told him that Legend understood everything. Hank Walkson was the strongest psychic ever recorded on any Earth-seeded planet. He'd used his abilities to cause a rebellion that had killed more than four million people.

Hudson wasn't his father.

But he was stronger.

I'm getting you out of my head, and then we're running. No one will believe we aren't planning something. The psych-officers already have plenty on us to cause doubt, and I did enough digging to know they falsified evidence in your case. They need to kill you to cover it up, and they've been keeping an eye on me since I was a child.

They don't have any idea how strong you are, do they?

No. They don't know about either of us.

The bed lights turned green, and Hudson looked back at the door. No one had come yet.

Here we go, Legend. Just a couple of minutes, and you'll be back in your own body.

How are we getting out of here?

They're afraid of me because they can't control me. I guess I'll have to show them why they should have kept on my good side.

Hudson, I'm glad you're on my *side.*

Hudson might have laughed under other circumstances, but instead, he typed in the emergency codes to start the transfer protocols. A panel opened, and he took the two psy-trodes and placed them on his temples. The third, he connected to the nape of his neck.

The connection was instant, and it took his breath away. Normally, the soul transfer was performed while they were sleeping to allow a smoother transition. This was a storm in his head. As consciousness left him, he felt empty and drained.

He stumbled against the stasis bed. He hadn't counted on the exhaustion. He lowered his head to the bed but jerked upright when someone touched his shoulder.

He hadn't heard Legend move, but he was sitting upright now, staring at Hudson with the same eyes that had been haunting his dreams.

Hudson took a step back and reached into a drawer in the bed. He pulled out two containers and handed one to Legend. "Drink it quick. We need to get out of here."

He downed his own, used to the bitter taste. Legend was looking at his like it was offensive. "Drink it. You haven't been in stasis long enough for atrophy to set in, but it will help your psyche connect with your body."

He opened another drawer at the end of the bed and found the clothes Legend had worn into the prison. "At least something is going our way," he said, as he pulled the items out and set them on the bed.

"What's that?" Legend's voice was scratchy as he croaked out the words.

"If we have to run, you have reasonable shoes." He smiled as he indicated the gym shoes underneath the clothes. "Get dressed. We need to leave before Andrew comes looking for me."

Legend tossed his legs over the side of the bed but stumbled when his knees buckled. Hudson grabbed him and steadied him. "Need help?" he asked.

"I got it," Legend said, pulling away. Hudson turned his back to him and took a deep breath. He couldn't hear anyone coming down the hallway, but he was beginning to feel cornered.

The few minutes it took Legend to dress took hours in Hudson's mind. When the other man touched his shoulder, Hudson looked him over.

"You don't look too worse for wear."

Legend smiled. "You don't look too bad yourself. Did that transfer kick you as hard as it did me?"

"Not feeling too steady on my feet, but it's time to go."

"You feel something out there?"

"No, I … I don't do that."

"Allow me then," Legend said.

Hudson saw Legend's eyes glaze over as the man reached beyond himself.

"Nothing yet. Looks like your friend Andrew got caught on a phone call and hasn't been able to check into your story."

"Alright. Back door. We're heading up to the locker room. From there, up another elevator, and out the front door."

"We're just walking out?"

"I'm not happy about it either, but if you can think of any other way to get your body out of here without killing it, I'd love to hear it."

Hudson didn't wait for an answer as he opened the door on the back wall that led to the emergency tunnels, which took them straight up to the locker room. Hudson grabbed a hat from his locker and handed it to Legend. The best he could do was hope that anyone who looked too closely wouldn't recognize the prisoner.

It was a slow time of day. Hudson breathed a sigh of relief when the door opened on an empty elevator.

The guard station was the problem. He glanced at Legend and started to make his way there. Legend grabbed his arm and pulled him to a stop. "Let me. You don't have to do this."

"I do," Hudson said. "I'm not letting them frame you as something you aren't."

"This isn't you, either."

"Apparently, it is."

He pulled his arm away from Legend and approached the desk. He didn't wait for anyone to speak. Instead, he reached out past his own mind and into the three guards at their stations. The first two, he turned away from his arrival. They were so focused on their screens that they saw nothing else. They would stay that way until he released them. The third he smiled at. "Let us out now," he said calmly. It was an order, though, and the guard smiled back at him.

"Have a good night," the man said.

Legend exited before him, and Hudson kept control of the minds he'd touched until they were at the car he'd rented. There were no records to tie him to that, either.

"You're good at this life of crime thing," Legend said as they pulled away from the prison.

"I spend enough time around criminals. I think some of it rubbed off."

Legend laughed, and it was the first time Hudson had heard it. He smiled in return. "I have tickets for a ship leaving the planet in two hours."

"And where to then?"

Hudson shook his head. "Then we decide if we're going to hide or get you home."

"You're going to come with me?"

Hudson laughed then. "You didn't think I let you loose without knowing whether I could follow this cause of yours, did you? If you go back to it, I'll help you. Not... psychically. I won't be my father. But I've carried you in my head. I know you. I'll help you protect your people."

"We'll make them see you are nothing like your father," Legend assured him.

Hudson wasn't so sure about that. As much as he'd fought against his father's legacy, he was still walking a path taking him to rebellion.

He looked at Legend, though, and knew neither was doing this for power or money. There was no pot of gold at the end of this quest. They were just doing the right thing, no matter the power that stood against them. In the end, that was a power in and of itself.

They should have known better than to pair him with a political prisoner. He was driven to undo the legacy his father had left behind, and Legend's people needed his strength.

He would make a legend of Legend, a man beyond the reach of corruption. He would stand at Legend's side and show them all just who they had made enemies of. And they would find both men unrestrained, unrivaled, and unleashed.

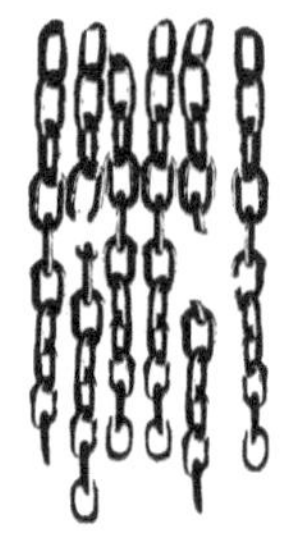

ANNABELLE
by
JOHN M. FLOYD

"YOU'RE A LUCKY lady," a man's voice said.

Helen Graham looked up at him from her hospital bed. The doctor had already informed her, when she finally opened her eyes, she'd broken both legs and her left arm and suffered a concussion. That didn't sound lucky—but she knew she was.

Both the doc and someone she'd not seen before stood over her now, looking like characters right out of network TV. White coat, solemn face, and stethoscope on one side of the bed; cowboy hat, beer gut, and sheriff's badge on the other.

"You're also an exception to the rule," the sheriff continued. "Not wearing your seat belt saved your life."

Helen blinked and managed to focus on him. His name tag said DRAPER.

"I was wearing my seat belt," she said. "I always do."

The only law she'd broken, she thought, was driving too fast. She did remember doing that, for what had seemed a good reason at the time: she was on her way to buy a last-minute birthday gift for her mother, a lamp she'd seen on a website for an antique shop out in the middle of nowhere. The problem was, her car's GPS had led her twenty miles off course. The last thing she remembered before the crash was a curvy dirt road with a tiny country church on one side, a deep ravine on the other, and a brown cow standing in the middle of the road just ahead of her. She would always wonder why she'd swerved left instead of right.

Afterward, only one thing stood out in her mind. The face of the man who had saved her.

She suddenly realized Sheriff Draper was talking to her.

"What did you say?" she asked.

"I said 'not this time.' Today, for some reason, you weren't buckled in. We found you lying on your back, twenty feet from your car. The vehicle itself was burned to a crisp—we figure it burst into flames when it hit the bottom, or shortly after." He raised his eyebrows. "You understand what I'm telling you, Ms. Graham? You were thrown clear, before impact. If you had been strapped in…"

Helen shook her head. "You're the one who doesn't understand. I wasn't thrown from the car."

The sheriff and doc exchanged a look. "You must've been," Draper said. "Even if the car didn't catch fire until afterward, your injuries would've kept you from—"

"Didn't anybody talk to the man who was there?" she asked. "An older man. Friendly face. Scar over his left eye." She started to raise her hand to touch her forehead to show them but found she couldn't. "He wore a floppy hat and overalls, like a farmer."

Draper frowned. "There was no one else there, Ms. Graham."

"This man was. He unbuckled me, picked me up. He carried me in his arms from the car."

Another glance passed between the two men. "I think it's time for you to rest a bit now," the doc said.

"Sheriff, listen to me. He must've left before you arrived—"

"No one carried you to where we found you, Ms. Graham. And you didn't walk there by yourself, either."

The room was beginning to spin. Helen tried to concentrate on what he had said. "How do you know that?"

"Because that gully was muddy. Everything was muddy—it rained yesterday."

"What does that—"

"That's enough for now," the doctor said. He gave the sheriff a hard look.

"No, wait," Helen said. "Answer me. What does it matter that it rained the day before?"

Sheriff Draper didn't move. His eyes stayed locked with Helen's.

"There were no footprints," he said quietly. "Not anywhere around you."

***

She stayed in the hospital for two more days, and at home for two months. Her boss at the bank's computer center allowed her to work remotely via her laptop, and her mother visited her often and did the grocery shopping. Not much else happened. Two broken legs can put a damper on one's social life.

No more was said about the accident. It was obvious nobody except her crazy great-aunt Winifred, who regularly embarrassed the family with things like palm readings and even seances, believed Helen's story about her phantom savior. At times, Helen almost doubted it herself. Such hallucinations were apparently not uncommon following situations like this, particularly those involving head injuries. And how could there have been no footprints?

But what Helen continued to see in her mind was too real, too clear to have merely been a dream. Footprints or not, someone had appeared from nowhere to rescue her that day in the gully, by that little church. She remembered feeling strong arms underneath her legs and back, lifting her right out of the driver's seat, and feeling the rough fabric of overalls against her cheek. Most of all, she remembered the way he looked. Grayish stubble, green eyes, jutting chin. A pale scar ran through and above his left eyebrow. A rugged but kind face. The owner of that face had saved her life.

And she planned to find him.

She did the preliminary snooping right there at home, between work and meals and network TV. She and Google Maps became close friends; from the comfort of her bed and her desk chair, she toured the crash site and the surrounding countryside. She wasn't too surprised to find that it was indeed the backside of beyond. The tiny church building and the gravestones in its cemetery seemed to be the only man-made structures anywhere close by. This was, after all, rural Mississippi. She saw that the road she'd been traveling dead-ended two miles south of the church, at what looked like a gravel driveway between a small barn and a farmhouse.

That would be as good a starting point as any.

***

One day in late September, exactly eleven weeks after the accident, Helen Graham was sitting in a rental car with a bottle of water and a state map—no more GPS for her, at least until she replaced her Honda, and maybe not even then, she thought—and heading west out of the city. She felt sore but functional, and ready to find some answers.

An hour later, she was on the dirt road she'd been driving the day of the accident. When she approached the spot, she saw the churned earth on the left shoulder where she had tried to brake after swerving to miss the cow, the tiny church and cemetery off to the right, and lush woods and pastures all around. Nothing else in sight.

She continued down the winding road toward the farmhouse she'd seen in the satellite image, the only one in the area. If the folks who lived there couldn't identify her guardian angel, maybe they'd know who could.

She located the house, parked, got out, and knocked at the screen door.

A woman in her fifties appeared in the doorway. At first, she just looked tired. Then she saw Helen and froze. Her eyes were wide, her bony hand clapped over her mouth.

"Annabelle?" she whispered through her fingers.

Helen just stood there. Before she could reply, the lady was grasped by the shoulders and gently pulled aside. Someone else took her place in the doorway and, as soon as Helen saw him, she forgot all about the woman.

This was the man who had saved her.

No, not quite, she thought. The face was a little different: wider, maybe, and more wrinkled. And there was no scar. It wasn't him—but the resemblance was unmistakable. The eyes were exactly the same. The knowledge thrilled her and chilled her at the same time.

He was studying her face as intently as she was studying his.

"Who are you?" he asked.

Helen swallowed. Pulling herself together, she glanced past him into the house. "I'm sorry if I frightened—"

"My sister-in-law," he said. "She's not well. What do you want?"

Helen took a long breath. "My name is Helen Graham. I'm the one who had the car wreck just down the road a few months ago. I wanted to..." She cursed herself silently. She hadn't given enough thought to what she intended to say. "I think—I think someone helped me that day. I want to find him." She swallowed again. "To find him and thank him."

The man seemed to think that over. Finally, he said, "I'm the only 'him' here, Missy, the only 'him' for miles around. And I wasn't there. All of us was here at home that day."

"All of you?"

"Me, my sister-in-law Martha, and her daughter Jessie. I'm sorry about what happened to you, and I'm glad to see you're okay and all, but we ain't the ones you're looking for."

Helen felt herself nod. But she couldn't leave, not without finding out something. This man looked so much like the person she had seen in her mind, over and over...

"You don't have any brothers in the area, then? Cousins, maybe?"

"He has a niece," a voice said. Helen looked behind her on the porch and saw a young woman about her own age. The new arrival smiled and thrust out her hand, her arm as straight as a ruler. "I'm Jessie Barlow. Sorry to sneak up on you. The grumpy man you're talking to is my Uncle Lester." As they shook hands, she added, "I heard what you said just now, and I'm glad you're all right."

"Thank you."

"Here, have a seat." Jessie backed up a step and pointed to a weathered porch swing. "It's cooler out here than in the house. Mama and Uncle Les don't believe in air conditioning."

Helen joined the young woman in the swing. Lester Barlow came out the screen door, stood there awkwardly for a second with his thumbs hooked in his overalls straps, then ducked his head and muttered, "Sorry if I was short with you, Missy." He stomped down the steps and around the corner.

Jessie turned to Helen. "We don't get many visitors," she said.

Helen gave her a weak smile. "Do most of them run off the road before they get here?"

Jessie grinned. "No, you're the first to do that." After a moment she said, "What is it you want to know?"

Helen hesitated. She really wished she had rehearsed some of this. "Like I told your uncle, I think somebody helped me that day. Saved me."

"Saved you how?"

"Saved my life. Pulled me out of a burning car. Carried me to safety."

"And then ran off?"

"I guess. The cops say nobody was there but me when they arrived."

"And this mystery man...you want to find him?"

"Just to thank him. And—I don't know. To see if he's real, I suppose."

Jessie Barlow studied her a moment. "You thought, at first at least, that he was my uncle?"

"Your uncle looks like the man I remembered. Too much so," Helen hesitated again, thinking, "too much for it to be a coincidence."

Jessie thought that over. "They all looked alike," she said. "The only person left who looks like Lester is his brother Nathan."

"Left?"

"They're the last of the Barlows. My daddy was the youngest, Nathan's the oldest—he's in a hospital up north. We haven't heard from him in years."

"You said 'was.' Your dad passed away?"

"Yes."

"And your Uncle Nathan," Helen said. "Is there any chance—"

"That he was here? No." Jessie paused. "It's not just a hospital. It's a mental institution. We were told not to visit and were assured he'd never be released."

"But it's a possibility, right? It could have happened."

Jessie finally shrugged. "I guess it's not impossible. But how could we not have known?"

Helen shook her head. "I don't know. But something strange is happening here, Jessie. Something's...not right."

Jessie just stared at her. "I don't know what to tell you, Ms. Graham—"

"Helen."

"I don't know what to say. Lester was here the whole time, the day of your accident. He was working on that gate over there, and Mama and I were shelling peas here on the porch. We only heard about it later that day, when the sheriff called us."

"Why'd he call you at all?"

"Looking for possible witnesses, he told us. Also, he'd found a cow wandering in the road, and wondered if she might've caused the wreck. Whether there might be a lawsuit."

"A lawsuit?"

"It was our cow," Jessie said. "A fence broke."

"Well, don't worry, I'm not suing anybody. I'm just trying to..." Helen paused. What *was* she trying to do? "I'm trying to figure this out."

"Closure?" Jessie asked. "Popular word, these days. You want closure?"

"I just want some sleep. I stay awake half the night, every night, thinking about this."

Before Jessie could reply, Helen had a thought. "What happened just now, with your mother? Who's Annabelle?"

Jessie's face changed. This time she was the one who swallowed. "That's a long story," she said.

"Did your mother—did she think I was…"

"You look like her," Jessie said. "Like Annabelle. Not a lot, but you're tall and thin, and blond-headed. Close enough that it must've scared her."

"Scared her why?"

Jessie shifted in her seat. "Because Annabelle died eight years ago. She was my sister."

Helen blinked. "Oh," she said. "I'm sorry."

Jessie started to respond, stopped, and then forged ahead. "The thing is…Mama's been a little on edge ever since we heard about your accident."

"Why?"

"Because it brought back memories, I think. Bad memories."

"What do you mean?"

A long pause. Jessie stared out past the driveway, into the green distance. "That gully you ran off into, where you wrecked your car? It's the place where Annabelle was killed."

Silence. In a hushed voice, Helen asked, "What happened?"

For a moment she didn't think Jessie would answer. When she did, it wasn't at all what Helen expected to hear.

Jessie said her mother, Martha, always entered jars of her plum jelly in the competition at the county fair in September. And she almost always won the blue ribbon—just a thirty-dollar prize, but, to the Barlow family, every little bit helped. The problem was, on that particular day eight years ago, Jessie's father Edgar wasn't around, and Lester was off at an auction upstate. None of the females in the family could drive—Annabelle and Jessie weren't quite old enough for a license, and their mother had never learned how—so after an hour of searching for Edgar, Martha decided to forget the contest that year. She tried to act as if it didn't matter, but her girls knew it did. So Annabelle had an idea.

The two teenagers waited until Martha was hoeing weeds in the back garden, then snuck the jelly jars out to the buckboard Edgar sometimes used to haul brush and lumber, hitched their old mule to it, and headed for the fair. The fairgrounds were five miles north of the church—a long trip for a mule and wagon—but almost no one traveled that road except on Sundays.

That day, though, someone did. A pickup full of kids blew through just as the girls were passing the church. The truck and the wild shouting spooked the mule, one of the wagon wheels slipped off the road into the ravine, and that was all it took. The buckboard went over the edge. Jessie was pitched aside and knocked cold, but Annabelle stayed aboard and was pinned underneath when the wagon overturned. The joyriders in the pickup kept driving and never saw what happened. The mule broke a leg, Jessie was unconscious for four hours, and Annabelle's chest was crushed. It was later believed that she died a slow and painful death.

Helen felt tears stinging her eyes by the time Jessie finished the story. Afterward, the two young women just sat there, saying nothing.

At last, Helen asked, "Where was your father? Why wasn't he here that day?"

"He was. He was passed out in the woods behind the house. Dead drunk."

The porch went completely quiet. Even the breeze seemed to stop.

"When he sobered up," Jessie said, "and found out what had happened..."

"He blamed himself?"

"Yes. For everything. I heard him tell Mama the next day, when I got out of the hospital, that if he'd been there he could've saved Annabelle, could've lifted that wagon right off of her." A shadow of a smile crossed her face. "He could've, too. He was that strong."

It occurred to Helen that his reasoning didn't make sense. If Edgar Barlow had been around, the girls wouldn't have had to take the buckboard in the first place.

Jessie seemed to read her mind. "He wasn't thinking straight. He kept saying, 'If I just hadn't been so far away.'" She stopped and shook her head. "Daddy never recovered. He died the following month. Most thought it was the booze that killed him, but the doc just said it was a broken heart."

Another silence. Then, suddenly, Helen had a thought.

"Where is he buried?"

Jessie looked up at her. "What?"

"Your father," Helen said. Somehow she kept her voice calm. "Where's your father buried?"

"In our church cemetery."

"The one beside the road where you and your sister had the accident? Where I had my accident?"

"Yes. Why?"

Helen felt sweaty; her stomach churned. She couldn't believe what she was thinking.

"They told me my driver's side door was gone, ripped off its hinges," she said as if to herself. "How could that have happened?"

"What do you mean?"

"I mean the car was going downhill, Jessie. There were no trees near, or in, that gully. No rocks. The car didn't turn over. How'd my door get torn clean off?"

Jessie let out a sigh. "Who knows? Look, Ms. Gra—Helen—you've been through a traumatic—"

"I have to ask you something. Okay?"

Jessie sat there, waiting. She looked drained.

"Do you have any photos of your father?"

"Photos? No. My family never was much on taking pictures." She smiled a little, remembering. "But he had a kind face, my daddy. A friendly face."

Helen took a long, shaky breath. She leaned closer and asked, carefully, "Did he have a scar?" She raised a finger to a point just above her left eyebrow. "Did he have a scar right here?"

Jessie's mouth dropped open. Her body had gone rigid, her eyes wide.

"How could you know that?" she murmured.

***

Helen stayed another ten minutes or so, there on the porch in the afternoon sun, the young city woman and the young country woman, lost in their own thoughts. Jessie, looking confused and upset but trying hard not to show it, did insist that since they hadn't seen her uncle Nathan in so many years, he could of course have a scar too by now. And now that she'd given it some thought, sure, he could have been released without their knowing it, could've come down here and maybe even left again without their knowing it. Who would've figured Nathan for something like that, she said, but thank God he must've been there, at the right place at the right time. Helen thought that explanation fell into the I-need-to-convince-myself category, but she had nodded politely and agreed. That could indeed have happened.

When she rose to leave and held out her hand, Jessie Barlow hugged her instead, hugged her hard and long. There wasn't much left to say.

Helen drove back down the dirt road to the accident site and parked in front of the church. It took less than two minutes to find the tombstone. A small, simple marker bearing the words EDGAR BARLOW, 1959-2007. As she had suspected, the grave was at the front edge of the cemetery, only about thirty feet from where Helen's Honda had plunged off the road.

You weren't too far away this time, Edgar, she thought.

Hugging her elbows and strangely at peace, Helen Graham sat down in the fallen leaves between Barlow's headstone and a similar marker for Annabelle. Helen stayed there until the shadows grew long and the crickets starting chirping in the woods across the road. Then she wiped her eyes and climbed into the rental and drove back to town.

Tomorrow, she decided, she would call Aunt Winifred. Maybe she wasn't so crazy after all.

Face Id
By
S. Faxon

Jesse didn't have a drink all night. She sat at the bar's table with Chelsea and me for two hours with nothing in front of her.

No beer, no cocktails, not even water. She just sat there, staring at me as Chelsea and I downed a pitcher and talked about the bullshit day at work.

When I ordered a round of appetizers for the table, she declined to take a wing or a cheese stick, waving her hand and flatly saying, "No, thanks."

My stomach was finally on the mend after enduring food poisoning last week, so I didn't think much of it beyond *You're insulting our neighborhood bar but, fine, more for me.*

But the longer we sat there, the more uncomfortable it became.

Jesse's buggy blue eyes, framed by camel-like eyelashes pointed *into* me. The feeling of dread her eyes bore into me made my stomach so uncomfortable that I almost didn't want to eat, but she was not going to ruin this night for me. I should have known this was going to happen. Jesse was a creep at work, but Chelsea was too nice and invited her out with us when Jesse pushed in on our conversation about our plans for the night. She'd said she knew the place, that she lived down the block from it, but that she'd never been here. Chelsea, in her typical sweet way, shared that we lived nearby it too and that she should join us.

Chelsea's own kindness left her blind and she didn't seem to notice the dirty-nailed creeper staring at me. Being watched while trying to eat, felt like everything I was doing was wrong and being hyper self aware while eating a sloppy food like chicken wings drained all the pleasure from it.

Ugh, Jesse. Why'd you have to come?

The pitcher of red beer ran out, and I couldn't wait to get out of there, but I couldn't leave Chelsea alone with Jesse. My desk was in between theirs at work and, in the rare times Jesse was actually at her desk, I'd see her listening in on Chelsea's conversations, watching her every move as she typed, stood up, walked away, walked back. At least twice a week, Jesse would leap across the office and skip to Chelsea's desk to sing her a high-pitched "Good morning!" which split the rest of our ears.

A chill ran down my spine.

It didn't feel like a healthy work-crush situation. Nothing about Jesse and her pale skin seemed healthy.

Why the hell aren't you drinking or eating? It's not like you're worried about paying us back. You make three times what I do, and you don't do shit. You eat this kind of stuff during the day; I know, because I have to endure listening to you smack your fucking food around in your mouth like a farm animal.

I wanted to slip Chelsea a text crying to her how I felt like a prisoner in a village of cannibals with Jesse, but the way she looked at me, told me that she knew what I was thinking. She and I had known each other for years at work. We'd worked our tails off in our marketing team to claw our way up the ranks, and then came Jesse, a cousin of one of our bosses and, of course, even with no marketing experience, she was suddenly somehow God's gift to our department. It had felt like the morale had been sucker-punched out of our entire team but, at the end of the day, we got to go home, and I didn't have to think about Jesse. And yet, here she sat, staring at me as I tried to eat my favorite wings at my home away from home.

Chelsea, please, *let's go.*

The waitress came over to our booth and pointed at our glasses. "Would you guys like another round?"

"No!" I shouted. I shrunk down in the booth and shot my eyes toward the sticky floor. "Sorry, Taz," I apologized to the waitress, but I couldn't pull my wallet out fast enough.

"Hey, Danny, you wanna split it?" I heard Chelsea ask, but I'd already shoved forty dollars at Taz and told her to keep the change.

Taz's brows raised. "You sure?" It was wing night, so the bill was probably only around half that.

Just take the money and let us leave.

"Yeah, yeah, I'm sure, Taz, thanks." My voice was shaking. Every part of my being was screaming at me to escape from this booth. Like my instincts were telling me that Jesse's silent face was actually a mask covering the bones of a demon.

"I'll send you what I owe you." Chelsea pulled up her phone and held it up so that it logged in with face recognition.

"No, no, it's all good." I pushed her arm down and motioned toward the door. "It's been a long day. Maybe it's time we head out?"

Chelsea beamed at me with her radiant smile.

God, you really are pretty. Fuck-face over there can just go crawl back in her hole if she thinks she's got a chance with you. Not that I intend to let her get anywhere near you.

Chelsea turned to Jesse and clapped her hands together. She was the perpetual cheerleader. "Thanks for coming out with us. Did you have a good time?"

Jesse broke her stare at me, and I felt like the weight of a building crumbled off my back.

"Oh yeah!" Her child-like voice sang out. She nodded with her entire body, her dirty-nailed hands clapping. "Yes! Let's do it again!"

Let's not.

Ever.

It wasn't natural, how she spoke. Like the demon inside was trying to pose as a four-year-old in the body of an adult.

Jesse's shoulders drooped, and her voice came to a more tolerable level as she said, "I really appreciate this, you guys. I haven't been out since, well, really *before*, my dad died."

I'm sorry, what?

My stomach clenched, I felt like I was going to throw up.

Your dad died?

"I was taking care of him for," she made a raspberry sound, "I don't know, my entire life. Mom didn't deal with either of us or much of anything, so, yeah." Her wide eyes turned up to Chelsea. She looked happy, but still in an unnatural, manic sort of way. "Thanks."

So I'm a fucking dick. Wouldn't anyone be a little weird if they were forced to take care of their parent their whole life? So maybe that's why her cousin has been so lenient with her at work; it wasn't just nepotism, he's letting her grieve. Would it be acceptable for me to excuse myself to go throw up? I'm the worst human on the planet.

Chelsea listened intently and then uttered a wave of supportive words I couldn't find myself. I nodded along and said something to the effect of, "I'm really sorry," and made a mental note to try to be nicer to her at work. To say good morning to her as opposed to grunting when she bursts into the room singing. And to just think of her as a human being who's hurting as opposed to a festering thorn in my side.

"Thanks, guys," Jesse said again. "It means a lot."

As Chelsea and I waved goodbye to Jesse outside the bar, I thought, *Is it really so bad for her to have a work crush on Chelsea? Chelsea is clearly not interested in her. Maybe Chelsea's the only bit of sunshine that tortured fucking soul has. She definitely makes my day better.*

I sighed, feeling the weight of the night rolling off my shoulders as I walked Chelsea to her car. She was parked behind the bar, next to my truck. We could have walked to our homes as we normally did when we drank here, but, as revealing as tonight had been with Jesse, I wanted to go for a little drive to process it all.

"Hey," Chelsea started, leaning against her car door. She held the handful of keys and various keyrings she'd collected over the years up to her heart, her lovely eyes glowing at me even in the dim light of this small alley. "Thanks."

"For what?"

She shrugged. "You know. I know Jesse makes you uncomfortable, but see, she's just been hurting."

It felt like my actual soul shrank and tried to hide in my gut. "I know. I feel so bad for being such a dick to her."

"Stop. She's fine. I know you may not want to, but we all live close by, so let's try to invite her out maybe like once a month or something?"

Chelsea could have asked me to invite Jesse out every night and, with her beautiful heart glowing like it was, I would have said yes.

I nodded.

Chelsea leaned forward, and her lips met my cheek. "Thanks, Danny. See you tomorrow?"

I felt like I was floating. Like I'd ascended from this parking lot beside the bar's smelly trash bins and was in the clouds.

Like a brainless idiot, I only nodded again.

Her bright smile radiated at me as she got into her car, reversed, and slowly drove away. The excitement within me was building. It needed to erupt out of me in a shout, a fist pump, a jump, anything, but I couldn't while I was still in view of her mirrors. I stood there, watching her car until it turned onto the main street and her taillights disappeared.

A white excitement started to fill me. I felt like I could fly.

A thud and the sound of glass shattering struck the back of my head, filling me with white pain instead.

My body hit the asphalt, sending thralls of pain against my entire side.

The parking lot swayed up and down. I tried to blink to make it straighten out. The pain in my head hurt so much, it felt like I was going to throw up.

I put my hand down on the rough asphalt, felt the bite of glass rip through my palm.

"Shit!" I tried to recoil my hand, but everything hurt so bad.

A second blow hit the side of my head.

My body went limp.

As a vignette of darkness began to take my sight, I heard a child-like voice say, "I think I *will* have a drink now."

***

Am I hungover? How much did I drink?

When I woke up, my head felt like it had been hit by a bus, and my throat was so dry.

I tried to lick my lips, but something was in the way.

I opened my eyes.

What the hell?

I tried to rip out the thing shoved in my mouth, but my wrists were bound, my arms stretched out away from my sides. My head felt like it was being stabbed, but I looked at my hands. My wrists were tied to what looked like a trundle bed's black posts.

Holy. Shit.

I looked down. My ankles were also bound to the black metal posts at the end of the bed.

My eyes shot around the space that surrounded me. There was a teddy bear-shaped night light plugged into the wall nearest me, but otherwise no light. It didn't even look like there were windows. On the far side of the room, I thought I saw a line of wooden stairs leading down into this room.

The space I was in was big, like a studio.

Is this a converted garage?

"Shit!"

Don't worry about what it is—just get out!

I started to wriggle my hands. The line was tight, but I was bound with rope, not metal cuffs.

I can get out of this. I gotta get out of this!

A door opened.

I froze.

The sound of shoes coming down the stairs echoed through the space.

Sweat poured down my face as I twisted my hands every which way I could. The right side was starting to feel like I was making progress, but then a light turned on.

Jesse stood in the center of the room. Below the light in the ceiling fan, the chain she'd pulled swung back and forth. Only one bulb was lit of the four, sending shadows across her face that made my skin crawl.

My gut at the bar had been right—she actually looked like a demon.

I tried to scream, "WHAT THE FUCK IS WRONG WITH YOU?" but the gag in my mouth stopped me.

She shook her head and approached, a hand behind her back.

What're you hiding?

"I really did mean thanks for taking me out tonight, but I know it wasn't your idea." She snorted. "I know you *hate* me." With one hand, she made air quotes when she said "hate." "I thought I'd be able to have a little more time with Chelsea after I slipped a little something in your coffee last week."

You poisoned me?

"And I guess it worked a little, 'cause she invited me out tonight, but I just…I know what I have to do." She kept walking closer. With every step, I felt my heart beating against my ribs so hard it hurt.

Frantically, I tried to wriggle my hands out of the ropes again. I didn't care if she could see me.

"She's clearly into you, so tonight I tried to memorize the little expressions you make, how you hold yourself, how you talk to her. But I realized that even if I can mimic you, it doesn't really matter, because Chelsea *still* hasn't given me her number."

You're insane. I'm not giving you her number. What the fuck *is happening?*

"I can't just mimic you. I need to *be* you."

She leapt toward me, swinging something silver at my face.

I tried to squirm away, but her claws grasped my jaw, her nails digging into my skin.

"Hold still!" she yelled, as my muffled scream echoed through my gag.

The knife pierced my flesh like ice biting into my skin.

My eyes flooded with tears as my nerves erupted. Every muscle in my body tensed and twitched as she cut beneath my ear, following my jawline.

Blood poured down my neck and into my ear.

It was as if I could feel the blade in my teeth, like chewing on foil.

I couldn't breathe. My body was trying to hyperventilate but, between choking on the gag and trying not to pass out from the pain, there was nothing I could do.

She drew her hand away and flicked it. Pellets of my blood shot out and landed on my face.

"Ooh, this is messy."

She put her bloodied hands on her hips and stared down at me.

I tried to scoot away from her on the thin mattress, but my arm was already as stretched as it could go. Beneath my shoulders, blood saturated my shirt and pooled on the mattress.

The room was starting to spin, like I was out in the middle of the ocean, the waves swelling and tossing me about.

This bitch is going to kill me.

She turned her back and walked toward a tall set of drawers that I hadn't noticed before.

It was taking everything I had for me to keep my eyes open. Maybe I could escape the pain by just passing out. It would be better, right? I wouldn't feel it. I wouldn't feel anything anymore.

The hell are you saying? Fight or you are going to die!

I looked up to my right hand. The bond was looser. I pulled and pushed, twisted back and forth.

Though my entire right side felt like it was on fire, I wriggled my wrist every which way, twisting this way and that. The rope bit into my skin, but it was slipping. The rope was slipping!

"Hey!" She was coming back at me, a shirt wrapped around her hand, the blood-stained blade shining in the light, level with her heart.

I twisted my hand as quickly as I could.

The bond loosened, just enough...

I pulled my hand free right as she tackled me.

***

The text Chelsea received a little after midnight said, "Hey, is it ok if I come over? I've had a really bad night."

"Of course," Chelsea texted back. "Everything ok?"

"I'll explain when I get there."

But I was already out front, standing in her driveway.

How did I get here? Did I walk? Did I drive? We only live a mile apart, but I wasn't home when I started, was I?

By the time my body made it to her front door, my feet dragging across the grass, I felt like I hadn't eaten or slept in days. Like I'd become subhuman, living in a fog, and the only thing that would revive me to my normal self would be to see Chelsea's face.

I drew my heavy hand up to her door and pounded my fist against it.

It took less than a minute for her to respond, but it might have been days as far as I could tell. I heard the locks click on the other side and, as the doorknob began to turn, I noticed the bloody stain I left on the face of the door.

The door opened.

Chelsea's expression went from excitement to concern to horror. She screamed, then collapsed to the floor.

I wasn't fast enough to catch her.

As I knelt to see how I could help her, I realized there was something in my other hand. It was squishy, sticky, and wet. I held it up over Chelsea's motionless body, and the fog cleared.

When Jesse had tackled me, my freed hand reached up. Her knife had slashed through my forearm, and blood ran up my arm, blending with the pool from my face.

But my fingers had dug into her neck, piercing her skin. With an animalistic force I didn't know was in me, I'd ripped my grasp back with all my strength.

She tried to take my face, so I took her throat.

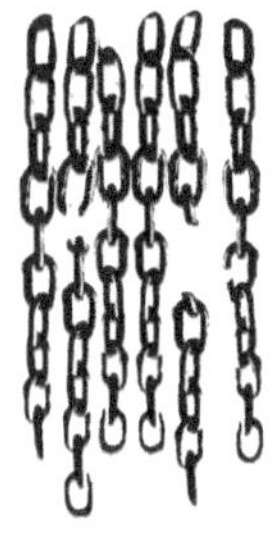

Gentle And Hate
By
Stephen Oliver

6th April, Hate

I hate my great-to-the-fourth grandfather, Henry.

What's happening to me is all his fault. If he hadn't been fiddling about, trying to split his good side from his bad, I wouldn't be in this mess. I wish I could kill him. Maybe I can, with a little help.

Anyway, Doc Chapman has told me to write down my thoughts and emotions. He believes it will help him heal me. He thinks that if the two parts of me communicate with each other, we'll be cured.

What does he know?

Oh well, it will give me something to do when I'm not hating Henry.

————————

April 7th, Gentle

It is my time to be me, again.

I dislike those periods when I am not in control. It is not even blackness, where I could at least think. Instead, it is as if I cease to exist. I blank out, and then I am back again, but time has passed. Time I am not even aware of. I never have any idea when it will happen, either.

Dr. Chapman came in earlier today and told me about the notebook on the table. He says he wants me to communicate with my other side. If he thinks it will help, I will give it a try. He promises he will not examine it until I/we allow him to.

I asked him again why I suddenly get blocked out. He finally relaxed enough and talked about the hyper and the alter personalities. The hyper may be aware of what the alter is doing, but not vice versa. The alter never knows what the hyper does.

Does this mean that I'm the alter?

————————

8th April, Hate

Ha! He thinks he's the alter. It's obvious that I am. After all, I just disappear whenever he wants to assert control. Lying little toad.

I was allowed out to join the encounter group again today. After I promised that I wouldn't try to tear anyone's face off with my teeth.

It was all that stupid cow's fault, anyway. If she hadn't made nasty jokes about my condition, I wouldn't have had to teach her a lesson.

At least I won't have to see her face for a while. Nurse Green told me the bitch is going to be in the medical ward for at least another month, waiting for her skin graft to take.

I'll just tear it off if I catch her making remarks about me again, so everyone else can see how horrible she looks on the inside.

————————

April 9th, Gentle

Wow! My other half is really vicious.

I suppose it should not be a surprise, given what is happening to us. After all, that was Henry's intention in the first place.

I had another session with Dr. Chapman this afternoon. He still believes that I/we am/are suffering from an extreme form of Dissociative Identity Disorder (which they used to call "Multiple Personality Disorder"). We had an interesting discussion about how the different personalities use different parts of the brain. He thinks I use some parts and they use others. He wants to prove this by doing MRI and MEG (Magneto Encephalogram) scans when each of us is in control.

I have given him permission, but I have a feeling that the other will not be so tractable.

————————

10th April, Hate

If that bastard Chapman thinks he's going to put me inside some machine, he's got another think coming.

I'll fight him every step of the way, so they'll get a crappy scan. That is, if they can even force me into that thing in the first place.

There's no way I'll agree to this.

————————

April 11th, Gentle

That was not so bad.

They injected me with a solution that makes the blood vessels and cells in the brain stand out better, then placed me in the machine. I had to lie still for half an hour while they moved me slowly back and forth.

Dr. Chapman showed me some of the images afterwards, displaying the parts of my brain that work the most. It was fascinating.

I wonder what he is going to have to do to get the other to go into the machine.

————————

12th April, Hate

OK, so I let them do it after all.

I mean, he went and did it, and I can't look as if I'm scared of doing anything that he does. The sissy.

Besides, Doc Chapman promised me I can spend more time with George, who's in the next room. I like him because he's nothing like me. I don't want to hurt him. Not like I want to do to most of the other people around here. They say he's just delusional. I think he's brilliant and they're too dumb to realise what a genius he is.

Lying still for half an hour wasn't so easy, but Doc Chapman only had to tell me twice to stop fidgeting, so I guess it was all okay.

I wonder what the scans showed.

————————

April 13th, Gentle

Today, they used the MEG apparatus to detect what my brain was doing when I was resting, walking, talking, writing, etc. It is supposed to be more accurate than an EEG because it can map individual neuron groups instead of whole complexes. They put something like a hairnet with hundreds of tiny sensors on my head, with the main cable leading down to a transmitter box on a belt.

I spent much of the day doing what I normally do but, every so often, one of them would ask me to do something completely different.

————————

14th April, Hate

They put that net with all the little bits in it on my head today. I must have looked like a right dork.

I caught a couple of the other inmates with sly grins. They looked away when I glared at them. I didn't hurt them because I've promised Doc Chapman that I won't.

If I do hurt anyone, then he'll stop me seeing George, and that won't do.

We've got a little plan to escape from this hellhole.

————————

April 15th, Gentle

I had another interesting conversation with Dr. Chapman this afternoon. He is utterly perplexed by the images. He showed me two of them. Apparently, when there are multiple personalities, some parts of the brain are used by all of them, for such things as movement, breathing, etc. Other sections are only available to one or the other.

Ours are unique.

It seems that no parts are shared at all! Moreover, they are mirror images of one another. I thought he had mistakenly brought me two copies of the same picture, reversing one of them, but he assured me that they are correct. The two of us are literally using only half of our capacity, because each is only using half of our brain, although scattered across both hemispheres.

He explained that, while I am right-handed, my other self is left-handed. He was sure what we see on these MRIs and MEGs accounts for that fact.

It probably explains why we are such opposites, too.

————————

16th April, Hate

Doc Chapman had to tell me what the pictures meant.

I finally understood that my other self and me, we're each only half a person.

Damn Grandfather Henry! He did this to us! I hate him even more now I know that half of myself is cut off from me. How could he be so stupid?

I asked Doc what the other side of me is like.

He told me that he's a gentle intellectual who couldn't hurt a fly. He loves reading and science and poetry and everything like that.

I told Chapman to describe me to my other self.

He thinks it might be a good idea.

————————

April 17th, Gentle

So now I know what the other is like. They are my exact opposite in every respect: emotional, destructive, harbouring spite and rancour. These are just a few of the words Dr. Chapman used to describe them. I am rational and perhaps too sane, he said, while they are driven by emotion.

Just like our great-great-great-great-grandfather and his alter ego. It is reflecting down through the generations, although I do not know whether any of our ancestors actually suffered from the split as badly as we do.

I have a lot to think about.

————————

18th April, Hate

Hey, other self, are you listening to me?

I have a proposal to make.

If Doc Chapman is right, and we're only half-people, so to speak, can't we still pool our resources?

I think I might know a way out of here. Would you be interested in helping?

————————

April 19th, Gentle

I have thought long and hard about what you have written, and I have decided that talk costs little.

I, too, am becoming very bored with life in this place. Everything is regimented, even to the times we are allowed to encounter other people.

I have read that you become angry when they look at you as if you were something terrible and strange. I must tell you that they look at me the same way, and I am deeply hurt by their expressions and harsh words.

What exactly do you have in mind?

————————

20th April, Hate

I know that they're watching us day and night, but George in the next room is a great inventor, even if they think he's as crazy as a loon.

He told me last month that his great-to-the-fourth grandfather was also an inventor. In fact, he invented the world's first real time machine. George knows all about it. Not only does he think he can duplicate it, but he believes he can actually improve on it.

What do you think of the idea of the three of us (well two of us, really, I suppose) using it to get out of here?

————————

April 21st, Gentle

Surely time travel is an illusion?

I have been reading about it on the Internet, and most physicists believe it is impossible. Something to do with relativity, reversal of world lines, and the Cosmic Sensor. How does George think he can get past these problems?

If we do succeed, what do you intend to do afterwards?

I mean, do we use the machine to move to a time when all the doors are open, or will we be going back to before the construction of the building? Then what will we do?

———————

22nd April, Hate

George says it'll work because it isn't a relativistic machine at all. It relies on quantum paradoxes and discontinuities, whatever they are. Either way, he's sure it'll work. We just have to be close enough when he starts it up.

I intend to go back over a hundred years, to the time Henry started his experiments. And then I'll kill him before he does.

Are you coming with me?

———————

April 23rd, Gentle

Are you sure this will work?

We are dealing with the so-called Grandfather Paradox here, after all. If we kill him before his children are born, then we will not be born either. If we are not born, we cannot go back in time to kill him, so he will be able to create his potion. And so on, around and around. Either way, it will not be possible.

Unless, of course, the attempt switches us to another timeline. I cannot be certain what will happen then.

———————

24th April, Hate

Dumbo!

I want to aim for a time after his children were born but before he started his experiments. That should be a timespan of around ten years. If we kill him then, we'll either cease to exist, or we'll be born as a normal person with no memory of the hell he's put us through. Either possibility is better than what we've got now.

By the way, I've hidden a sheet of paper at the back of this notebook. It's a list of items George needs to complete his machine. I'm not sure what they are, but he says they're vital. They won't let him near the workshop anymore, and they don't trust me because I'm too friendly with him.

Can you get them for us?

———————

April 25th, Gentle

I have started to collect the pieces together and have hidden them in a hollow book I found in the library.

However, I believe I may have found a flaw in your plan. While I was reading up on Henry's case, I found a hint that things were much more complicated than we first thought.

I have to research further before I am sure. I will let you know in two days' time, when I am back.

———————

26th April, Hate

What's the problem?

Do you think that we won't be able to travel through time? Won't we be able to kill Henry? Or is there something wrong with us, so we won't be able to carry out our plan?

Let me know, for God's sake. The thought that I might be stuck like this for the rest of my life is enough to make me want to kill myself.

And I don't think you'll like that.

———————

April 27th, Gentle

Calm down, please. Do not do anything drastic until I have had time to explain myself.

I have done more searching on the Internet, especially on the Blacknet. That is a part of the Deep Web that concerns itself with the supernatural. Your friend George was able to show me how to circumvent the censorship software on the library computers without being detected.

Apparently, Henry's experiments are well known there. Many have tried to replicate them, but to no avail.

It seems that, in his desperation, he resorted to more drastic means than chemistry. It would appear at least one component of his elixir came from a supernatural source. In other words, he used Black Magic.

It was this factor that led to the release of his alter ego in the first place, and its lack later that prevented him from suppressing that other self again.

It is because of this that the curse has come down the generations to strike us, since supernatural entities are timeless.

————————

28th April, Hate

Oh crap!

Does that mean we're going to be stuck like this forever? I don't want to have to kill myself just to get away from myself.

Take a deep breath. That's better.

Look, let's forget this problem for the moment, shall we?

How's the search for those components going? George says he's got everything else ready. All he'll need to do is insert them in the right places, and we can go.

He'll make a short shift to a time when our doors are open because we're both at the encounter group. Once he's in my room, he'll hide and wait for me to come back. Then we'll make the big jump backwards.

OK?

————————

April 29th, Gentle

I have placed the components in George's room, next to the rest of his machine.

It is not very large, is it? I assume that it generates a field around itself that isolates the people nearby from the flow of time. I do hope that it works.

I am pleased to tell you that I have discovered the name of the entity that Henry contacted. It is my hope we can persuade it to provide something to make the elixir into an effective means of merging us into a single person.

No matter what happens, I want you to be aware that I love you, because you are the half of me I have never known.

————————

30th April, Hate

This is for you, Doctor Chapman, because I know you're going to read this after I've gone, you prick!

A few minutes ago, just after George and I were locked into our respective rooms for the night, I found him hiding under my bed.

That shows that his time machine works!

I'm writing this so you'll know that we've beaten you.

Once I've got all of great-to-the-fourth grandfather's secrets out of him, I'm going to kill him.

After that, I think I'll find out who your ancestors are, and I'll kill them too.

When that's done, George and I will set out on a great adventure, travelling to wherever and whenever we want to.

Goodbye, you bastard. I hope you rot in the same hell as Henry!

————————

1st May, 20 - Notes from Doctor Carmichael Chapman-Eddowes, psychiatrist in charge of Bedlam Hospital for the Insane.

This has been the most perplexing case of my career.

Patient Z was delivered to this facility after the deaths of their parents, presumably at the hands of the patient. There was no way anyone else could have entered the premises.

It was evident from the first that they were suffering from Dissociative Identity Disorder, although this is the most extreme form I have ever heard of.

They both refused to communicate their names, stating that they had never been given any. As a result, the staff took to calling them "Gentle" and "Hate," after their most prominent traits.

The switch between them was so regular that I could almost have set my watch by it. Every day, between nine and ten in the morning, there would be the shift from the one to the other, taking no more than a minute to occur. I have been reliably informed that this was the time of their birth.

What has made this case so confusing are the changes in the state of the patient as their personality altered. I know that physiological changes can manifest themselves as different aspects come forward. In most cases, this shows itself as variations in the tension of the muscles of the face and body, making them look like different people.

I am also aware of more pronounced changes. The most interesting are those of a patient of a friend of mine incarcerated in a psychiatric penal ward for the murder of her spouse. The woman in question is a diabetic when personality A appears, but not when B or C are manifested.

However, this one was even more extreme. "Gentle" was a fully-functioning male, capable of producing viable sperm, while "Hate" was equally female, ovulating and menstruating regularly during their stay with us. Blood tests confirmed the change was all the way down to a biochemical and even chromosomal level.

Their disappearance is a matter of grave concern, as the "Hate" phase is particularly dangerous.

There is no known way they could have absconded. Patient Z was locked into her room (she was in her female phase at the time) at 19:07 by Nurse Green. The CCTV system confirms this, as do the computer records for the doors.

At 8:00 the next morning, the room was empty. The bed had not been slept in.

Equally worrying is the absence of the patient from the adjacent room, one George H. Wells.

Roman and Romana
by
Lara Yamada

It was one of the worst hotel rooms she'd ever seen.

Room 116 was on the first floor facing the parking lot. Massive cracks ran along the drywall in the ceiling, the dark carpet had stains that left even darker streaks and swirls, and a musty odor blew out from the air conditioning unit under the window.

I can't believe we're paying for this, Ramona thought. *He's paying for this,* she amended. She lifted a small luggage trunk onto the bed and unclipped the orange buckles. She'd wanted to travel for so long, but this was not a welcome first stop.

Her eyes traveled lovingly over the old luggage. She kept it rubbed with leather conditioner and ready to go since she had found it at a thrift store a decade ago. It barely fit two days' worth of clothes, but she made it work. She just wished she had asked Roman to clarify what he meant when he told her the job included travel benefits "within the United States."

Despite the motel's remote location far from the freeway, they still had Wi-Fi, and she could log into her bank account. It gave her a thrill to see money in her checking account. The short written contract hadn't seemed real when she'd signed it a month ago, but the payday proved it wasn't a scam.

"$2,000 a week for each week of travel. Hotels, meals, and all travel expenses covered. Bonus commission for every energy anomaly identified."

Before Ramona could plot too far into how she'd spend her first paycheck, she noticed movement from the side of the bed. Something small and fast. She should try to identify it before calling the front desk to complain so the maintenance man would know if he had to bring a mousetrap or insecticide.

Why had Roman picked such a dump?

She swung her legs off the bed and crouched on the floor. The bright light of her cell phone illuminated old wrappers, dust bunnies, and a crumpled magazine. Then she saw something else and froze.

The reflection from the floor-length mirror on the other side of the bed showed an upright pair of nondescript brown pants with uneven and tattered pant hems and scuffed shoes.

She'd only been on the floor for three seconds, and the person stood on the opposite side of the room from the door. With this logic in mind, she knew the person she saw wasn't alive.

Her nostrils flared. Several inhales filtered oxygen through the musty debris in the air and helped her through the routine she practiced to stay calm. She pushed the unwelcome feeling of panic to the back of her mind, and she steeled herself with the knowledge that *this* was the real reason she'd accepted the gig.

Ramona suffered from severe anxiety. Therapy was limited because the root of therapy success relied on honesty, and her therapist believed the ghosts she saw were hallucinations. Whether real or imagined, the path to peace required control. If she was hallucinating, she had to stop her mind from seeing the ghosts or, if they were real, she had to stop the ghosts from appearing.

She didn't think the latter was possible until she met Roman.

He had sold her with two lines. "We will eliminate the spirits completely. They will cease to exist."

The only way to avoid most unpleasantness with ghosts was to pretend like she didn't see them. She rose from the floor, kept her eyes averted, and dialed Roman's number with her back turned to the ghost.

"It's Ramona," she said in a hushed voice. The man started to shuffle closer to her side of the bed, and she corrected her tone. "Let's meet in the lobby," she said more forcefully.

She remembered his sales pitch now and wondered if the money would be worth it.

When Roman had picked her up this morning, he'd arrived in a Jeep Wrangler with off-road additions. The massive front bumper was splattered with bug guts, and the treads on the double-size tires caked in dried mud. She had stood on the curb outside of her trailer and wondered how she was supposed to get in. Her neighbors, watching from their windows, were probably wondering if she *should* get in.

He had immediately informed her that their first stop was in the middle-of-nowhere desert in southwest Arizona, in the Yuma Territorial Prison State Historic Park. His mannerisms were calm and controlled. He didn't say anything when a truck driver cut him off, nor when they passed a four-car accident. He seemed deep in his own thoughts and drove mostly in the middle lane. Despite the appearance of his Jeep, he was not an aggressive driver.

There wasn't much talking, so she snuck looks at him from the passenger seat and gave in to petty thoughts. He was average height, average weight, and wore average clothes. She'd seen him three times, and he'd worn the same dark t-shirt and jeans combo each time. His face, however, was exceptional. He wore his dark hair in a ponytail, and his heavy eyebrows and brown eyes were slanted into a discerning gaze. She had wished her friends could see her and wonder where she was going with him. But since arriving at this motel, that thought had vanished.

Once she had passed at least four room doors, she allowed herself a quick backward glance. The headless man hadn't followed.

Relieved, she waited by a potted fig tree, touched the tip of one shiny leaf to see if it was fake, and watched Roman emerge through the main lobby doors. The door caught on the curled edge of a welcome mat, and the 110-degree heat and the smell of hot asphalt lingered until the woman at check-in kicked it closed with one expert whack.

"You saw one," he said bluntly.

"Room 116. Here's the key."

"That was fast." He looked at her directly for the first time all day. "What can I do?"

"Nothing. Wait for me here," he said, and offered her his room key.

She had expected him to retrieve equipment for the spirit extraction. It would be something large and bulky, as new technology prototypes seemed to be. But Roman headed for Room 116 without any gear.

Roman's room was cleaner. The AC unit wasn't a yellowed hunk of plastic with faded buttons, but it didn't seem any more effective. Both rooms were simultaneously cold and damp. With a sigh, she sat in the armchair by the window. She had given up on a semester of community college classes for this. He had explained little of the process, and now she wasn't even part of it.

He was too secretive.

Ramona eyed the black bag on his nightstand. She knew almost nothing about him. In a moment of sudden conviction, she sprang for the bag and zipped it.

She looked down at a neatly folded pair of dark jeans, socks, a black shirt, and white underwear. She took a moment to revel in the fact that Roman wore tighty-whities. But still no tech and no gear. She swept her hand along a side pocket and pulled out a white envelope.

There was a thin bundle of hundred-dollar bills, a pair of keys, and a passport-sized photo of Roman. There was also one of her.

She nearly collided with him on her way out the door, and she was careful to position herself into the hallway before she held it up for him to see.

"Why do you have a photo of me?" she demanded.

"That's from our employer."

"I thought you were my employer."

"There's someone funding both our efforts."

"Who?"

Roman looked down the end of the hallway. "Let's continue inside."

She didn't budge. She'd seen plenty of TV shows that warned her of these moments.

"I got your info from our employer. Name, campus, and the photo. How do you think I found you?"

"You told me you were researching ghosts."

She'd met him on campus, and he had approached her in the library and asked her about the Mercer Hall ghosts. She didn't tell many people about her ability, but she had admitted more than she should have to the economic professor's teaching assistant the previous week. Her evening class took place on the third floor of Mercer Hall, one the oldest campus buildings, and it was frequented by a disturbing pair of ghost siblings. She couldn't outright say why she wanted to drop the class, but when the professor's teaching assistant had joked if it was because of the ghosts, she had answered him seriously.

After that conversation, Roman was the third guy in a week to approach her about seeing ghosts, but before she could retort with a snippy rebuke to leave her alone, he introduced himself. His demeanor was mature and his questions were sincere, and she remembered that she had been eager to confide in him.

"I never said I was researching ghosts."

"Are you even a student?"

He reached a hand into his shirt at the collar and pulled out a black necklace line with clear, glass stones. One of the stones was raised and filled with a charcoal gray mist.

"Look. That spirit is gone, just like I promised," he told her.

"The ghost is in there?"

"No. Just its remaining life-force."

Ramona gave him a skeptical look. "I thought you were going to destroy the spirits."

"I did. And I took the life force it had before it disappeared."

"And it's in your necklace? I'm not an idiot!"

"Our employer will repurpose the energy."

"How do you—"

"Either my room or yours, but I'm not going to continue this conversation in the hallway."

An older couple with several pieces of luggage approached, and she moved out of the way.

As they passed, Roman's fingers grazed against her forearm.

When he touched her arm, she felt a rush of exhaustion. He wrapped an arm around her back and carried her inside. He set her down on the bed, and she spent ten long seconds crumpled forward in an awkward position before her limbs responded and she pushed herself upright.

"What did you do?" she accused.

"Calm down. I'm not going to hurt you," Roman said and raised his hands. "Sorry. I was going to wait to have this conversation with you. Today's only your first day. This is *my* gift. This is how I drain the spirits. Now that you know my secret, you can stay with me when I do it."

She glared up at him, and he stared down at her.

"Don't ever do that to me again," she said hoarsely. "Or I'm going to quit."

He turned to his bag.

"Here," he said, thumbing through the cash. "A bonus for your trouble." He tossed the entire bundle in her lap.

That brightened her mood. "How long are we staying here?"

"Another night, tops. We need four more spirits and then we can go."

"Who's the employer?"

"No one you'd know. I've only met him once. When we collect enough, you'll meet him."

"Where?"

Roman pulled the nightstand light on and a small cloud of dust floated from the inside of the lampshade and onto the pillow. Maybe his room wasn't cleaner after all.

"He has a thing with water. He has to be on an island or a boat, so, we'll meet him on one or the other. I'll make the arrangements. I used your photo to get a passport, in case we need to cross any borders."

"What does he want with the energy?"

He put a hand on the necklace bulge against his chest. "We all have life-force. Some of us have less—a shorter life—some of us have more, which would mean a longer life. There's one more person on our team. She can transfer this to him."

Ramona raised her eyebrows. She thought this adventure was about destroying the haunts of the world to make it a better place. No one wanted a ghost around. But this operation wasn't altruistic. This was about harvesting the value of ghosts. She had never thought of them as valuable, but she didn't know that their life-force could be extracted and transferred to someone else, either.

"So he pays us to find the ghosts and give him their life-force so he can live longer?"

"Yes."

He obviously had a unique gift, but so did she. If Roman wasn't her employer, then he wasn't her boss. She rose and limped to the door.

"After this, no more dumps. Marriott or better."

He passed her and opened the door. "Remember the contract you signed. Not a word about this to anyone."

Back in her room, she noticed her luggage ajar on the floor. She heaved it back onto the bed and opened it for a second time. Right on the top were her new undies from Walmart... white, high-waisted granny panties.

They shared a preference for practical undergarments, but she had been searching for clues about him. What had he been doing? She was leery of his draining gift, so she suppressed the urge to go back to his room and ask.

Roman knocked on her door an hour later. It hadn't been a restful hour, and instead of showering or relaxing, she'd been thinking about how the ghost she'd seen in her room had disappeared into his necklace. Or rather, had vanished from existence. She put a fist under her chin and leaned forward, gazing without seeing, and thought hard about it. She thought of her ability to see ghosts as an intuitive gift, but his seemed like magic. Or even aliens.

"Ready? We can get dinner somewhere first if you're hungry."

"Of course I'm hungry," she wanted to retort. They'd been to two gas stations since the bright and early pick-up. She didn't know lunch would be canceled and had failed to buy something more nutritious than a Snickers bar.

She kept a few feet of distance between them as they walked, but that amount of space wasn't possible in the car. She waited for him to buckle himself in before she reached down to her own buckle, her fingers a dangerous two inches from his elbow.

She hated conflict, but the only way she knew how to tackle a problem was to go right through it. "Why did you go through my bag?"

He adjusted the mirror and set the GPS coordinates on his phone. "I added something."

"Don't you think you should have told me before doing that?"

He gave her a long look and, as the guilty party, she dropped her gaze first.

Roman refrained from digging in the point. "It's for your protection."

"Protection from what?"

"The spirits will start to notice that something is snuffing them out of existence. After surviving decades or centuries as an echo of life, they'll figure out what's going on. And like living humans, the dead ones don't like change."

"You're the one snuffing them out. Don't you need protection?"

He lifted a hand. "I can protect myself. I put a device in your luggage that will deter them from approaching while you're resting. During the day, you'll be alert enough to avoid the worst."

"It sounds like you've done this before."

His silence was suspicious.

Roman drove them to a roadside diner, but they didn't stay. They ate mediocre Reuben sandwiches in the car, and Ramona maxed out the AC so the swishing sound of the vents would cancel out her loud swallows.

When he started driving again, she rolled down the windows. The sky was a deep blue with pretty white stars, and the 90-degree heat felt like a warm embrace.

"I get that you want to tell me as little as possible," she said, staring at distant hills. They were like bumps in a dark blanket, with all the little shrubs and dips of the desert erased. "But this would work better if we coordinated on the ghost hunting."

"What do you mean?"

"It seems like you came to Yuma because you think there are a lot of ghosts. Former prison, I get it. And we're driving around at night to the old prison because you think midnight or early morning is the best time to catch ghosts."

"I've worked with other ghost hunters. I know a few things about it."

"But I'm here because I'm the expert on this. I'm the one that sees them. Right?"

"Sure."

"I wasn't going to say anything because I really want to travel. But there were plenty of spirits where we came from. And I see them at all times, day or night. People are just more aware of them at night because it's dark and they're feeling jumpy and get hyper-aware of everything out of the ordinary."

Roman kept driving, but she felt the car slow.

"You think we should go back?" he said finally.

"Yes."

"You don't like Yuma," he surmised.

"I don't see the point in clearing out the ghosts here. I'd rather work somewhere it will actually matter."

"In your hometown."

"Exactly. You get the energy you want, and I get rid of the ghosts I've hated seeing for the past twenty years."

"It took six hours on backroads to get this far in," he pointed out.

"We can still check out the town I researched."

"Fine," Ramona relented. "How many ghosts do we need total?"

"Probably eighty. Each spirit has a different amount of leftover life-force."

She made a surprised sound and leaned forward. "We're going to be at this for a long time."

"I know."

"That's a lot of road trips."

"Yes." Roman turned on the high beams, and a small outcrop of shadowy buildings loomed ahead. "Our first stop."

He parked next to a broken tree but kept the car and the high-lights on.

"Ready?" he said, pulling the necklace out. "Just point to the first one you see."

They'd gone nearly twenty feet when Ramona stopped walking and held out an arm.

A sea of dull, opaque eyes glistened back at her. Perspiration pooled out of every pore of her body. Her heart churned like a drum, and every ticking pulse was a boom in her eardrums.

"Looks like you saw a ghost," Roman whispered next to her.

She blinked, turned, and ran back for the Jeep.

He barely made it inside with her before she locked it. She shoved her hands under her bottom to stop them from shaking in an embar-rassing display of fear.

"What's the matter?" He pressed. "What happened?"

"For—for—" she stuttered, and her eyes smarted with angry tears. Why couldn't she control herself?

"Four ghosts?" he guessed, squinting back towards the town.

"For—for—TEE!" she gasped, forcing out the last syllable with great effort.

He made an impressed sound.

"Payday." He reached for the door, and she launched herself over the seat to stop him.

"Don't!" she cried. "They'll get in. They'll know I saw them!" She was beside herself with angst.

"Alright, calm down," he said.

She lifted a hand and placed it on his cheek.

No relief came, and he gingerly pried her hand away.

"It doesn't work like that," he said. "I control it."

"Oh," she said weakly.

He turned off the headlights, and she leaned back in the seat and closed her eyes.

She spent the next ten minutes in a meditative silence, taking deep breaths. Her audible breathing no longer bothered her, and she absorbed the relief of the extra oxygen until she could speak.

"Just walk around with your arms out. You'll connect with them," she said.

"Do you want me to take you back first?"

"No!" She shifted in the seat. "I'll just wait in here."

"Are you sure?"

She nodded and then realized he couldn't see her in the dark. "Go."

When he was out of the car, she relocked it and sank to the generous space under the glovebox to hide from sight.

Her first day of ghost hunting wasn't going so great. She hadn't thought through what it would feel like to pursue what she feared, and she didn't expect to feel so vulnerable.

It felt like she crouched for hours, but only forty minute had passed when Roman knocked to let him back in. It was a quiet drive back to the motel, and with sore knees and hurt pride, Ramona shuffled back to her room. Whatever mysterious trinket Roman had put in her luggage she was going to repurpose it into something she could carry with her day and night.

When she flicked the lights on, the room was in total disarray. She rubbed her tired eyes and stared at the glass strewn over the air conditioning unit and the floor and connected the debris with a hole smashed in the window by the latch.

To her dismay, her luggage was gone. Room 116 was the absolute worst.

Roman wasn't pleased.

"It took me months to make that."

"Obviously, someone thought it was valuable."

"It was."

"And you just obliterated an entire town of ghosts tonight…"

"So you'll definitely be targeted," he finished.

Neither of them wanted to sleep on the floor, so for the second time that night, she found herself scrunched up with her knees tucked in close.

In the darkness, on her edge of the bed, she felt the oppressive weight of silence again and spoke one more time.

"So, Marriott or better, right?"

"Yep," Roman said from across the pillow barrier she'd placed between them.

She couldn't wait to get back home and start tackling the onesie-twosie ghosts in her town—after tonight, she felt like it would be easy. They'd begin with Old Town, and then The Hotel Del, and then the lighthouse in Point Loma. One by one, she'd say goodbye to every shadowy face that had haunted her childhood and teen years.

She didn't bother to think if it was right or wrong. Ramona was far too enthralled. Together, she and Roman would eliminate the scourge of spirits that had overstayed their welcome in the world of the living. Eventually, she drifted into a restless sleep.

Roman, on his side, was wide awake. The item he had placed in her luggage could not have been mistaken for jewelry. The thief knew exactly what they were taking, and no matter how cheap the motel, he was convinced the break-in wasn't random. He had already lost two ghost hunters, but he had confined the person responsible for those deaths—although he now believed those efforts had failed.

He had been meticulous about finding the third ghost hunter. She was young enough to adapt, easy enough to stay close to and protect, and inexperienced enough not to ask the right questions.

His necklace was full of life-force energy, and although he had expended much of his energy draining every ghost he could reach among the ruins in that depressing town, the young woman who slept beside him was his ticket to much greater possibilities. Extending their employer's life was only a fraction of what they could do with the life-force and, at the right time, he would pitch his ideas to her. But today was only her first day, after all.

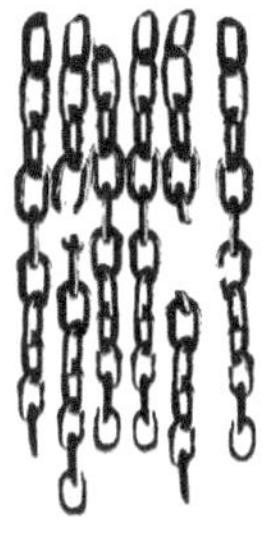

Horse Guts Horse Guts
by
Tobin Elliott

Journal notes by (name redacted)

My therapist, Dr. Morrow, tells me it would be a good thing to get it out, to write out what I remember. I don't necessarily believe her. It's not going to bring back my feet, my leg, my friends.

Then again, it's not like I have dick-all else to do in here besides hanging with the droolers. Probably a problematic, negative term for them, but I'm pretty much one too, so I figure I have permission.

I'll give it a shot. You ready, Dr. Morrow? If I was a Lovecraft character, I'd say something about this being my recount of the indescribable thing escaping its cyclopean lair buoyed on the rising tide through the stygian darkness. Might even get a racist comment in there, too.

Anyway, fuck that guy. Here goes.

It was a Sunday, it was raining, and I was bored. Mind-numbingly, achingly, titanically bored. Around eight, I gave my best friend Al a call and asked him if he wanted to catch a flick. Al's a good guy, a bigger nerd than me, and crazy smart. Not so much in the looks department, but he compensated by maintaining a well-clipped full beard that hid his chubby cheeks and weak chin. Kinda pissed me off, that luscious beard, because I could only manage tumbleweed on my face. Al also nerd-compensated by being a funny bastard.

I obviously hit him up at the right time. Apparently, in his world it was also Sunday, it was also raining, and he was also titanically bored, because he agreed gratefully. We settled very quickly on the least-shitty movie we could find and made plans for me to pick him up shortly in my Stutter Bunny. By the time I got there, he'd rounded up his brother Ian, and another friend, Steve, for the night.

Yeah, yeah. Sunday. Raining. Bored like the Titanic. You getting the picture, Dr. Morrow?

Though most of the time a tagalong younger brother would suck, it was cool if Ian tagged along. He was the opposite of Al. Shorter and more athletic than his brother. Less nerdy. Still not much in the looks department, but then, with a face like mine, who the hell was I to judge? Where Al would jump in with wisecracks at any opportunity, kind of like throwing shit at the wall to see what sticks, Ian was the type that sat back and listened, missing nothing. But when he had something to say, it was ninja quick, scalpel sharp, and surgically targeted. Although a couple of years younger than Al, Ian seemed the more experienced of the two. Maybe wiser, or more worldly, is what I'm trying to say. Don't get me wrong. Like I said, Al was smart, just more in a schoolbook kind of way.

Steve was more a friend of Al's than mine, but we got along fine. He was a nice enough guy, with a stone face that cracked into an easy laugh surprisingly often. I didn't know him well, just through our few times hanging out and Al's stories. He was very likely gay, but hadn't come out yet. No biggie, we'd be there for him when he did. For the purposes of tonight's mission, he—like Ian—was a welcome addition to the ragtag team.

We got drenched waiting in line at the movie theater, because our town had the big movieplex and one struggling local theater with better prices and better popcorn, so of course we went there instead. The rain was also a good excuse to talk to the peroxides with the umbrella in front of us. Not that that went anywhere. Four nerdy-looking guys and four really blonde women, with all the stereotypes that entailed. We were well aware the only reason they were interacting with us was an equation involving time and proximity.

Still, they laughed at our jokes, and we laughed when it was obvious they did not smell half of what we were cooking. Yes, they were good-looking but vacuous. Yes, we were funny but obnoxious and self-important.

The movie was all those things, too. One of those big, dumb, violent wastes of time that are so much fun to make fun of, which was just a bonus. Money and time well spent. Afterward, the four of us went for pizza, the peroxides long gone.

There is nothing like going to a restaurant and having a steaming hot waitress serve you a steaming hot pizza. Didn't matter that she only pretended to like us—she earned her tip when she didn't get disgusted when I referred to the pizza as roadkill on toast. No rolling of eyes or pursing of lips equaled tip, in my book. I mentioned the whole smoking hot thing, right? We spent a good hour skewering the movie, the peroxides, the actors, and mostly each other.

In the end, even though it was pissing rain, and it was too damn cold for August, and there were no girls (or guys, in Steve's as-yet-undeclared case) that were serious prospects—hell, there never were, because, let's face it, we were less than average looking, well above average nerds with little in the way of social skills—we had a blast. If this was to be our last night together, this was the way to do it.

We just didn't know about that whole last night thing at the time. Maybe that made it better.

Does not knowing about impending tragedy increase or decrease the pleasure of the events preceding it? In five hundred words or less, Dr. Morrow, explain and defend your argument. Use examples.

Yes, I'm avoiding getting to what happened. Sorry about that, doc.

Goddamn, I miss those guys.

***

Around one, we decided to call it a night. Steve and I had to be up early for work. Both Al and Ian had finished their summer jobs and were killing time until school started again.

The rain had accelerated exponentially by the time we were heading back to the car. There's heavy rain, there's biblical rain, and then there was what was coming down now. Stupidly thick, blanketing waves of water.

Air rivers.

Insane rain.

By the time we got my car unlocked and piled in, we were all soaked again. Al and Ian had tussled over the shotgun position but, as usual, Al pulled rank. In protest, Ian got in the back seat, leaned toward his brother in the front seat, barked, and shook the rain from his shaggy hair like a dog.

"The fuck are you? A Dalmatian?" Al said, emphasizing the last couple of syllables. *Dal-maysh-IAN.* It was an old joke between him and Ian. As he said it, he wiped his glasses clean with the leg of the stuffed moose that had ridden my dashboard since last February when a bunch of us had driven to Lauderdale.

"That joke was abysmal," Ian said, pronouncing it *ah-biz-mAL.*

"Ah, crap," Steve said, rolling his eyes. "Here we go."

"Sim*IAN.*"

"Bacteri*AL.*"

Then, the rain somehow scaled up even *higher*, hitting with both barrels, taking no prisoners.

"Shit," I said, "I knew I should've bought those plug wires yesterday." Vehicular maintenance was not one of my strong points.

Okay, full disclosure, I have very few strong points.

"Oh, beautiful," Al said. "Is this thing gonna crap out on us again?"

See, the problem is my car doesn't like the wet weather too much. A little rain doesn't bother my VW Rabbit—lovingly called the Stutter Bunny —too much, but all this Noah's Ark shit we've gotten this summer was just too much. I mean, there's only so much you can ask of a car that's been around twice as long as its owner.

I crunched the key into the ignition and, wonder of wonders, the car started, first try. There was much rejoicing. Once we got going, the streets were deserted, like something out of an apocalyptic *Twilight Zone* episode. Granted, anyone with half a brain wouldn't go out on a night like this, but no one ever accused the four of us of sporting more than half a brain. *This*, though. Goddamn. This wasn't just rain—this was solid sheets of water. It was like being underwater. Or, at least under Niagara Falls. But the Stutter Bunny worked fine.

Until about a mile from Al's house.

We had just entered Al and Ian's suburban neighborhood, a wasteland of cookie-cutter homes side by side by side by side, repeat *ad infinitum*. Heading up the main artery, the road took a fairly severe dip that made me a touch nervous, considering the rain. Sure enough, we reached the bottom of the dip, pounding through a particularly large pond of water when my car coughed once, then simply died, essentially thumbing its German-engineered nose and telling us to take a hike. Literally.

I tell you, when I get a car, I get one with a personality.

Steve said, "You're kidding, right? Tell me you're kidding." I gave him a look. "You're not kidding," he said. "Fuck me."

"Relax," I said. "It always does this." I turned the key, pleading under my breath.

Al gave me a withering side-eye. "'Always does this,' he said. Like there's nothing wrong with that."

"C'monbabyc'mon..." I pleaded.

And it caught!

And it died.

"Aw man, why don't you get a real car?"

"Hey! Your mama..." I really had nothing. "Should...um...get a real car." Okay, even I knew that one was weak.

"Leave my mama outta this."

I tried again.

Waited...

And again.

Waited...

And again.

Nope. By now, the battery was dying.

***

I gave it ten minutes and gave it one more shot. All it gave me was that belated...*whoa* that happens when the battery is almost gone. The rain increased its tempo. I would have guessed that would have been impossible until it actually happened. Al opened the door and checked the water level. In an overly-dramatic voice, he said, "By Odin's beard!" The water was only about two inches from the door now.

It had only taken ten minutes. "We are well and truly fucked," Steve said.

Al closed the door again. The car smelled like wet dog.

Then Ian said, "Hey. Check it out. Here comes a car."

"Ask him if he's got a raft, man."

I quickly blinked my lights, hoping there was enough juice. There was, judging from the illuminated washes of water in front of the headlights. The car stopped beside me, and the window sank into the door. I rolled mine down. A shaggy blonde head stuck itself out of the window, seemingly oblivious to the rain.

"'Sup?" he yelled over the thunderous downpour.

"Hey, man, any chance you can give me a bump start?"

"Sssuurrrrrre, man. Noooo prob," he slurred.

"Dude's faced," Al said. Al was not wrong. Dude was stoned out of his gourd.

One arm wildly gesticulating at me, he said, "Jez let me ged turned around, and we'll gedja right outta there, man." With that, he drove off.

And kept right on going.

"Probably got a sudden attack of the munchies," Steve said.

"Probably gonna come back and rear-end us doin' eighty," Al said.

We sat there joking about the faced surfer dude, my car, and our predicament for a while, but it soon became obvious the guy wasn't coming back. And that the rain wasn't slowing down. It had progressed so far beyond biblical, it was now a poly-denominational onslaught.

"Welp!" Steve said. "Screw it." He slapped his palms against his wet thighs and said, "Sorry guys, but I gotta be at work in five hours. I hate to ditch you, but I gotta bail. I'm walking back to my car. Al, you want me to get your dad to come rescue you?"

As none of us had the scratch for a tow truck, it seemed like a plan to us. Al leaned forward to let Steve out. From the look on Al's face, I could tell he wasn't looking forward to seeing his dad at two in the morning. Nobody should have to face their parents at two in the morning. For any reason.

Steve got out, became instantly drenched, flipped up his collar against the rain, and gave us a jaunty wave as though he was actually digging getting a power wash. We watched him do a little *Singin' in the Rain* routine that was funny as hell, especially with him up to almost mid-calf in water. It only lasted a few seconds. Then, with a final wave, he turned and headed for his car.

He got ten feet before he disappeared.

He just vanished into the water. We laughed our brains out. The stupid ass fell in the water. *Ha ha, wot a maroon! Wot an ultra-maroon!* Al and I thumped the dash and howled.

Then Ian said something, and we sobered up.

"I don't think he fell, guys. Didn't you notice? There wasn't any splash. It almost looked like he was *sucked* down." As soon as Ian said it, we realized the truth of it. It looked like he'd fallen. But no, there was no accompanying splash. Comparing notes, we realized he'd dropped straight down, as though into a hole. Maybe an open manhole or something?

And as we sat there watching, he wasn't coming back up.

Al and I both opened our doors to go help, but Al was faster. He was out—and he was gone. Straight down, just like Steve.

He barely had time to get out a small, abbreviated scream.

I yanked my foot back in. I'd seen something dark—black on black—in the water, level with the doorframe, before I shut my door.

Ian was screaming something unintelligible.

Then a hand came up as I thought, *Al? Steve?* and it grabbed the passenger-side door frame. It was wet, shiny, glistening, and human.

And then—

Then—

***

I'm sorry. I can't write what happened next. I just can't.

***

Hypnotic regression audio transcription (portion)
Dr. Morrow and (name redacted)

"Ian reaches down, grabs, pulls, and screams because all he has is a hand and wrist...just a stump of a hand, completely bloodless and clean and wet from the rain but there's no fucking blood on it at all so it looks so fucking fake and I think, one of those practical jokes, right? Shake? Ha ha hahahahahah!

Then the car kind of *flexes* and makes this weird groaning noise. I think it's the car, anyways. I think, *whatthehellisunderus,* and I see movement from the passenger door where Ian is and I yell at him, I yell shut it shut it shut the fucking *DOOR*! But Ian's just holding his brother's hand and I know it's his because of the scar across his knuckles he got when he was eight, and we were playing in the park together, and Al fell off the monkey bars headfirst, and he landed on his hand teethfirst and chomped down on his knuckles, and chipped his tooth and broke his wrist and now he's gone and broken it again, and his mom's never gonna let him play on the monkey bars again, oh god oh god ohmygod, I'm so scared I grab at the seatbelt. Thank you, God, for seatbelts that latch into the door and I haul on it, and I pee myself, and I hear the door slam shut."

(Sound of patient crying)

***

Journal notes by (name redacted)

I don't know how long we sat in the car, the rain pounding the roof, the windows steamed up. Ian was curled up in a ball in the back seat, quietly sobbing. He still held his brother's hand.

And me. My pulse pounding in my ears, the quiet hiss of my breathing, the taste of copper, the smell of wet velour, piss, and fear. I stared at the interlocked VW symbol on the steering wheel. I blew out a long breath and closed my eyes...

Something roared and slapped the windshield. Water splashing hard. My eyes snapped open in time to see the red tail lights in my fogged rear-view mirror.

We had to get out of there. Checking on Ian again, I realized *I* had to get us out of there. Now.

I reached down, grabbed the key, and twisted. The goddamn car started without a hitch. Of course it did. Ian let out a hopeful whine as I put it into gear, and we slowly inched forward. Slow and easy. Relief flooded through me and I started to shake. It was hard to concentrate, hard to not just stomp on the gas and try and blast out of there.

But we were okay. We were more than halfway across this massive puddle, this lake of rainwater.

My leg exploded in pain. I yanked my foot off the clutch and the car stuttered to a stop and died. I thought, *nonononononononononononononono.*

I tried to pull my foot up to where I could see it and, as it thumped against the bottom of the dashboard, it seemed almost weightless. Then I knew why. When my leg came up, there was no foot. There was no fucking knee. It looked like there was a wet black leather purse wrapped around my thigh. I squealed and grabbed it.

I've never actually held a human lung in my hands, but I can imagine what it would feel like. Cold wet heavy squishy slippery. This was worse. This had teeth. Small sharp ones. I pulled and pulled, digging my fingers in, with it digging its teeth in, pulling, ripping, tearing the skin off my leg. I kicked at it with my good leg and realized there was a lot of it. From what I could see—and I swear all I could think was *horse guts horse guts*—it looked like eviscerated organs all over the floor. Black and shiny and wet and cancerous. I opened the door to kick it out, but the water started to pour in so I shut it quick. One was enough.

The pain seemed to clear my head. By this time, I was up with my feet—fuck, my *foot*, my single remaining foot—on the seat.

"Ian, man, keep your feet up on the seat. There's one in here with us." Ian's eyes reflected white in the streetlights. I could see the entire pupil in each eye. He nodded, two quick jerks. Good. He was still with me.

Suddenly, there were twin suns behind us, and a bang that knocked us both into the seat backs. Someone was pushing us!

We stopped about a hundred feet farther up the road, on a rise. We'd been pushed completely out of the pond. Faintly, I heard a car door slam. I opened mine and frantically kicked at the horrible thing on the floor. It slopped out on the pavement with a wet slap like spaghetti, then slid under the car.

"Sorry, man, I was lookin' fer a place t' turn ar—"

I grabbed the steering wheel and angled the top half of myself out of the car and screamed at stoned dude to get the hell away. "It's under the fucking car!" I wailed. The half-lidded eyes snapped wide under the shaggy blond mop, and he jumped back like he'd been punched. Probably saved his life.

I took a breath. "Call 911," I said, as calmly as I could. He nodded with that goofy whole body nod that only the supremely stoned can do. I saw his eyes flick to my missing leg, the stump pissing blood. He loped off to the nearest house even though I could see the shape of a cell phone in his back pocket. I probably fucked his shit up until it was almost as bad as mine. I shut the door, knotted my jacket tight around my half-gone leg, looked at the floor, and then back at Ian.

Then I passed out.

***

I woke up in this bed. Missing most of my left leg and most of my right foot. I hadn't noticed it at the time. Guessing the Lung Beast (what would *you* call it, doc?) took the rest as I kicked the shit out of it. Steve and most of Al gone. I'd heard what had been left of Al's handhad to be pried from Ian. He, incidentally, got out without a scratch. He hasn't talked since and won't go near water. He can't even face a toilet, from what I hear.

I know the feeling.

Outside my hospital window, it's clouding over. The stygian black thunderheads roiling over a cyclopean skyline.

Thunderclouds that remind me of the thing under the bed...no, that's not right. The thing under the car.

I gotta call the nurse to drop the blinds.

I clutch at my pillow.

It's time to be sedated again.

I gotta stop writing now.

Rise of the Diva
by
Dennis K. Crosby

The hairline crack in the windowpane started in the bottom left corner and moved slowly on an angle until it reached the midway point in the glass. A tremor hurried through the concrete walls, and the crack in the glass splintered, moving in five directions. Each new crack formed three of its own. As the tremor in the walls increased, the window's integrity failed, causing an explosion of glass. That explosion was mirrored in adjacent windows as the intensity of the tremors increased. The concrete that made up the walls chipped away little by little. The fluorescent bulbs overhead flickered, then exploded in a haze of glass and mercury vapor. The desks in the library shook. All but the largest in the center. That desk was still, as was the jar resting on top of it. The jar glowed. First a golden hue, illuminating the exquisite glyphs that decorated it. Then a reddish hue, which highlighted the letters. All that began when a graduate student translated, from Ancient Greek to modern English, the last word on the jar.

"Release!"

As chaos reigned around it, the jar glowed white. The light expanded, filling the room. The grad student and her boyfriend cowered in a corner, frozen in fear, unable to escape the scene. Heat filled the immediate area, and an audible sizzle was followed by a large pop and a gust of wind. The light dimmed, and a swirling cloud escaped the jar. Gray smoke rushed to the ceiling, then spread in tendrils across the tiles. Mouths agape, the pair watched the tendrils coalesce into a human form next to the jar. As it solidified, they saw bare legs forming, then arms, a torso, breasts, and finally a head. The woman standing bare before them had smooth mocha skin, a crop of jet-black hair in a pixie haircut, and tattoos of various shapes and patterns across her midsection. Her eyes were closed. As the last of the rattling stopped, a single shard of glass fell. As if awakened by the noise, the woman opened her eyes.

Eyes that glowed an ethereal blue.

She looked around, unphased by all that had just occurred. When her eyes settled on the pair, she smiled.

"Thank you," she said.

And then she shimmered out of view into nothing.

***

"It just…got out," said Mia.

"It just got out?" asked Jacen.

"Yeah. Just like that," said Josh.

"Just like that?" asked Jacen.

"Yeah," said Mia.

Jacen stared for a moment, waiting for the break in eye contact that would inevitably arise when someone wasn't completely forthcoming. The bigger the secret, the faster the eye averted—

There it is.

"That's all you have to say about it?"

"Look, we didn't know that—"

"You didn't know? You are doctoral candidates specializing in not only ancient literature, but occult studies, and you didn't know? You didn't think that messing around with a jar specifically designed to contain the worst things in the world could potentially cause an issue?"

"I mean…it was a jar. It wasn't the box, it was a jar. The text, the lore, all talks about the box and all the things that were in it. But…all that is just legend anyway. It's superstitious nonsense people made up to explain what they couldn't understand. I mean...look at the thing. It's just a decorative jar," said Josh.

"Seems to me that the events of the last half hour would say something different, no?"

"We...we...we didn't know," said Mia.

"Every legend starts somewhere, with some grain of truth. My friends, you've unleashed a very deadly truth today."

"But it was a jar. Not a box. Why would we even question it?" asked Josh.

"Because if you'd bother to dig a little deeper in your studies, you would know that the word 'box' was mistranslated. Pithos, the original word, which means jar, was changed to pyxis, which means box. There's still no clear reason as to why this was done, but it was, and it's documented. Pandora's box is, in fact, a jar," said Jacen.

"Why a jar? What the hell would they keep things in a jar for?" asked Josh.

"What do you think an urn is?" asked Jacen.

Again, Jacen simply stared at Josh, waiting for an answer, but also allowing the depth of his hubris to fully take hold. Jacen was not trying to scare him—mostly. He recognized he tended to get overly excited about things. But in this case, it was warranted. In this case, the world had the potential to be turned upside down by what the pair had unleashed. Something so powerful it called to him from across the miles and woke him from a deep sleep.

"Are you at least sure she's still in the building?" asked Jacen.

"We think so," said Josh.

"Well, that's something. Good to know she's at least maintaining her original form. Don't know if that'll make it easier to find her, though, since no one has laid eyes on her in several thousand years," said Jacen.

Jacen closed his eyes and stretched out with his senses. There was a lot of interference in the old building, and that was a good thing. If he was having challenges, hopefully she would, too. Though, given who she was, that challenge might not be as long-lasting as he needed it to be.

"Dammit!" exclaimed Jacen.

"What? What's wrong?" asked Josh.

"This building is blocking me. I can't get a bead on her."

"Wait, what *are* you?" asked Mia.

"I'm complicated," said Jacen. "Where's the jar?"

Josh and Mia gestured to the table. Jacen walked toward it, each step a struggle. The closer he got, the more he felt its power. He felt heavy, sluggish. The jar, seemingly sentient, did not want to be touched. Inches away, he felt the resistance ease. Magical static, which he felt on his skin, filled the air.

"Dude, what the hell?" asked Josh.

Jacen ignored him as he slowly reached out to grab the jar. It vibrated lightly in his hands. After a few beats, it stopped. The magical static was gone. Jacen felt the weight lifted from him and his own powers strengthening.

"The jar was created to hold great power," said Jacen. "When it feels threatened or uncertain, it pushes back. Especially against something that also has great power."

"But you're holding it now. So it knows you're not a threat?" asked Mia.

Jacen nodded.

"It's...alive?" asked Josh.

"It's aware," said Jacen. "That's vastly different."

Jacen inspected the jar and the script etched into it. Unlike most jars of the time, it was made of metal and not clay. Likely adamantine, a common substance used by the ancient gods. It was the strongest substance on Earth and, when infused with magic, it was indestructible.

Usually.

"How exactly did you get this open?" asked Jacen.

Josh and Mia stared at each other. Jacen felt as if an hour-long conversation was being held between the two in the seconds their eyes met. In the end, it was Mia who finally spoke up.

"It just...opened," she said with a shrug.

"Just opened? Just like that? A jar made thousands of years ago by ancient gods just...opened for a couple of doctoral candidates in the Chicago suburbs?"

"Dude—"

"Young man, if you call me dude one more time, I will fold you up and stuff you into this jar," said Jacen.

Jacen was no telepath or empath, but he was certain he felt Josh's response. The kid was scared. Scared people say stupid things. Particularly after they've done something stupid that's now causing them to be scared. He felt some sense of concern and empathy for the two. They truly didn't know better. Still, this is not how he expected his Friday night to go.

"Which one of you opened it?"

Josh's eyes immediately went to Mia.

Mia's eyes immediately went to the floor.

"Well, that answers that," said Jacen. "All right, Mia, you're up. Consider this your promotion to demon hunter."

"Demon!" they both shouted.

"Oh no. That's just a very generic title for what we're about to do. Trust me when I say it's much worse," said Jacen.

"How much worse?" asked Mia.

"Wait, let me guess. She's like a witch? Or a sorceress?" asked Josh.

"A god," said Jacen. "You let a god out of Pandora's box."

The initial shock at Jacen's statement was broken by a loud crash and subsequent shriek down the hall.

***

The Reaper stared down at the body lying face down on the floor next to the shattered display case. The bloodied face, crimson-stained trophy, and sea of broken glass around the young woman spoke volumes about the way she'd lost her life. What truly stood out to him was her missing clothes. The fact that she still wore underwear indicated that she wasn't assaulted in any way other than physical. At least…he hoped that had been the case. Reapers weren't supposed to care one way or another. Their sole function was to escort souls to the afterlife. Good people went to the Beyond. The other people, well, they would end up in the Void. It was hard to say what that was like. No one had ever been there and returned.

Not even the Primus.

As the Reaper prepared to escort the young woman's soul, he was caught by a shift in the air. Turning slightly, he noticed another woman walking in his direction. He was not too concerned because, unless he willed it, no human could see him. Still, her eyes seemed almost fixated on him. It was as if—

"Hello, Reaper," said the woman.

His jaw dropped and his eyes widened.

"Oh yes, I can see you."

There was nothing overtly remarkable about her. She was of average height, for a woman. Her mocha skin and short hair were not of note. Her clothing was normal, though it didn't quite fit. And she was barefoot. The Reaper looked back to the body on the floor, then to the mystery woman now in front of him.

"Yes, I killed her," she said. "I needed clothes, and I also needed…you."

Again, the Reaper's face betrayed him.

"Well, to be honest, any Reaper would do," she said.

"Why?" he asked.

"Because I need to speak to the Primus."

"What do you know of—"

The Reaper's words were cut off as the woman moved with preternatural speed. She grabbed him by the throat and pressed him against the wall. He attempted to dematerialize into vapor to escape, but he found himself unable to do so. He was trapped in his human form.

That's not possible, he thought.

"Don't bother trying to escape," she said.

"Who…are…you?" he managed to get out through a restricted

airway.

She did not respond. As he continued to struggle for his freedom, he noticed a change in her eyes. He thought, when he first saw her, that they were brown. But now, they appeared blue. Even stranger, the more he stared, the brighter the shade. Until...they glowed.

The mark of a god.

"You're...a..."

"Yes," she started, "and if you do as I ask, I won't have to make an example of you to get what I want. Now, I need you to reach out to your Primus. When he arrives, I'll be more than happy to—"

"Our Primus is unavailable," said a voice from behind. "But you can speak with me."

The Reaper looked past the woman to find Senaya, a Wraith, and lieutenant of the Primus, Azra-El. Senaya was similar in appearance to the woman currently holding him by the throat, only a little taller with a more athletic build.

Both women scared him.

The Reaper felt himself being lowered to the ground. He gasped as the woman released the hold on his neck. He backed away quickly and tripped over the dead body.

"Jesus, Anthony," said Senaya.

"Hard to find good help sometimes, isn't it?" asked the mystery woman rhetorically.

"I'm sorry, who are you again?" asked Senaya.

"Take me to the Nexus, and we'll talk."

Anthony looked to Senaya, then the mystery woman, shocked at her knowledge of the Reaper world. Then again, she was a god. It should not have shocked him too much, yet it did. The mystery surrounding this woman was unsettling. Her knowledge. Her power. Her confidence. His fear of Senaya's ferocity was inconsequential compared to what he felt about this god before him.

"Anthony, carry out your duty," said Senaya.

He nodded. Allowing his eyes to go silver, he placed a hand on the body of the dead woman next to him. Within seconds, everything around him took on a greenish tint, and tendrils of smoke swam across the floor. He had entered the Nexus, the place between the real world and the final resting places of souls. He would help this woman transition, and then he would leave and try to forget everything else.

As he prepared, he heard low laughter, and a voice echoed in his head, "I'm sure I'll see you again, Reaper."

***

The trio rounded the corner to a macabre scene. On the floor, a woman lay half-naked, surrounded by shattered glass. Opposite her, the mystery woman, now in an ill-fitted dress, seemingly talking to herself. When she turned to face them, Jacen froze. She was just as she'd appeared been on paintings he'd seen. Her features flawless. A palpable energy filled the room, and the intensity of her metallic blue eyes increased.

"Don't look at her!" shouted Jacen.

But it was too late.

***

Mia heard Jacen say something, but it was drowned out by her screams.

At the age of five, Mia had been fascinated by spiders. She loved the intricate webs they spun. Marveled at the way they scaled walls. She was even captivated by the look of them in illustrations. Tarantulas were her favorite. The legs, the eyes, the tiny hairs. Mia studied them relentlessly, and when the day came for her to finally see one in person, she was ecstatic.

Until the case holding it shattered. Until the spider skittered along the broken shards and leapt to her leg. When it crawled up, it seemed to do so at an almost supernatural pace. It leapt from her leg to her arm, then moved swiftly to her shoulder, then jumped to her head.

That was the day her love of spiders died.

What she saw now did nothing to reignite her fondness for the creatures.

The body of the dead woman burst open, and hundreds of spiders escaped, each of them scurrying toward Mia. Frozen in fear, she could not move. Her mind shouted for her to run, her screams an unconscious attempt to cry for help and shock her body into action. But it was no use. She remained still, watching as the army of spiders crawled and leapt their way to her.

The first wave covered her shoes and moved up her body. She could feel the tiny legs of the arachnids through her jeans, then on her skin as they reached her bare arms. Her screams continued, but her fear paralyzed her.

The last sensation she felt was that of tiny hairy legs skittering across her tongue and down her throat.

***

"Mia!"

Josh screamed her name, but nothing seemed to shake her. He put his hands on her shoulders and felt nothing but cold. He stopped shrieking her name when he saw the vapor escape his mouth. Looking around, he saw ice forming on the walls. Glancing up, he watched snow flurries drop down. Then he heard a distinctive crack. The crack of ice. More specifically, the crack of ice on a frozen lake. Daring to glance down, Josh watched as clear ice cracked beneath his feet. With one last shout of Mia's name, Josh fell through into an ice-cold lake.

The water seemed to grab at Josh as he struggled to reach the opening he'd fallen through. He watched in horror as the hole froze over. He pounded his fists against the ice, but to no avail. His arms felt heavy. Swinging them expelled energy that he didn't have, but the desperation for air kept him going. With one last burst of energy, he punched, and the ice cracked, giving him renewed hope.

Until he felt the tug at his leg.

He reached out, instinctively, trying to grasp something, anything, seemingly forgetting he was underwater.

Josh's lungs burned. The energy he expended trying to escape left his body begging for oxygen. He fought the instinct to open his mouth. As he kicked, trying hard to pull away from the unknown force dragging him down, he finally gave in.

His underwater scream sent sound waves against the icy ceiling above.

***

Jacen agonized as he watched the young grad students succumb to, well, nothing. Mia stood frozen one minute, staring only at the dead body on the ground, only to choke to death not long after. Josh fell to the ground, clawing at empty air, holding his breath. When he finally let it out, he simply died. He went to both and tried to revive them, but his efforts had no effect.

"Amazing how fragile the human mind is, wouldn't you say," said a voice behind him.

"What did you do to them?" asked Jacen.

"Nothing really. Just made their greatest fears come true. At least... in their minds."

"But if it was all in their minds, how—"

"How are they dead? The human mind is quite formidable. They'd know that if they truly took the time to study it. It gives power to so many things. Without it, the body does not function. Their minds believed they were dying, so their bodies followed suit."

"Why?"

"Why?" repeated the woman. "Because we need souls."

Jacen spun around and looked directly at the woman, no longer concerned about the consequences of her power. Her eyes were still an ethereal blue, but she was not using her power against him. Her smile sent waves of discomfort throughout his body. She was gleeful and self-assured and bore no remorse.

"Why do you need souls?" asked Jacen.

"She doesn't," said a new voice. "I do."

Another woman, a taller version of the god standing before him, appeared. Her onyx-black eyes identified her.

"You're a Wraith," said Jacen.

"Senaya," she said, with a slight bow.

"What is going on?" asked Jacen.

"The Primus was recently wounded in battle. His injuries are severe," said Senaya.

"The Angel of Death?" asked Jacen.

"Yes," said the goddess, letting the word drag on. "I have given them the secret to restore him. And when he does, he'll take vengeance on the one who hurt him, absorb her power, and ascend to godhood."

"But...Thanatos—"

"Will be taken care of," said the goddess.

"He won't allow it," said Jacen.

"You know who I am?" asked the goddess.

Jacen nodded.

"Then you understand that I know things about him that most do not. I have advised Senaya here on how to capture and imprison him. Everything will fall into place with him out of the way."

"But...why?"

"Because the world is in chaos. The world needs change. It needs healing. Isn't that why you became an Advocate?"

Jacen recoiled, shocked that she knew about him. He'd only recently become an Advocate, a being with almost limitless power. Not quite a god, but not so unlike them either. To be among their order meant they could only guide, and never interfere in the events of human history. They'd been around for several millennia, the answer to balancing the unbalanced scales of power in the supernatural world. He had become an Advocate to help right wrongs. He wanted to fix the world, broken thing that it was, and give hope back to those that inhabited it.

But he could only do so much.

"Without Thanatos, there will be no balance in the natural order," said Jacen.

"Balance will be restored, when Azra-El heals and ascends," said Senaya.

Jacen looked back and forth between the two women. He felt the heat of their stares. The goddess stepped toward him, eyes illuminated, and she took his hand.

"You want to do more for this world, yes?" she asked.

Jacen nodded.

"Then help me," she said.

"I'm forbidden to interfere. Advocates are only guides to help people become who they're meant to be."

"And that's all I need from you."

Jacen looked at her and then looked down at the ground. He thought back to the person he had been when he was simply human. He'd worked hard, day in and day out, to help others. To help those who couldn't help themselves. Giving a voice to those who didn't know how to speak up and advocate for their needs. He fought for people to get housing in sub-standard slums just so they would have a roof over their heads, only to watch them be kicked out months later for drug use, theft, or prostitution. He fought hard with police, state's attorneys, and judges, trying to educate them, influence them, and get them to see in some way that these men and women just needed some additional help to get where they needed to be; just a little extra support to reach their potential. He argued that they would never achieve that in jail or prison. He fought hard, and he won, only to watch them return to jail and then be told by the judge, "I told you so," with one condescending look. He was yelled at. He was threatened. He was largely unappreciated by his clients, collateral supports, and at times the very agency he'd worked for. All he wanted was freedom to do and be who he wanted to be. To be appreciated. He wanted the things he did to matter. Not so much to him, but to anybody.

And so he became an Advocate.

Yet nothing changed.

Perhaps now, things could be different.

***

Jacen Lucas stood in Potter's Field, people-watching, something he enjoyed frequently. He found it much more pleasing in recent days then he had before. Since his return, the world seemed different. Smaller even. Definitely more fragile.

"They never cease to amaze, do they?" said a familiar voice from behind.

"No. They certainly do not," said Jacen.

"Where have you been, Advocate?" asked the goddess. "You seem… different."

"A vision quest, of sorts. And I *feel* different."

"Color me curious."

"I projected myself back through time," Jacen said.

"Such is the power of an Advocate. A power that's frowned upon. Especially among your brethren," said the goddess.

"True," he said. "But I found a work-around. It's kind of how we do things here in Chicago."

Jacen smirked when he said that. He noticed that the goddess did, too.

"And what did you discover on your vision quest?"

"That perhaps you're right. Perhaps a change is what the world needs."

"So you're on board?"

Jacen nodded.

"Good. Very good."

"What's next?" asked Jacen.

"The Wraiths will work to imprison Thanatos. They will lead the Reapers and use souls to regenerate Azra-El. His wounds were extensive, so it will take some time."

"The natural order will be thrown out of balance."

"Yes, and as he heals, her power will grow," said the goddess.

"Her?"

"Yes, her. The key to everything."

"Who is she?"

"Her name...is Kassidy Simmons. She is Death's legacy."

Jacen took note of the name, then turned his attention to the people in Potter's Field. He watched the children play. He watched lovers walk hand in hand. In the distance, he watched people argue, and heard foul-mouthed screams between the blaring car horns.

He saw these things through a different lens now.

Soon the rest of the world would, too.

"What should I call you?" asked Jacen.

"Call me...Diva."

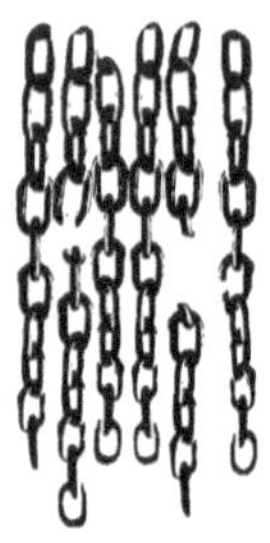

Eyewitness
by
Christina Hoag

David Shatzkin blinked. Summer sun rays slashed through the slits in the teak blinds and flayed his eyes. He rolled over and picked up his phone from his bedside table. Nine thirty-seven. Crap. He had hoped to sleep until noon. What time did he get home—four-thirty, five? He vaguely recalled the cabbie flying through a string of green lights up Park Avenue.

His mouth was as dry as stale pound cake. His temples throbbed. It was a helluva night, alright. It seemed like he hadn't missed a beat from three years ago, when he and his three roommates were NYU seniors, starting weekends on Thursday nights and getting shitfaced around Greenwich Village.

Mindful of the spears of pain in his head, David swung himself to a sitting position and belched. Stale beer and stomach acid. *Yech. Into the shower, dude. And coffee. Lots of coffee.*

He stretched. *Holy shit, what was that?* He looked in alarm at his forearm. There was a bulge on the inside, just below the elbow. He pressed it. Firm, but not solid. Some kind of bruise? Had he hit his arm last night? If he did, it must've been a real wallop to create such a lump. He couldn't remember doing anything like that. It seemed like he should recall something that significant.

But considering how many shots of Jack Daniels he'd tossed back, maybe not.

He staggered into the bathroom and turned on the shower faucets, twisting the hot water a notch higher than usual, as if the extra heat would purge his hangover. It didn't, but it helped. As he lathered himself for the second time to wash off the stubborn night, fragments emerged from the quicksand of his drunken memory. Making out with a brunette in a hallway. Was that the second or third bar they'd gone to? Puking on McSorley's sawdust-covered floor. Jesus.

Fucking embarrassing. That must've been when he bailed.

It was his own fault, though. He'd kept ordering shots as his friends compared progress in their careers. He'd landed the most prestigious job after graduation and was easily making the most money—close to a six-figure starting salary—as an equity research analyst for a Wall Street investment bank, but he hadn't moved beyond the entry-level position. The others were already climbing the ladder. Alex had won prizes for his series in a Nebraska newspaper about contaminated drinking-water fountains. Jake was clerking for a federal judge. Jason had just been promoted to copywriter at an ad agency in Chicago. And David, well, now he was going to do what he had always vowed not to—go to work for his father, one of New York's biggest commercial real estate developers. He had told his friends last night. They'd accused him of selling out, of being a hypocrite, of taking the easy path. It was all true.

He slid the soap over his left arm and was immediately reminded of his new contour. Was it a tumor? Some kind of ridiculously fast-growing cancer? He leapt out of the shower and grabbed the towel. Heart pummeling like a boxer's fist, he switched on his desk lamp and studied it. It was the size of a mouse. David poked it. It didn't hurt, but it jiggled slightly. A herniated muscle? Was that possible? A cyst? He'd make an appointment with the doctor first thing Monday.

He dried the rivulets of water dribbling down the nape of his neck with the towel. As he lowered his arm, the skin over the lump peeled back. David froze. A brown eyeball stared at him. He yelped and reeled back, tumbling onto the bed. He saw his blanched face, the purpled crescents under his eyes, the overhang of hair covering his ledge of a forehead. He squeezed his eyes shut and reopened them. It was like looking into a mirror.

The eye was seeing *him*.

He shook his arm like a rag doll and the eye closed. Was he really awake? This had to be a nightmare. If it was, he needed to wake up. *Now*.

He bit on a forefinger.

Hard.

He was awake.

The eye fluttered open. Panic seared him, then an uncontrollable jitter. *Stay calm, dude, think.* He was hallucinating. Could someone have slipped LSD into his drinks last night? Who would do that? Did he fight with someone?

Possibly.

Caffeine. That would clear his cobwebbed brain.

He pulled on shorts and crossed his studio apartment to the kitchen. As he heaped a couple extra spoonfuls of coffee into the filter, he glanced at his arm. The eye opened, shut, opened, shut. The flash of vision made him dizzy.

"Stop it!" he yelled. "Fuck off!"

He was losing it, shouting at a figment of his imagination. *Get a grip, dude.* He could go to the emergency room. Maybe they could give him something. A straitjacket, that's what they'd give him. No. If this was a bad acid trip, he'd have to wait for it to wear off. How long could that be—a couple more hours? He must've slept through most of it already.

He poured the coffee into a mug with "Shatzkin Commercial Real Estate" striped across it and took a whiff of the milk. He recoiled. It was way past its expiration date. He'd have to go to Gristedes. He could use some fresh air anyway. He threw on a T-shirt and a Yankees cap and headed down in the elevator.

The Upper East Side was tranquil on Sunday mornings. Polite

clinking and chatter buzz from brunch bistros, locals walking kennel-show dogs and wheeling high-tech strollers, the five-inch-thick edition of the Times tucked underarm. He felt calmer until perspiration bloomed in his armpits. Manhattan in mid-July. The heat turned into a stinking, cloying vapor as it rose off the asphalt. He should've gone to his parents' in Southampton, skipped this fucking reunion.

Flip-flops slapping his heels, David crossed Third Avenue to the Gristedes. A homeless woman with a foam of matted hair and wearing lots of clothing layers stood outside the store. Her rank smell hit his nostrils as he tugged the door handle. Why don't these people go to a shelter, for god's sake?

He stopped.

He was in a hospital.

The woman screamed as two orderlies tried to restrain her on a gurney. A doctor waited, holding a hypodermic needle aloft. She kicked off the sheet. Her legs were dotted with oozing sores. Fear shot through David. He didn't want to be jabbed with that needle. He wanted to go back to the street, be left alone.

He was leaning against the wall outside Gristedes, staring at a window ad for a sale on organic Bulgarian yogurt. He straightened and wiped his forehead with his T-shirt sleeve. This acid trip was really intense. How long could it last? On flimsy legs, he entered the store and bought the Times, milk, and a one-pound bag of Twizzlers on the notion that he should eat something despite his nausea at the thought of food. On his way out, he paused in front of the homeless woman, then offered her the remaining twenty dollars in his wallet and the Twizzlers.

"Don't ever go the ER," he said.

She snatched the bill but not the candy, muttering what sounded like gibberish.

His cell phone chirped as he rode the elevator up to his apartment. Caller ID read "Jason."

"Where are you, dude? We're all waiting for you."

Brunch with the guys. He had forgotten all about it. "Go ahead without me. I'm not feeling too great."

"Aw, come on. Hair of the dog. We've got the Frisbee football challenge in the park this afternoon, remember?"

Shit. "I'll meet you over there."

"Don't forget. We want to hear about that hardbody from last night." He laughed. "See you later."

"Jase, wait. You ever drop acid?"

"You mean like LSD?"

"Yeah."

"Can't say I have. Why, you thinking of doing it?"

"I think someone dropped LSD in my beer last night. Or maybe mushrooms or some weird shit like that."

"What? You really are tripping, man. You got one wicked hangover, that's all. Take a couple Tylenol PMs. It'll knock you out for a few hours. When you wake up, you'll be back on track, guaranteed."

That was a damn good idea.

***

David stirred. His eyelids were heavy with the residue of three pills. He remembered why he'd taken them and checked his arm. The mound was still there. The weight of worry descended upon him. David closed and opened his eyes again. Still there. It seemed to be mocking him.

Fuck.

He got up and looked out the window, thirty-six stories high. Starbursts of late afternoon sun glinted off the glass and metal of the skyscrapers. Glare washed out the Chrysler Building's peak. Down on the street, minuscule cars glided along as if shunted by an invisible force.

David lurched into the kitchen. As he downed a glass of water, he looked at his arm. Maybe this thing wasn't a bad acid trip. Maybe it was some bizarre disease that affected one-in-thirty-million people.

His cell phone chimed. He jumped.

"Dude, where the hell are you?" Jason shouted above the crowd-buzz in the background. "You missed Frisbee football. We're on happy hour now."

"I crashed. Just woke up."

"We're at Sugar Reef on Second and Fourteenth. It's like a Caribbean beach shack kind of place. Real cute servers. Get your ass over here."

The day was passing him by. Fuck this thing. He was going to party.

David walked into a paper lantern hanging too low from the restaurant ceiling. He batted it from his face, which was then assaulted by a dangling fake liana. He yanked on it, and a clump of it fell to the floor. Ignoring the other customers' stares, he walked to the guys sitting around a corner booth, a pitcher of beer and the debris of nacho demolition on the table.

"You finally made it!" Alex cried over the too-loud salsa music.

"Where you been all day, dude?" Jake slapped his back and poured him a glass of beer. "Here, get this down. Best hangover medicine there is."

David guzzled the beer. It plummeted down his gullet and splashed into his stomach like a log flume. He was relaxing already. "Let's get some food. I'm starving." He snapped his fingers at the server. She scowled at him but came over and took his order of buffalo wings.

"So, what about that girl last night? Did you get her number?" Jason said.

"I don't think so. Honestly, I don't remember much about last night."

"If you didn't, you passed up a golden chance, dude," Jake said. "She was all over you. And she was cute."

David took a long cool draft of his beer. Then he saw it.

Jake and a girl were lying amid a tangle of sheets. The cascade of curls sweeping her shoulders looked disturbingly familiar.

David sputtered on his beer.

Alex thumped him on the back. "Take it easy, big guy."

So that's who Donna dumped him for? Sonofabitch. He'd

introduced them, for crissake, at a party, one of the few times he'd seen Jake while he was at Columbia Law.

David drained his beer and banged the glass down on the table. "So how's Donna, Jake?" he asked as he grabbed the pitcher for a refill.

Jake's face slid off his skull. So it was true.

"Ah, good, good," he croaked. "She's good."

Fucking asshole. "Yeah, she's a good fuck, right?" David said feeling a rising tsunami of resentment and rage.

Jake looked into his glass and cleared his throat. "Listen, dude, I…

"Here comes the food." Alex made a boisterous show of making room for the platter of buffalo wings. "Let's eat."

David scraped back his chair. "Catch you later, guys."

They called for him to wait, to come back, not to be like that. He ignored them. He trudged up Second Avenue into the gauze of dusk. He wasn't hallucinating at all.

The eye saw the truth.

***

The next morning, David dragged himself off the elevator that served floors fifty through eighty and entered the glass doors of McClenahan Grasshill. Suit jacket hooked on a finger over his shoulder, he shuffled through the warren of cubicles, replying to his co-workers' greetings with a limp smile.

He entered his cubicle, where towers of 10Ks, 10Qs, proxy statements, and other assorted SEC filings awaited his perusal. The week's assignment was to write a market outlook on the aluminum industry for the Mergers and Acquisitions Department. Some big hush-hush deal was undoubtedly going on upstairs.

"Hey David, how was your reunion?" Delia's glacier-blue eyes drilled him from over the shared wall of their cubicles. He had asked her out for drinks twice, but she had made excuses both times. He got the hint.

"Great. Partied down and all that." His voice trailed off as his vision swept him into an office.

The M&A vice president was banging Delia on his desk. Her flailing arm knocked the photos of his wife and twin toddlers to the floor. Delia lay on a sheaf of papers headed "Trompe d'Oeil, Inc. CONFIDENTIAL."

"What's the matter? You look like you just saw a ghost." Her voice sounded like she was in a tunnel.

"What? Oh, nothing. How was your weekend?"

As she babbled about some indie movie, his brain whirred. Trompe d'Oeil. The cosmetics company. On the M&A veep's desk.

"David, are you listening to me?"

"Yeah. Just got a lot on my mind."

"You need more coffee, dude." Her head disappeared.

David pivoted to his computer entering "Trompe d'Oeil," into a stock market search engine. The company report popped up. The stock price had crashed to a five-year low and the majority shareholders were pressuring the board of directors to oust the CEO. The CEO was also the company founder, though, so he wasn't going easily.

David leaned back in his chair. The shareholders and the board were probably looking for a buyer to recoup their investment. Hence, the documents on the M&A veep's desk. That meant its stock price would skyrocket in short order. A tremor of excitement rippled through him.

Should he?

What the hell.

He placed an order for $5,000 worth of Trompe d'Oeil shares and settled in to review an aluminum company's 10K.

Maybe this eye was useful after all.

***

By the following morning, the bulge had disappeared. With a huge sense of relief, David canceled the doctor's appointment he'd made and attributed the hallucinations to either a bad reaction to a mickey someone had slipped him or some odd stress thing. As for Jake and Donna, he'd known it all along at some unconscious level, just didn't want to face it. And Delia. He must have overheard a mention of

Trompe d'Oeil, seen her talking to the M&A guy. He debated selling his Trompe d'Oeil shares but the price had dropped even lower. He decided to hold for the time being. It was only five grand.

On Thursday, a blurb cropped up on a stock watcher website that Trompe d'Oeil was in takeover talks with a multinational consumer products corporation. The stock price zoomed. David watched the ticker-tape crawl across the bottom of his screen with glee. By late afternoon, his five grand was worth fifty. He waited until just before the closing bell and put in his sell order. He made another twelve grand and change. He punched his arms in the air in victory.

"Knock knock. I take it that means you're almost finished with that aluminum report." Geri was standing at his cubicle doorway.

"Almost done," he said. His vision flashed. *Shit. It was happening again.*

He was in a bathroom.

Geri bent over the counter. She straightened, sniffing as she pressed a finger to a nostril. She swept a forefinger along an open compact mirror, dabbing up traces of white powder. She licked her finger, snapped the compact shut and walked into the equity vice president's office, her eyelid twitching. The guy looked up. "I need everything about retrovirals on the market and in R&D by Monday morning. That's when PharmaRay is filing their patent. This is going to be big."

Geri felt a shot of hope. She needed cash to pay her dealer.

He checked his arm. It was there. The bulge was back. An electric current of anxiety pinched him.

David?" Geri squinted at him, sniffing. She did that a lot, come to think of it. How had he not noticed that before? "Bad news. I need that aluminum report by tonight."

"Don't worry. Under control."

"Thanks." She left, swishing as her chubby, panty-hosed thighs rubbed together.

He swiveled back and forth in his chair. *Shit. How could this thing have returned? But wait. What had he seen?*

Geri was a coke fiend. Interesting. More interesting was PharmaRay. He typed the company name into a stock search engine. It was a small-cap pharmaceutical R&D company in Bangor, Maine, of all places, formed by a couple of twenty-something MIT PhDs who were obviously about to hit the big time.

David invested all his money from the Trompe d'Oeil deal in PharmaRay shares, then strolled to the break room. Delia straightened from the water cooler.

"Big plans for the weekend?" she asked in a bored, making-conversation tone.

His smile was saccharine. "No, but I bet you do—desk-jockeying with the M&A veep perhaps?"

Her eyes grew as big as an owl's. "Gotta get back to work." She practically sprinted out of there.

David felt a gleam of satisfaction as he sauntered back to his desk, fresh coffee in hand. Behind the pinstripes, McClenahan Grasshill was a pretty interesting place. Who knew?

At five o'clock, the cubicles emptied out like a toilet flush. He ordered pad thai noodles on a delivery app and wandered over to Geri's office, where she was watering plants.

"I'll have that report for you shortly."

She didn't bother looking up. "Great. I've got to pull an all-nighter. Equity wants a report by Monday morning so I need the aluminum thing ASAP." She plucked brown, crinkled leaves from a tendril of ivy drooping from a cabinet.

"By the way, how do you manage to stay awake all night?"

"Oh, I'm used to it by now."

David lowered his voice. "Know what helps? A few lines of Bolivian marching powder."

She hesitated for a fraction of a second, then yanked a fistful of green leaves off the ivy. "I've never been into that stuff."

"Really? I thought you might have some in those things women carry in their purses, you know, makeup mirror things?"

Geri's eyelid twitched furiously. "I don't know what you're talking about."

David bounced on the balls of his feet. "I've been meaning to talk to you about my career path. I'm way overdue for a promotion. I'd like to get into M&A."

Geri stared at him with a set jaw. "Let's talk about that next week."

"Sure."

Score one for Shatzkin. He returned to his cubicle. When PharmaRay hit, he'd buy a Porsche Boxster. Or maybe a Carrera. And make sure he swung by Donna's place. He'd make a couple big hauls in M&A, then he could leave research reports in the dust. And Shatzkin Commercial Real Estate. He'd strike out on his own.

Several mugs of coffee later, a squealing noise came down the hall. The janitor wheeled his cart outside David's cubicle and stopped to pick up the trash can. David looked up in annoyance. His vision flashed.

The janitor was huddled in a crowd on a rickety wooden boat rolling on a nighttime sea, the white of his teeth and eyes stark in the darkness. The smell of vomit and body waste was acrid. A wave crashed over the boat. People screamed and clutched each other as the frigid water doused them.

David gasped. His teeth chattered and his stomach roiled.

He grabbed his jacket and, shoving aside the surprised janitor and his cart, fled.

***

It was close to eleven. The subway was baking with the day's grime-laden stuffiness. David slumped in the plastic seat, gazing at the blackness through the window as the train rocketed with a soothing rhythm. In the glass pane, he caught the reflection of a man entering the car from the one ahead. A chill gripped him.

The man was being stabbed in the neck in an alley. Blood spilled over his hands as he tried to wrest the knife from his assailant.

David gulped for air and erupted in a sweat. An angry red scar laced the man's neck. Wiping his clammy palms on his thighs, he averted his eyes. A woman with stringy hair and the complexion of a sponge sprawled on a seat. She seemed fixated on a gum wad on the floor.

She jabbed a hypodermic needle into her upper arm below a rubber tourniquet. The liquid in the syringe swirled with blood. She depressed the plunger. Her head dropped like a rag doll's.

A tide of nausea churned David's stomach. He clapped a hand over his forearm. He didn't want to see this stuff, this human flotsam and jetsam. He really, really didn't. It had nothing to do with him but it was all around him.

***

David woke to the sound of his alarm. He had to get to work early and finish the report before Geri arrived. He felt drained. The eye's visions had crackled in a ghoulish kaleidoscope in his mind all night. He flung off the bed covers and padded to the bathroom. The solution came to him as he peed. He'd keep rolling up his sleeves at the office, but not in the street. That way he could stop the eye from seeing what he didn't want to see. Easy.

Dawn was breaking as David hailed a cab. He didn't feel like chancing the subway again. He settled into the back seat and relaxed as the cab hurtled down Park. David looked at the taxi license on the glass partition.

A bearded chin peeked around the door of a dark room. A little girl woke in her bed but remained motionless, her senses sharpening like a blade as the man crept into the room and folded back the blanket. His hot breath was foul with tobacco. Dread bunched her stomach as he lifted her nightgown and passed calloused hands over her thighs.

David screamed. The driver braked at a red light. David chucked a twenty at him and flung open the door in the middle of traffic. He skipped around the cars until he stood panting on the sidewalk. That had been the worst vision yet. He looked down at his arm. It was covered by the sleeve. Had the eye seen through the fabric? Then he saw it.

A lump on the back of his hand.

His legs crumpled.

Eyes stared down at him. A scream blasted out of his lungs.

"Take it easy, buddy. Paramedics are on the way," a man said.

All he could see was a forest of shoes and shins. He was lying on the sidewalk. He scrambled to his feet. The eye. He had to rip it out. He clawed at it.

"I don't need a paramedic."

"Calm down. You're going to make yourself bleed like that," the man said.

"I'll be okay!" David shouted. "I just have to get this out of me!"

"Buddy, there's nothing there."

"Leave me the fuck alone!" David glared at the man, who took several steps back, hands in surrender pose.

David ran. He spotted the mouth to a subway station. He dived down the steps as a siren wailed behind him.

It was so early, the office still had that hollow feel. David shoved his file cabinet into the doorway of his cubicle. He didn't want to see Geri or anyone else. He didn't want the eye to see them. He didn't want to know anymore. He had almost finished the report's conclusion when he heard Geri's voice.

"David? Are you in there? What are you doing?" A shadow filled the crack between the filing cabinet and the cubicle wall.

"I'm finishing the report like you wanted me to, remember?"

"What's with the filing cabinet?"

"I don't want to be disturbed. I'm getting this done." His voice was as taut as a violin string.

Silence. David thought she'd left, but then she spoke. "Are you all right? You've been acting a little weird lately."

"Of course, I'm fucking all right. Are you? Snort enough coke last night?"

"David, maybe you should go home. I think you're stressed out. Don't worry about the report. I'll take care of it. You take care of yourself."

"I will stay until I finish this fucking report."

A beat of silence passed. "Take a deep breath. I'll be in my office."

David typed the last line of the conclusion. He emailed the report to Geri along with a note that he was taking the rest of the day off, as she had suggested. He had to take care of the eye. He knew what he had to do.

Hugging the wall, David raced into his apartment building. He beelined for the huge potted palm in the lobby and squeezed himself behind it. He could hear the doorman whistling in the package room behind the concierge counter.

"Hey, Felix!"

Felix stepped into the lobby and peered around. "David? That you?"

"Yeah. Listen, here's a fifty." David extended the bill through the palm fronds. "Can you get me a fifth of Jack Daniels and bring it up to my apartment? Keep the change."

Felix frowned as he took the bill. "Sure. Everything all right?"

"Fine. Now go back in the package room until I go upstairs. When you come up, just leave the bottle outside the door and knock, okay?"

An hour later, David lowered the empty bottle onto the coffee table but it missed and clunked onto the hardwood floor. His head spinning, he wobbled into the kitchen, bumping into the furniture. The floor was tilting like a carnival ride. He slammed into the wall. The blow reverberated but it didn't hurt. Just what he wanted. He lay his hand palm down on the counter and fumbled for the butcher knife.

A meteor shower of pain streaked through his arm. David's eyelids flicked open. The haze of light from the moon and neighboring buildings illuminated the room through the window. He smelled something faintly metallic and realized he was lying on the kitchen floor in a thick puddle. Blood. He was naked except for his skivvies.

Then he spotted them. Two lumps on both his arms. The skin slid back and baleful eyes glared at him.

In double vision, he watched his mouth yawn wide in a scream.

Red Perfection
By
Douglas Ford

When she opened the hotel room door, Levisa felt it again—something in the tree on the edge of the hotel's parking lot, crouching in the low-hanging branches.

Just tiredness, she told herself, the result of too much coffee and not enough sleep.

She shook it off and stepped aside for the man who knocked, the one who had introduced himself as Louis. Likely an alias, she imagined. She held open the door a moment longer after he came inside and began shaking off his raincoat. The rain that refused to abate dampened her, but she wanted to make sure he brought no one else with him, as per their agreement. The nagging feeling something watched her from the trees persisted. She closed the door and turned to regard her guest as he dropped his raincoat onto the bed.

He paid her no mind at first, his attention on the covered object in the room's far corner. He looked even thinner than the first time she met him, at the prayer meeting, like he hadn't eaten in days.

"That it?" he said, his attention fixed on the object, as if he spoke to it, not her.

So right to business. Fine with her. "It's sleeping. Cash?" she said.

"I want to see it first."

You've seen it already, she wanted to say.

He had approached her after the prayer meeting, just after she led the ritual that had become a well-rehearsed routine. With the rise of the Evangelical Movement came a surge in the belief in demons, and Levisa knew enough about human nature to know those who claimed to hate and fear demons also harbored a desire to *see* one, to witness one suffer, perhaps even touch one if they could. For years now, she had traveled the circuit, visiting the innumerable churches that have sprung up in strip malls or fairground tents—she didn't care where so long as people opened their wallets to see what in years past they might have called "spectral evidence," a true sign of the kingdom beyond, as well as the forces that sought to inhabit corporeal bodies.

This man attended her last one and approached her afterwards with an offer to buy. Having decided she'd had enough of this game and hearing the figure he proposed, she'd agreed, as long as he kept it quiet.

And why not, of course he could see it first. So she edged past him and removed the cage's covering, a black shawl adorned with stitching from traditions wide and varied in nature, some ancient Sumerian, some Kabbalistic—protection, she told people who asked, and if pressed she would explain some of the meaning behind the markings.

She stepped back so the man could see the cage and the Capuchin monkey inside.

The man regarded the cage's occupant. He took two steps forward and crouched, maintaining what he probably considered a safe distance.

Levisa waited for him to say something. She wanted to leave this place and get away from the intensifying wind and rain. Coming here to the Vissaria Springs Hotel, marked a homecoming of sorts. The springs were situated a half mile away, a deep body of water whose richness in healing minerals once attracted visitors but now sat fenced off and abandoned. Go deep enough into their waters and you encounter the source of the springs, a hot plume of water, hot enough to melt the skin from your bones. Artifacts and fossils used to turn up around it, many without any apparent connection to known species or settlements. Some of her family still lived in the area, rooted by her ancestors who migrated there long ago, and perhaps that alone proved enough to draw her back and conclude this chapter of her life.

Still no cash forthcoming. Instead, only a look of skepticism. He said, "You're sure it's—"

"You were there. And it goes by lots of names."

"You called it Abyzou," he said.

The demon of miscarriages and infant death, fodder for the evangelical crowd, nearly all of them political zealots. Lucifer's grandmother in some lore. Levisa just called it the Capuchin, no other name. "It's her," she said. "I'd like to see cash. Please."

Doubt in his face. This man didn't want to part with money, and Levisa scolded herself for not insisting on money up front. Lately, she found herself losing the hardness that carried her through life. She had learned the hardness from her grandparents, exiles from the old country who brought with them their traditions and beliefs and used them to frighten her with stories about the springs. They used to take her right up to the fence circling the ring of trees and the unseen waters beyond, telling her to stand very still and listen. And she would obey, listening and dreading, until she heard the screaming.

That, they said in their old tongue, *that is the screaming of unwanted children, thrown into the water by parents unable to care for or feed them. The Drekavac. You don't obey us, we'll throw you in as well.* As their bodies sank below the surface, a plume of steaming water hundreds of meters below roasted their young flesh, causing it to fall away from their bones like a holiday turkey. The image always haunted her. In hindsight, Levisa suspected the screams she heard came from local wildlife, but from her grandparents she developed her inclination toward the occult, as well as an education into what frightened and fascinated others. The power of belief.

"Let me ask you a question," she said.

"Only if I can ask you a question first."

Levisa hesitated. "Ok, shoot," she finally said.

"How did you catch it?"

The industry secret: how does one capture a demonic entity inside a physical form? Levisa maintained many different answers, having explained so often she never needed to rehearse. Just know your audience, she reminded herself. Only she still didn't quite know this one. He bore a quietness that set him apart from the last group of evangelicals, already so unquestioning of the existence of devils and demons. She settled for the old stand-by.

"It's a lot like how you trap an actual monkey. Get a small object—a gourd of some kind, just big enough for the monkey to insert her hand. Put something inside it the monkey can't resist, something sweet and tasty. Once the monkey puts her hand inside and gets her hand around the delicious morsel, she won't let go. Meanwhile, the hole you made is just big enough for her hand, but not the fist she makes once she's holding something. Then, voila, you have a monkey simply because the monkey refuses to open her hand. She would rather you capture her than let go of her reward."

A beat passed as he considered this explanation.

"Demons are like monkeys. You're telling me this with a straight face," he said.

"No, not exactly. But once they get their hands on something—or someone—they don't like to let go."

"So what's inside this animal just needs to let go, and it's out? That sounds dangerous."

"It won't let go," said Levisa. "It doesn't want to. That's the trick. To make it want to stay."

"A filthy demon, and you treat it like a guest."

Levisa felt her heart flutter, something that happened whenever she got nervous (and had become worse and more painful over time). She thought of rolling up her sleeve, doing the spiel she performed in front of the faithful as she showed the scars. *The Capuchin didn't cause these. The demon inside of it did.* She felt herself close to calling off the whole deal. Her and the Capuchin together forever. Instead, she said, "My turn to ask you a question."

He nodded at her to continue.

"What do you do? You don't seem like the kind of person I should be dealing with."

By way of answer, he turned to the bed where his coat lay in a heap. Once again, Levisa thanked her stars she didn't intend to sleep on those sheets when she saw how sopping wet it was. She also saw what she failed to notice before, something bundled up in its folds. He meant to keep it concealed, she realized, as he held it out for her to see.

A ceramic work of art, twisted and snake-like, with long strands of hair ending in viper faces and dragon wings fixed to its back, the whole thing a glossy red. Levisa recognized the likeness: Abyzou, its female form unmistakable.

"I'm an artist," he said, extending his work out as if he intended it as an offering. She made no gesture of acceptance. Not only did its serpent tail seem delicate, but its redness made her uneasy.

As if he could sense her thoughts, the artist said, "I'll trade your monkey story for an industry secret of my own. Something I learned from one of my mentors a long time ago that stuck with me. A Chinese emperor, not the easiest person to please, demanded an artist in his court produce a special shade of red in his work. I'm talking about the medium I work in—ceramics—and, like everything else, it comes with its own special challenges. After experimenting with different dyes, the artist presented the emperor with every shade of red he could imagine. The emperor rejected them all. None of them were good enough. The artist's life and reputation were at stake. Can you guess what the color red signified?"

Levisa thought of death. She paused, formulating an answer. "Sacrifice?"

The artist nodded. "The artist returned to his studio despondent. Nevertheless, he tried again with materials he prepared the night before. This time he managed a remarkable red, something that astounded even himself. When he returned to the emperor's palace, he prepared himself for another rejection. To his delight and aston-ishment, the emperor met this newest display with joy. He ordered the artist to produce several creations in this shade. The artist took the praise home to meet his master's demands. When he opened the kiln, he saw something that horrified him."

From outside came the sound of wind and rain, the storm heightening. They both paused to listen. The sound of a branch breaking met their ears. Levisa thought again of how she had sensed something in the tree. "Go on," she said.

"He saw what he was unaware of before. Two nights prior, a cat had crawled into the kiln, perhaps old and sick. Whatever the case, the firing of the kiln destroyed the animal. That was what produced the shade of red. Nevertheless, the artist cleaned the kiln and set about reproducing the color, but he simply couldn't do it. Finally, in his despair, he threw himself into the kiln and left instructions to his successors, knowing from his flesh, the proper red would result. He would die horribly but preserve his reputation."

Levisa regarded the work of art held by her visitor. She asked the next question with her eyes.

He understood. "Yes, this red is similar. I know a doctor who lets me have—well, let's call it medical waste. The glaze is similar but different."

She didn't know what he meant by glaze.

"The shine," he said, "the finish. You need calcium, and human remains will do." He paused, adding, "Ashes."

She felt a perverse urge to touch it now, and he let her. Without discussing the matter, they both kept it out of the Capuchin's line of vision. As her fingers grazed it, she heard another sound, a creak of what was certainly a tree branch. The wind's roar increased.

"And these ashes you used in the glaze—I'm guessing they have something to do with Abyzou."

He nodded. "I don't have much. Never did. But I had someone I loved, and she got taken away from me."

"And this has what to do with my Capuchin? You need what possesses it to admire your art?" She felt as though she had truly seen and heard everything.

"I need closure," he said. "She died after an ectopic pregnancy."

Levisa laughed at him. She tried to stop herself and could not. He watched, mystified.

"Oh, you stupid man," she said when she could finally speak. "You stupid, stupid man. You think a miscarriage happened because of a demon?"

The way his mouth set challenged her to continue.

"That's science, a natural failure of the human body. That's not the work of a demon, even one known to cause stillbirths and miscarriages. And you wanted to meet this Abyzou for what—revenge? Stupid, idiotic man." The work of art gripped in her hand made the rest come clear. "And you created this—this fantasy—to confront it. Used the remains of that poor woman in the hopes of creating a spell, a summoning. Because of course, that's what you artists think—you can create magic through your enfeebled imaginations."

The set lines of his face answered her. Everything she said was true. Another crack from outside, and both of them jumped. The wind blew the door open. Levisa, thinking she hadn't closed it well, made sure it latched properly. A quick glance outside told her that two branches had indeed fallen. Turning, she said, "And you don't have money, do you? You thought I'd be persuaded by this sad story and just give the Capuchin to you."

The mention of the animal caused them both to turn. Ravaged and old, it regarded them from the security of its cage.

"And that's just a monkey," she said, pointing. "Not something housing a demon or revenant or any other kind of supernatural entity. It doesn't cause miscarriages or stillbirths or ectopic pregnancies. It eats fruit and leaves, maybe an occasional frog or small bird. It doesn't eat souls, and it doesn't cause anyone's death."

Levisa made it to the end of her speech and suddenly felt her chest go heavy. More cracks from outside, definitely not thunder, and she wondered if the whole tree had just fallen, or if something huddled on its branches, looking for shelter from the storm, getting wetter and wetter until the growing mass had caused the whole thing to collapse. She touched her chest and thought of her grandmother's fatal heart attack, how she clutched the space between her sagging breasts, took two heaving breaths, and died right in front of Levisa so long ago.

She wanted to call out but could not, could only fall back onto the bed, onto the soggy raincoat, the man watching her, not even turning when the door blew open again. The sculpture fell from her hand to the floor beneath the bed, out of sight.

The artist didn't reach for it. He only watched her. He disregarded the door still hanging open and approached her. She wanted to tell him to go out into the rain, to find help, and perhaps her own vision began to fail her as her heart thumped hard, because she saw a disturbance in the air where the rain burst in. Watery shapes with large heads, and she thought again of her grandmother and the stories from the old country. The melting flesh of unwanted children thrown into the hot springs. Would the artist, who now approached her, wonder what sort of red their ruined bodies made, what he could make with them?

He seemed not to see them. Instead, he began pulling up her shirt, and she wondered if he intended to perform CPR. Again, she wanted him to run for help. She tried flailing her arms, but something held them fast.

At the side of the bed, she saw the outline of one of the giant watery heads, and she again remembered the term used by her grandmother. The Drekavac, the spirits who cried terrifically from inside the fence surrounding the springs. What sort of dying vision did her grandmother inspire, what sort of curse did she deserve because of this act she performed, this ruse she played with the Capuchin, parading it before people who clung to absurd beliefs? She became good at it, pretending to believe in invisible forces along with them, displaying this spectral evidence she arranged for them to see, to part them with their money, nodding and shaking in fear and ecstasy along with them. It proved a good game, never as dangerous as she pretended, as long as she ignored their fanatic politics. She never hurt anyone.

But this artist, she realized, meant to hurt her. He pulled up her shirt not to help her. He did so in order to place his face close to her abdomen. "You're carrying," he whispered to her bare flesh, "in labor." At that, she realized his delusion and what he'd done or intended to do—not just taking medical waste to create his special shade of red. He meant to harvest her and a baby he imagined she had inside of her. The importance of his story struck her, the unthinkable things that went into making his shade of red.

Her arms refused to move, and she heard it then—the scream her grandmother urged her to listen for, right now, from beside the bed. The head appeared again and jerked away when she turned to see it more clearly, an obscene game of peek-a-boo. Something sharp grazed her abdomen, and she knew he held a knife or scalpel there. She looked for something to use to fight him off, and turning, saw something she couldn't explain.

The Capuchin, sitting on the dresser. Something—perhaps the room's invaders?—had set it loose, and it watched her. She saw its misery and hate for all she put it through, and she couldn't blame it. She wanted to yell to it to run, to escape this place before this mad artist put its body along with hers inside a kiln to make his red. But it sat still, its suffering having made it resigned and wise.

Something shone in its eyes, though, and it held up the statue of Abyzou, as if for her to see.

"Break it," she managed to say, feeling the blade slice into her. Instead, still holding the object, the Capuchin leaped onto the bed and approached her. An intelligence she never recognized before glimmered in its eyes. It held her with its gaze as it approached her, a shimmer of hate, and she thought, yes, maybe all she'd done before to it managed to create an actual possession. Its gaze never left her as it broke the ceramic over the headboard, as if to say, *Mercy doesn't compel me to do this, but to help you defeat a common enemy.* As the pieces broke, a black-red ichor flowed forth, and the Capuchin held it over her face so she had no choice but surrender her last gasps to drink it, take it all in, the remnants of countless dead.

As the man emptied her insides, she felt something else fill her, something that dulled her pain.

Something pushing through her back, something growing.

She looked down at the redness covering the lower half of her body—a translucence, like glaze.

It was beautiful.

The artist began collecting the spoils of her body. He had brought plastic bags to carry it home.

Her arms felt free now. A pressure from her back forced her to sit up.

She felt the wings unfold, leathery like those of a bat.

So occupied was the man with the parts of her body she no longer needed, he did not at first see her stand up and allow the wings to extend to their full glory. When he did, he froze. Her hair began changing too, the cords thickening and extending into little viper faces. One bit her face, and she answered it with a kiss.

What must her eyes look like? She wanted to see.

The artist dropped her liver and fell to his knees. She knew what he intended to do with the Capuchin—throw it into his kiln and bake its flesh into the reddest of reds. To create a work of even larger stature, his need for revenge growing into a need to summon and see. To serve and to earn blessings.

She didn't have to wait long for his prayer.

"Give her back to me," he said, still kneeling. "You took her, I gave you form. Now reward me." He would have bowed his head, too, if he could have pulled his eyes away from her magnificence, but he couldn't look away. Did he imagine he created her? Such egoism.

She allowed him to gaze just a bit longer before tearing him apart. The vipers needed to feed. So too did the Drekavac, those lost children. Unsatisfied with the body of the artist, they turned to the wastage in the plastic bags, the organs she no longer needed or wanted. Once they finished their feast, she ate the Drekavac herself, swallowing their gigantic heads, for they had served their purpose, and their screams would inhabit her now.

Her feast completed, she stepped out into the rain, having shed the remainder of her clothes. The blood of the artist made the sheen of her new body complete and so perfect.

The Capuchin followed her in supplication. She regarded the tree, where some branches still remained. There in the rain that would soon end, she touched the head of the Capuchin with the forked end of her new tail. "Go," she said, and, having earned her permission, it found its way into the tree. She watched it climb high and bid farewell to her former host.

Behind her, the door to the hotel room hung open, suspended by the wind. She set forth to find the springs.

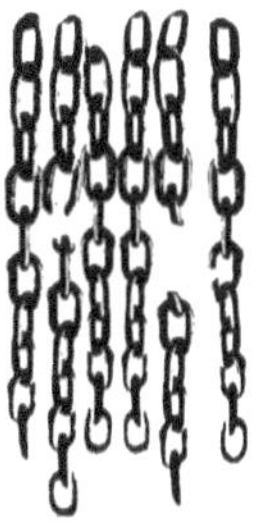

With Wings, I'll Make You Fly
by
Theresa Halvorsen

The shutters in my laboratory blew open, and I cursed. Darting across the room to pull them closed, my hip hit the massive worktable I'd bought in town for ten dollars. Glass beakers and tubes fell to the ground, and papers from my journal flew in a cyclone around me. I yanked on the shutters, splinters cutting into my fingers, straining to pull them closed as pollen and dust from the dry Kansas morning swept around me. I heard the flames on my Bunsen burners sputter and hoped they wouldn't go out.

I strained as the wind tried to sweep the shutters from my grasp, my blonde hair whipping out of its braid to stream behind me. For an instant, the wind died, and I yanked the shutters closed, throwing the latch. The wind howled, straining against wood, bits of pollen blowing through cracks, but the latch held.

This time.

Go to the United States, Professor Stewart had told me, exactly 32 days and six hours ago. *Get on the first train out of London and then onto the first boat heading to the United States,* he'd told me, passing me the giant crate with all his journals in it. *Get out, didn't matter where,* he'd said, carefully packing the microscope, beakers, and other breakable equipment. We needed to be gone before the authorities found our laboratory and what we had been doing.

So he'd gone to Brazil, and we'd come to the United States,

promising him not to use human specimens until I didn't have a choice.

But the papers in New York, Boston, Washington DC, and Philadelphia had stories on the front page about Professor Stewart and his experiments. Frustrated, we'd set out west, aiming for San Francisco. I figured by the time I made it there, the papers would have forgotten, but I'd run out of money halfway there.

As it turned out, I didn't have anything to worry about in this backwards Kansas town, judging from the education level of the locals. No one had even heard of The New York Times when I'd tried to get a subscription. I could set up a lightning rod and raise the dead, and they'd have no idea.

Though it wasn't like it was possible to raise the dead. I'd tried. Never worked.

Securing my hair back in its braid, I surveyed the mess of my lab. Glass sparkled on the floor, mixing with the yellow Kansas dust, the blood specimens, feathers from numerous birds, and the various chemicals I used to create my brother's medications. The smell was nearly caustic, with an undercurrent of copper, and I took a few light breaths until my nose adjusted.

The wind howled again, pushing more dust and pollen inside, and I sneezed. The windows should've had glass, but the most recent "twister" had blown them out before we'd moved in. Jeffrey Todd, my landlord, had told me last week he'd only consider replacing the glass if I stayed a year.

"You see, Ms. Adderly, Stella, if I can call you that—" He ignored the shake of my head, his eyes on my chest where I dabbed at perspiration with a handkerchief. "Glass 'round here's 'spensive with the twisters blowing out windows every spring and summer. But I like your London accent. Like your London outfits."

Yes, of course you would, I'd thought at the time. I wasn't wearing a faded gingham or flowered dress like the other women, but jeans and a man's shirt with the sleeves rolled up, like I always wore in London.

"Maybe we meet at Joe's for a drink, see where the night goes,"

Jeffrey Todd had said, grabbing my hips and pulling me against him, "I'll see 'bout replacing the glass sooner."

Luckily, it had only taken a stomp on his foot to get him to release me—but I wasn't getting glass in the windows anytime soon. And now Jeffrey Todd liked to drive down my dusty driveway in his rusted pick-up and blare his horn in the middle of the night.

Flicking on the radio, I hummed along with Elvis singing All Shook Up and squatted on the floor, trying to pick out the usable feathers from the gore on the floor. The damage from the wind was worse than I would've expected. At least fifteen test tubes full of bird blood were lost. They would take weeks to replace. Birds, especially the tiny ones like hummingbirds and sparrows, were nearly impossible to catch and drain the blood out of, too. But for some reason, my experiments had gone better on the smaller birds than the bigger crows and rooks.

My eyes flicked to the empty cage the latest experiment rested in. At least I was making progress. It had survived the surgery and, with luck, the transplant would hold.

The empty cage.

The empty cage.

The empty cage.

My mind repeated the phrase over and over. Where had it gone? Ten minutes before, the cursed hummingbird was resting on the branch I'd set in the cage for it.

I vaulted across the laboratory space, tripping on a set of metal pliers and falling to the ground. Glass bit into my hands and knees, my own blood joining the pool of animal blood and chemicals on the floor, but I barely noticed. Crawling to the cage, I pulled myself up, staring inside.

It was gone.

I shook the cage, but nothing happened. No vibrations, no chirps, no hums. I held my breath, listening. I'd replaced its wings with my creations, and they made a faint squeaky sound.

Nothing. It had been fine ten minutes ago. Had the wind blown the wings off or given it a heart attack?

The flowers I'd placed in a little floating bowl for the bird to drink nectar from had wilted and curled in on themselves. Maybe it had fallen into a fold of newspaper? Even if it hadn't survived the latest experiment, its body would still be in the cage.

I opened the cage, patting around in the newspaper. Maybe it had simply passed out; I needed it to survive so I could move to the next phase of my experiments.

Something darted past my face, so quick I barely saw it. A high-pitched squeaking sound filled the air, so loud it was almost painful. Apparently, the green and purple-streaked hummingbird, with its transplanted wooden wings, had been hiding the whole time in a newspaper fold.

Stupid cursed thing.

The hummingbird darted around my laboratory, the high-pitched squeak from its wooden wings replacing the thrum most humming-birds made. I felt a grin stretch my facial muscles as I watched it dart around the room.

Finally, a success! Hopefully, it would live longer than Professor Stewart's human subjects had.

It dive-bombed my worktable, and more blood-filled tubes hit the ground—the dog and cat this time. I winced as more blood pooled under the table, though it didn't put a damper on my elation. The hummingbird flew by my head, almost hitting me, wisps of hair blowing into my face. It was fast! So much faster than the hummingbirds I'd observed and collected from the wild.

I'd be able to fix my little brother!

Grabbing the net I used to capture my specimens, I swiped at the tiny bird. Miss. My notebook, with its meticulous notes, joined the blood, dust, and glass on the floor. Exclaiming, I dived to grab my notes before they got soaked and sliced my hand further on a shard of glass. I cursed, even more blood joining the mess on the ground.

Bloody brilliant. Tying a cloth around my hand, I swung for the bird again, hitting the radio to the ground. The station switched, and Sh-Boom by The Chords blared out of the speakers and then cut off in a stream of static.

I hoped the radio hadn't broken; Mathew would never forgive me.

Swipe, miss.

Swipe, miss.

Swipe, miss.

Surely the cursed thing was getting as tired as I was!

I took a quick break, leaning against my worktable to catch my breath, turning off the Bunsen burners before the hummingbird set the house on fire. More feathers floated through the air to stick to the floor. But the goose feathers—the giant wings I'd been stitching together for Mathew—those were still fine.

The DJ came back on the radio out of the static, introducing Johnny B. Goode. The opening guitar riff came on. I turned up the sound, expecting it would improve my mood; Americans had better music than we did in London.

"Stella! Hurry!"

With a stifled groan of frustration, I grabbed the radio and hurried around the mess of blood, chemicals, feathers, and glass to bolt out the door. I slammed it shut behind me; I couldn't afford to lose my one successful experiment. The slam shook through the ancient Kansas farmhouse, and something from the kitchen hit the ground, probably the one good pot I had left.

I opened Mathew's bedroom door, reeling at the stink of urine and unwashed body. Johnny B. Goode cut out in a burst of static, and my brother screamed in rage. I went to the bed where he struggled to sit up, but he shooed me away, shouting, "Fix the music!"

I put the radio on a table and played with the dials until his favorite song came through. I helped him into a sitting position, pushing several pillows behind him. He shimmied his shoulders to the music, raising his hands into the air, a smile on his lips. I was glad he still had control of his shoulder muscles; he needed his upper body functioning to make my plan work.

Six months ago, on his fourteenth birthday, my brother had been run over by a car. Professor Stewart and I found the driver, and she became the first of our experiments. While Mathew's decimated legs and broken back would never allow him to walk again, I was hoping to make him fly, hoping to make all the boys and girls like him fly. I just needed more time.

And money, but that went without saying.

Jailhouse Rock came on, and he smiled at me, his head bobbing back and forth in time to his arms. "Dance with me, Stella," he requested. I'd never been one for dancing, but even I knew how to do The Twist, and my booted feet twirled back and forth on the threadbare rug in his room.

For a moment, this was all that mattered. Mathew was happy, and I was closer to getting him healthy.

The song ended with a drum crash, and a commercial came on for a washing machine. I turned the sound down.

"That was fun," I said. "How are you feeling today? Want to get out of bed?"

He eyed the straps on the chair I'd cobbled together so he could sit upright out of bed. It worked, but the straps cut into his skin and caused bruises, so it was always a war between getting out of bed or being comfortable. Between my experiments to give him wings, I'd been working on tinctures to ease his pain but help keep his wits. That was the only good thing about Kansas—the weeds that grew all over had pain-dampening properties if mixed correctly.

But I hadn't been very successful. Sometimes my concoctions removed his pain, but he'd hallucinate or throw up. Other times the tinctures increased his pain or made him sleep for days with horrible dreams.

"I can put you in the chair and give you some of the purple drink." I was pretty sure that beaker hadn't broken. "You didn't seem to mind that one as much."

He made a face. "I'll stay in bed," he said.

I took a comb out of my pocket and slicked his hair back. "Just like Cary Grant," I told him. "Ready for breakfast?" I wasn't sure what food we still had, but I'd gotten good at making it last.

"I heard crashes," he said. "Is everything all right, Stella?"

I shrugged and started to tidy the bedsheets, tucking him into bed more firmly and plumping his pillows. "Minor mistake. On one hand, the hummingbird is flying well. So well that it got out of its cage, and I can't catch it."

"But it worked?"

I nodded. "I think the key was using hummingbird blood when I swapped out the wings and injecting it a little bit at a time into the bird. I don't think cat or human blood worked well. I hypothesize that's what caused the problems before."

"You'll need blood to make my wings work?"

"Yes." I tucked a plumped pillow behind his head. "And it's going to have to be human. And I think it's best if it's yours or mine. And I need to run some more experiments. Add the wings to a mockingbird and a crow. Then I'll try on a rat, dog, and cat. They don't have the muscles like birds do, so it's going to be a bit of trial and error, but people don't have the same muscles either."

I picked up his half-eaten plate from the night before. I never said I was a good cook, but the dumplings and stew I'd made the night before had been passable. "You have to try—"

Mathew ripped the plate from my hand and flung it against the wall. Congealed stew, dumplings, and pottery flew across the room, scenting the room in old food and covering up the urine stench.

"You promised it would only be a few weeks once we got here!" He screamed, spittle flying from his mouth.

I put my hands on my hips. "That's not how to behave. I'm doing the best I can."

"Professor Stewart would've done it by now."

"I doubt that." I had his journals, and I remembered how the human experiments had been a disaster. No one had survived, and the only reason their families hadn't come after us was because we'd chosen subjects from the workhouses and asylums. "Getting the wings to work on the hummingbird was a huge accomplishment today." I took a deep breath. "You need to eat. I'll bring you some breakfast."

I started to leave but stopped when Mathew tried to wiggle himself back to lying down. I went over to help him, turning him so he lay on his side away from me, facing the wall.

"I promise," I said, leaning over to kiss him. "You will fly. I just need time."

"I don't want breakfast," he mumbled to me. "Not hungry."

He needed to eat, or there wouldn't be any muscle left to make the wings function. I looked at the mess of food and pottery on the ground, trying not to let my frustration show. I couldn't force him to eat either.

"Ok. I'll come back to clean up after I catch the hummingbird. Maybe you'll want to eat then."

"Clean it up now," he ordered. "Or it'll get flies. And you know I hate them."

I had to breathe to control my temper. Mathew was right, and I knew he was frustrated and bored. The Kansas flies were huge and bloated and liked to land on his destroyed legs.

I turned up Johnny Cash on the radio, got some rags, and cleaned up the mess. He didn't speak to me when I closed the door behind me and headed back to my laboratory. It was indisputable his temper was getting was worse. I had to hypothesize it was the painkiller I was giving him. Maybe it was changing something in his brain. It was too bad I couldn't experiment on that without killing Mathew.

I went back into the laboratory, carefully opening the door and quickly shutting it behind me. The smell hadn't gotten any better, the acrid chemicals warring with the coppery blood. Coughing, I tied a handkerchief around my nose and mouth. The high-pitched hum had stopped—maybe the hummingbird was resting. I picked up the net and tiptoed around the room, trying not to step on the broken glass and blood.

There it was! The hummingbird was on the ground next to a puddle of congealing blood, its beak stuck deep into it. Was it drinking the blood? Was this normal behavior for hummingbirds?

It spotted me, turning its head, and lifted off the ground, the high-pitched humming filling the air. Then holding its eyes with mine, it shot at me. I screamed and darted out of the way, waving the net wildly. The hummingbird spun in midair and flew toward me again, its beak sharp, deadly. I screamed and darted again, but this time felt sharp scratches against my neck and arms.

I swung the net, and a box of gears hit the ground with a crash, adding to the mess. Experiment or not, I was going to murder this bird once I figured out how I'd made its wings work.

Suddenly the shutters flew open again, and wind howled into the room. The hummingbird shot out through the opening.

"No!"

Leaning out the window, I searched the clouds. But it was gone, lost in the dark gray sky. I slammed my good hand against the windowsill and cursed as pain shot through my fingers.

I'd lost it. The proof of my experiment. The evidence that the wooden wings I'd added to its tiny body actually functioned.

With a sigh, I sat down in a chair, massaging my temples.

At least I still had my notes.

I spent the next few hours cleaning up the laboratory. My stomach rumbling and feeling a bit light-headed, I went into the kitchen. Opening up the cabinets, I found a bottle of ketchup, a dusty can of condensed mushroom soup, and several moldy beets. I didn't even have flour or yeast to make bread.

I was going to have to go to town, or we wouldn't be eating today. And Mathew needed to eat. I looked down at my blood-spattered overalls and threadbare shirt.

After applying a real bandage to my cut hand and pulling on an old dress and oxfords, I yelled goodbye to Mathew and climbed into the truck I'd bought for fifty dollars from one of the locals. It needed a tune-up, and the left front tire was patched, but it was still enough to get me into town. It wasn't as if there was anywhere else I could go, not with Mathew. And there was nothing to see in Kansas anyway.

I drove slowly down the dust-strewn road toward the town, falling behind a rust-coated truck. I sighed, recognizing the rusty patches as belonging to Jeffrey Todd, my landlord. Hopefully, he wouldn't see me and insist I join him for that drink at Joe's. I switched the radio station away from Patsy Cline and looked up to see Jeffrey Todd swerve into a ditch, bumper first.

Heart pounding, I jumped out of the car and ran to his driver's side window. Jeffrey slumped over the wheel, his mouth open and blood dripping from his temple. There was blood on his neck, thick enough to drip onto his collar and stain his shoulder. I leaned closer, inspecting the gouges. I smelled beer, but not the strong scent of whiskey. He couldn't be that drunk.

I shook him. "You ok?"

A high-pitched hum made me step back. I knew that sound. The hummingbird—my hummingbird with the wooden wings—darted at me from inside the truck.

It had been inside the truck with Jeffrey.

The hum of wings surrounded me, and I ducked again. Dozens of hummingbirds flew out of the open car window, surrounding me. I screamed, waving my arms around and protecting my face with my pocketbook. Yelling and ducking, I ran back to my truck and got in, slamming the door. A pained chirp told me I'd caught a bird in the door.

The birds circled the truck so thick I couldn't see through the windows. I blared the horn and flashed the lights until they flew away.

Breathing fast, I waited to see if they would come back. But they didn't.

What was that?

Heart pounding, I stared at Jeffrey Todd's truck. What if there were more birds inside of it? What if they attacked me again? It was a reasonable hypothesis they'd caused Jeffrey Todd to crash along with whatever had made the marks on his neck. I was curious, but not stupid. What if a rabid dog was wandering around? The best decision was to get to town and send help. I wasn't a doctor, only a scientist, and if Jeffrey only bumped his head, he'd be ok. He didn't need me, just the doctor to clean him up and apply some bandages.

I continued down the road, Heartbreak Hotel playing on the radio. I searched the sky for more birds, but there was nothing, just the gray sky.

I pulled into the main street with the grocer's, hardware store, women's clothing store, and bar seemed oddly empty for noon. A dark cloud zoomed down the road, seeming to chase three people. Was that dust? I started to get out of the car and then sat back down, pulling the door shut as someone yelled a warning. The odd cloud surrounded a group of people. Someone fell to the ground, and the cloud covered them while the other two people ran into the hardware store and slammed the door.

Putting the car into gear, I drove closer and rolled down the window to hear over the engine. Parts of the dark cloud darted and weaved within it. Were those hummingbirds? I turned down the radio and heard a familiar high-pitched screech over the low hum. My hummingbird broke away from the cloud surrounding the person on the street and hovered before my windshield, meeting my eyes.

It gave a chirp and went back to the person on the ground. I couldn't see much, but blood pooled under the body, and it had stopped moving. Hummingbirds perched next to it, dipping their beaks in the blood. My hummingbird landed on the neck of the poor soul. It leaned down, its beak impaling the main artery. I watched, frozen, as the hummingbird drank its fill, then the other hummingbirds attacked the person's neck. The blood beneath the body spread.

Had I caused this? And could I replicate it?

With a deep breath, I reminded myself to go back to what I knew, not jump to wild conclusions. My fingers shaking, I started to count:

1. I'd replaced the hummingbird's wings using a combination of light wood, gears, and blood drained from other hummingbirds.
2. The replaced wings worked, and the hummingbird could fly.
3. I'd seen the hummingbird drinking the spilled blood off the floor; the mixture of cat, dog, rat, bird, and human blood along with the chemicals I'd used for Mathew's medications.
4. Those chemicals were increasing my brother's erratic behavior.
5. The hummingbird had escaped through the window and was now in front of me.
6. It was drinking the blood of a human.
7. Other hummingbirds were now attacking and drinking the blood of a human.

A crow landed on the outskirts of the pool of blood. Crows were carrion birds, and I expected it to land on the human and start pulling flesh away. But it leaned over, drew up a beak-full of blood, and, tilting its head back, swallowed.

I'd never seen behavior like this in birds before. They didn't drink blood. Meat and insects, and dead things, of course. But not fresh blood.

Someone yelled, and I gunned the engine. Maybe I could get them into my car, get them...I didn't know where.

I turned into an alley, chasing the screams. Several cats turned their heads to stare at me. They stood on top of something—something moving, but barely. Dark liquid pooled under it. I flicked on my headlights, and dozens of cats reflected back at me. The grocer's neck was nearly severed from scratches and bites, blood pouring from it. I put my hand over my mouth as a brown tabby leaned over to lap the pooling blood.

Rats came running, bending their heads into the pool of blood to drink their fill.

A newscaster came onto the radio. "This is Casey from Kansas City. Return to your homes immediately; we're receiving reports of birds attacking people. Shoot to kill and seek shelter immediately."

Through my windshield, a massive cluster of birds darkened the sky. As I watched, they dive-bombed a store owner who had cracked open his door. Hundreds of birds streamed in. Screams sounded from within.

What had I had done?

I switched radio stations, and Great Balls of Fire came on. Gunning the engine, I shot out of town back to my farmhouse. I had to bottle up the chemicals on my laboratory floor. They'd go to the highest bidder, and Mathew and I would be out of this Kansas town in no time.

***

AUTHORS NOTE: I have the wonderful Semi-Sages of the Pages to thank for the idea of vampire hummingbirds for this one. Thank you, amazing friends, writers, and idea-fairies!

Don't Open the Door to the Dollhouse
by
Stephen Johnson

Isabelle pulled at her mother's hand, insistent on leaving the thrift store. "Mama, I am bored. Can we go now? This place doesn't have any toys!"

Isabelle's mother, Charlotte, knelt down and spoke softly to her irritated daughter. "Isabelle, you are not being very nice, honey. Remember our talk this morning about thinking of others and not ourselves." Charlotte stood up and gave Isabelle one last stern look that said, *Cut it out!*

Isabelle took the cue and stopped her tantrum, easing her grip on her mother's hand. She reluctantly followed along through the endless aisles of recycled glasses and dishes. Isabelle's father, William, walked around the corner, excited to show her mother something. Charlotte looked down at Isabelle.

"Honey, why don't you look around over here while I see what your father has found?"

William led Charlotte away, and Isabelle idly wandered past display shelves of old Christmas dishes—until she heard a soft voice whisper, "Would you like to see my dollhouse?"

Isabelle looked around, trying to locate the voice, when she heard the whisper again. "Would you like to see my dollhouse, Isabelle?"

Isabelle jumped back, excited. "Did someone just call out my name?" She peeked around the end of the large display cabinet and nearly jumped when she saw an old doll standing on the top shelf looking down at her. The doll had matted red hair and faded clothes, musty with age. She wore a red sweater, frayed in the back, over a blue coverall dress. Both of her shoes were still in place and were slipped over two socks now turned a dirty grayish color. The two-foot-high doll stood next to its well-worn box.

As Isabelle stood gawking, straining her neck to look at the doll, a lady walked out from the employees' break room and noticed her staring. "Want to have a closer look?" the lady asked.

Isabelle smiled as the lady pulled the doll from the top shelf and handed it to her. "There you go, sweetheart. She even has these disks you insert so she can talk. Want to see?"

Isabelle's hands shook with excitement and the lady smiled as she placed the small disk in a slot under the doll's left arm. The woman pulled the string on the doll's back, and a sweet voice rang out, "Would you like to see my dollhouse?"

Isabelle let out a shriek of laughter, and the woman giggled along with her as Charlotte and William walked around the corner. William knelt down to see the doll. "What have you got ther?"

Isabelle shoved the doll toward him, almost knocking him over. "Look, Daddy. She talks, and she even knows my name! Watch!" She pulled the string again, and the doll repeated the same phrase, eliciting laughs from the group.

"Can I get her? Please, Daddy?" Isabelle bounced up and down with anticipation as the saleswoman nervously laughed while looking at the parents.

Glancing from William and Charlotte up to the price on the box, she said, "Well, it says $40 but, just between us, how about we make it half-price today. Does $20 sound alright?"

William looked up at Charlotte as she nodded. "Awesome, sounds like a great deal," he said sarcastically as Isabelle grabbed him around the neck.

The ride home was joyous for Isabelle. She insisted her father place

Dorothy in a seat belt next to her.

"Who is Dorothy?" he asked, helping Isabelle into her seat.

"Daddy, Dorothy is my new best friend!" Isabelle laughed and pulled the string on the doll's back.

"Would you like to see my dollhouse?" The doll repeated her famous question as both Charlotte and William closed their eyes, searching for patience.

"How about we learn how to put another disk in there so she can say something else," Charlotte said in a low voice from the front seat.

William pulled the rest of the disks from the bag and showed Isabelle how to change them out. "Looks like we have a whopping four different sayings to choose from." He sat down and started the car. Looking over at his wife, he raised his eyebrows and grimaced as the doll spouted out her new phrase behind them. "Let's have some tea!"

That night, Isabelle placed Dorothy in her bed before brushing her teeth. Her dog, Rosie, an auburn chihuahua, jumped up into the bed close to her. Spotting the doll under the covers, the small dog backed away suddenly, then quickly jumped down and ran away. Isabelle called out for the small dog, but then returned her attention to Dorothy. She climbed into bed, pulling the doll close to her and giggling. Charlotte came in to say good night.

"Wow, you never go to bed without being told before eight. Are you feeling all right?" Charlotte checked Isabelle's forehead for a fever.

Isabelle laughed softly. "I feel fine, Mama. Dorothy told me I should go to bed with her right now."

"Oh, is that right? Well, for once today, I think Dorothy had something good to say." Charlotte laughed as she kissed Isabelle on the cheek. "Sleep well. I love you."

The next morning, Charlotte and William awoke to the sounds of Isabelle talking with someone in the kitchen. They entered and found her sitting with a bowl of cereal, talking with Dorothy seated in a chair next to her.

"Well, good morning, honey. Did you sleep well?" Charlotte walked over to kiss the top of Isabelle's head, but the girl drew back suddenly, startling Charlotte.

"What's wrong, Isabelle?"

"Nothing. Dorothy just said…" Isabelle's voice trailed off. She looked confused for a moment, staring at the doll until finally she stood up and hugged her mother. To Charlotte, it seemed reluctant. "I'm sorry, Mama. I think I was just still a little asleep when you came over."

Charlotte hugged her daughter back, clearly concerned, but tried to play off her anxiety. "It's alright, sweetheart. Want me to fix you something else to eat?"

The rest of the morning ran without incident. Since it was July, school was out, and Isabelle had a swim lesson at the YMCA. That day, she was a little nervous in the car because she would be tested on her backstroke.

"Don't worry, sweetheart. You will do just fine," Charlotte told Isabelle as they arrived at the swimming pool.

Charlotte was helping Isabelle check-in for class when her phone rang. She answered, said a few words, then bent down to talk to her daughter. "I have to run by the house for a minute. Your father left a folder for work at home, and he needs me to bring it to him. I will be back in a few minutes."

Isabelle bit her lip, clearly nervous, and Charlotte hugged her. "I will be back in time for your test."

"Promise?" Isabelle whispered.

"I promise. See you in a minute."

Charlotte arrived home and found the files on the end table next to the recliner in the living room. As she left the room, she heard whispering coming from the dining room. Charlotte rushed quickly toward the room, only to find the shades drawn and the room pitch dark. She stepped in, flipped on the light, and shrieked loudly, falling back against the wall. There, in the middle of the room, standing on the dinner table, was the doll staring intently at her. Charlotte moved diagonally across the room, trying to escape its creepy eye, but the gaze stayed hauntingly on her no matter where she went.

Charlotte reached down to pick up Dorothy and felt other eyes watching her from across the room. She stopped to look around, hand outstretched, but saw nothing. Shaking and nervous, she grabbed the doll and went upstairs. As she walked up the steps and into Isabelle's room, the doll stared steadily into her eyes. Its disconcerting look made her feel nauseous. For some reason, Charlotte did not want to be alone in the house with this doll.

She placed Dorothy on Isabelle's bed and hurried back downstairs, breathing a little easier as she neared the door to leave. As she walked out the front door, she heard a noise from upstairs, but the house was quiet when she stepped back inside. She stood in the doorway and listened. *Probably just my imagination,* she thought. But as she started to close the door, she heard a faint muffled voice from upstairs.

"Would you like to see my dollhouse, Charlotte?"

Charlotte stopped dead still at the doorway. She stood for another moment waiting to see if the voice came back. This time, the house remained quiet. She closed the door behind her, shaking her head in disbelief and muttering about how stupid she felt at letting her imagination run away.

Later that evening, Charlotte and Isabelle returned home from swim practice and celebrating Isabelle's test with a cookie-dough ice cream treat. Charlotte had delayed as much as possible before coming home. She had no interest in being in the house with the doll without William. Silly, she knew, but nonetheless, she couldn't deny it.

Isabelle burst through the front door, bounding for her room and cheering, "Dorothy, I'm home!"

Charlotte anxiously yelled up to Isabelle, "Wait a second, sweetheart. Let me come up with you."

Walking up the steps, she heard Isabelle whispering softly and, for a short moment, she seemed to be crying. Charlotte could not make out what she was saying but, through the crack in Isabelle's door, she saw her daughter kneeling submissively on the floor and staring up at her small tea table. Her face seemed stressed and confused and Isabella bowed her head down close to the ground.

Greatly concerned now, Charlotte swung open the door, screaming to Isabelle. At the sound of her voice, Isabelle looked up suddenly. Charlotte saw her daughter's eyes dart to the table, pleading. Isabelle looked back toward her mother, and the door instantly shut. But Charlotte had caught a glimpse of the table and, for a fraction of a second, she thought she had seen the doll hovering above the small table and chairs. With tears streaming down her cheeks, she beat rapidly on the door, screaming, "Isabelle, open the door. Open the door right now!"

The front door opened, and William walked in, calling up, "Hey, I'm home. How is everyone?"

As the downstairs door shut, Isabelle's door immediately opened, with the girl standing on the other side looking as if nothing had happened. "Hey, Mama. Why are you crying?"

Charlotte barged past Isabelle toward the table but stopped when she did not see the doll.

"Where is that doll, Isabelle?" Charlotte screamed.

"What's going on?" William asked, walking into the room with a confused look.

Charlotte ignored her husband and resumed looking for the doll. She found it lying on Isabelle's bed and grabbed it by the leg, flipping it up to carry it out of the room. Isabelle screamed like she was in pain, "No, don't take Dorothy, Mama. Please don't take her away."

William stepped in front of Charlotte. "What is going on?" he repeated.

Charlotte halted and took a deep breath before describing the events from earlier in the day. William listened with a slight grin but changed his expression as he saw the seriousness on her face. He put his hand on Charlotte's shoulder gingerly. "Whoa, whoa, let's just relax for a minute. Everybody just calm down, and let's go downstairs and talk."

In a few minutes, the family met downstairs. Isabelle sat across from Charlotte, still crying. William asked Isabelle what she was so upset about. Isabelle spoke, hurried and panicking, "I have to see Dorothy right now. She wants me to do something for her. She wants me to leave a door open tonight for her."

William's mouth dropped open, and he looked at Charlotte, fear plain on her face as she returned his stare. William composed his thoughts and turned back to Isabelle, "What else does Dorothy tell you to do?"

Isabelle looked from Charlotte and back to William, lowering her eyes and rubbing her forehead with her hands. "I promised her I wouldn't tell. I promised! She said if I told anyone she would..." Isabelle's voice trailed off.

"What did she say to you?" Charlotte interrupted calmly. "It's ok, sweetheart. You can tell us. Dorothy will not mind if you tell your parents."

Isabelle looked up quickly—with the most severe look Charlotte had ever seen from the young girl—and said, "Yes she will. She said if I say anything to you, she would kill you and Daddy."

Charlotte and William sat up in their chairs, speechless. William finally broke the silence. "I think it is time we take that doll out of the house." He got up and left the room as Isabelle screamed in protest, but Charlotte came to comfort her. "It's going to be ok."

They listened as footsteps overhead creaked along the floor. William was careful not to let Isabelle see the doll as he walked out to the trash can. He re-entered the house a few seconds later, saying, "Listen. It's late, and I know everybody is tired. How about we all try to go to bed early tonight? Isabelle, you can sleep with us, and we can watch cartoons while we fall asleep. How about that?"

Isabelle nodded with tired eyes as William kissed her on the head. He looked at Charlotte, and she nodded. "Maybe we all need to get a good night's sleep tonight," she said.

After a quick bath, Isabelle settled into bed between Charlotte and William. They watched Isabelle's favorite cartoons as Isabelle cuddled Rosie. William looked down later to find Isabelle asleep. He began to say something to Charlotte before he noticed she too, was fast asleep. He sighed softly, turned off the television, and closed his eyes.

***

Isabelle tossed in her sleep as she dreamed of running through the house and back to her room. There she found Dorothy standing next to her bed, waiting for her.

"Are you ready to open the door, Isabelle?"

The doll smiled invitingly, but her eyes glowed a fierce red as she opened her mouth, exposing a ragged row of sharp teeth. The doll's voice changed to a deep growl. "Now it is time to open the door, child. Do it now, or I will kill everything you love."

Isabelle cried and tried to leave, but she found herself in an endless black space as she turned around. The rest of her room was gone, the only things existing were her, Dorothy, and a small door hovering in the pitch-black darkness. The doll pointed toward the white door.

"Open it now, child!"

Isabelle dutifully walked toward the door and touched the handle, twisting it and pulling the door open. Behind her, a low, gravelly voice said, "Good, now step back."

Isabelle looked over her shoulder to find a tall, skinny man with long, slender arms—much longer than was normal for his height—replacing the doll. He wore a long black trench coat pulled tightly around him. A black bowler hat kept his face hidden, except his glowing, dark-red eyes. As he reached the open door, he looked down at Isabelle, a terrible wide smile splitting his face. His mouth grew to the size of Isabelle's head, and a loud shriek filled her ears as he leaned down to swallow Isabelle up.

Isabelle bolted upright in her parents' bed. It was morning. She rubbed her eyes, trying to clear her head. Rosie backed to the edge of the bed, barking relentlessly. William entered the room and swiftly grabbed the small dog, asking, "Rosie, what is wrong with you?"

He put the dog outside as Charlotte came in to check on Isabelle.

"How did you sleep? You seemed to be tossing and turning all night." She noticed the dark circles under her daughter's eyes and checked her forehead. "Are you feeling alright? You don't look well, and you are burning up."

Isabelle reached up and grabbed her mother's hand. "I am fine, Mama. I just didn't sleep well. Could I get something to eat? I am starving." Isabelle jumped out of bed and headed for the kitchen.

Charlotte stood in the bedroom for a moment longer, still concerned about her daughter. She sighed deeply, then turned her thoughts to making a special breakfast. Perhaps a good hot meal would make everyone feel better. She entered the kitchen and stopped, finding William standing with his back to her in the middle of the room, his arms at his sides.

"William, what are you doing?" she asked, walking up to him, wondering if he was playing some a game with Isabelle.

He ignored her as she approached. Charlotte placed her hand on his shoulder. William's gaze was locked on the dining room, and tears flowed down his cheeks. Charlotte's smile faded as she saw his tortured face, and she, too, looked toward the dining room.

"Where is Isabelle?" Now she grabbed him by the shoulders, yelling loudly. "Where is Isabelle, William?"

William kept staring into the dining room with no change of expression. Charlotte ran over and flipped the light switch—and screamed. The doll was standing in the middle of the dining table. Isabelle stood before it, her head slanted down toward the floor. Her eyes were closed, and her body slouched. A tall man loomed over both Isabelle and Dorothy. He opened his large trench coat wide, like a large bird taking flight.

His unnaturally long arms extended the length of the table as he looked down at Charlotte with a devilishly sly grin. Under his coat, he was nothing but pale skin wrapped around a skeletal frame. Swirling wisps of smoke flowed around his body, each smoky wisp carrying a face that strained to pull away from the strange man. One of the faces looked toward her, looking just like her William.

Charlotte turned quickly to see William still in his trance as the sound of hundreds of voices rang in her head. The ghostly white wisps crawling around the man all twisted their heads in unison, crying out in suffering. Charlotte put both hands on her ears to block out their cries. She fell to her knees, looking up at the pale man. With a leer, he directed Charlotte to a small white door that sat oddly in the corner of the room. His voice rattled and gargled between sinister laughs. "Would you like to see my dollhouse, Charlotte?"

Squeezing her eyelids shut, Charlotte summoned the strength to combat the creature who held her husband and daughter captive. When she opened her eyes, the dining room was gone, and she was in darkness, with the tall man and the doll standing in front of her. The tall man leaned in close to Charlotte's face, so close she could smell the rot from his breath as he whispered, "Open the door for me, child. It is the only way out." He laughed, and she felt rancid droplets of spittle fall on her cheeks.

"Open it now, and you can join your husband and daughter. You can join all of my family!" The tall man roared with sadistic laughter as he shoved Charlotte towards the white door.

She reached down and pulled the door open but, instead of backing away to allow him to go through, Charlotte jumped in front of him and entered the door. From the other side, still in darkness, Charlotte looked out to see the tall man screaming in anger. The fiery red eyes no longer pulsed but seemed to dim as he frantically scratched his way toward Charlotte and the door. "No, what are you doing? The door is for me!"

The tall man reached out with a withered hand but, as he neared the handle, Charlotte pulled the door shut on her side with a powerful bang. She heard screams from the other side, and the darkness around her dissolved as hundreds of voices rang out loudly and then dissipated. Charlotte felt the blood rush out of her head. Her legs collapsed and she fell to the ground. She closed her eyes and lost the desire to remain conscious.

***

Charlotte opened her eyes, expecting to see the terrifying smile of the tall man but was surprised to see the beautiful blue eyes of her daughter. William sighed loudly as he saw Charlotte stir from the floor. "Oh, thank goodness you're alright!"

Charlotte reached for Isabelle, embracing her. Isabelle cried quietly in her mother's grasp and held her tightly.

"Is it over?" Isabelle whispered.

"I think so," Charlotte replied, though not as assuredly as she intended.

The next few days passed uneventfully as the family stayed home together, each one afraid of what they might see when they turned a corner in the house. After a few weeks, William returned to work, but the family had not gone out for anything since what they all referred to as "the break-in."

One Saturday, Isabelle asked Charlotte if they could go out to a movie, and she happily agreed. Later that afternoon, Isabelle finished getting ready in her room and ran downstairs. The house was quiet.

"Mama? I am ready," she called. "Where are you?"

After a few minutes, Isabelle started to run through the house. She came through the living room and stopped around the corner from the dining room, still hesitant to go in. She took a deep breath and walked around the corner to the entrance of the dark room. Isabelle reached up and turned on the lights. She froze in the doorway, unable to scream or talk. In front of her on the table stood the doll, Dorothy, staring back at her. Tears streaming from her eyes, Isabelle looked past the doll to a large, familiar trench coat. The black jacket opened wide, revealing not the tall man, but a woman beneath it, her face hidden under a bowler hat.

Isabelle stepped back when the woman in the trench coat lifted her head, smiling broadly. She shook her head in frightened disbelief.

Charlotte stood looking down from the table, laughing cruelly. She looked at Isabelle and rasped, "Would you like to see my dollhouse, Isabelle?"

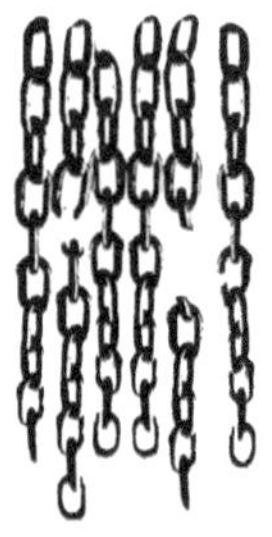

The Resonance
by
M.S. Ewing

The Captain didn't look at me.

Which was impressive, considering they had thirty-eight eyes.

"Envoy," the Captain thought. Their Resonance darted around panels, stopping briefly to dip a wing at me in greeting, but didn't add anything.

Envoy. It was a pointless, honorary title. I'd never even studied diplomacy. But, if I hadn't picked this, I'd have become one more passionless bureaucrat on the home planet. Here, I'd carved out my own place and purpose. Our exploratory ship filled in the blank spaces of the star charts, and whenever we encountered another species, I managed those interactions. I kept us safe, avoiding any miscommunications or unintended slights that could launch us into an intergalactic conflict.

"We've received a distress signal from a Claxrion ship," the Captain thought, their sinewy limbs moving across displays. I wondered, not for the first time, if they'd selected their form for spiritual comfort or simple convenience. The Captain's trunk rooted to the bulkhead, their body receiving all its nutrients from mechosynthesis. There they stayed, overlooking the operation of the entire ship, never missing anything. "Perhaps this is something you'd be interested in, Envoy."

That's why I liked the Captain. Why we'd been able to work together for so long without incident. They managed the delicate balance of never giving me an order while always finding me work.

"Distress?" I responded, letting interest leak through my thought. Out here in the Deep Dark, there were so few ships that, if someone called for help, you helped.

"Yes. The Claxrions claim a prisoner has escaped," the Resonance answered. They flitted through the air, maneuvering through the crowded space with ease. Their thoughts matched the Captain's in tone and tenor so closely, it was difficult to tell the two apart.

Growing up, I'd always been told that finding a resonance was rare. But as we pushed the boundaries of exploration, throwing our race more into the universe, the rate of occurrence increased. These two had been together, sharing the deepest corners of their souls, long before I'd boarded this ship.

I hated the idea. How horrible to have freedom, to have a whole universe of possibilities and challenges stretched out before you, and then be unexpectedly, forcibly anchored to a single person for the rest of your life.

Not wanting to insult the pair, I suppressed the thought and drew my focus back to the present moment.

"I didn't realize Claxrions had prison vessels." I sat back on my haunches, idly scratching behind an ear with one of my tails.

The Captain waved a few of their primary stalks, the body language equivalent of a negative. "They don't. The Claxrions are in a Planet Skipper."

"Curious," I thought, even more intrigued. Everything about this situation was strange. Claxrions were notorious "explorers." At best, they could be considered collectors. At worst, thieves. On average, voracious hoarders, nabbing anything sparkly, shiny, or novel. But their ships were only designed to hop between planets or close systems. How had they gotten out here in the Deep Dark? And carrying a prisoner...

A shimmer of bioluminescence flashed down the Captain's side. A wave of self-satisfaction escaped their thoughts, amplified by the Resonance. They both knew I couldn't resist investigating this mystery.

***

I greeted three Claxrions as they boarded our ship, their articulated exoskeletons clicking with every movement.

"Welcome," I thought to them. "How may we assist?"

"PRISONER," the middle creature responded. I suppressed a wince at the abrasive thought. Claxrion brains were barely capable of mental communication. Individuals on the other side of the galaxy probably heard them. "BROKE FREE. TOOK WEAPON."

I glanced behind me to my two crewmates, Engineer Six and Security Thirteen. Both kept their thoughts locked down. Either they had no opinions on the matter or didn't care to share them. I watched Engineer Six's membrane take on a gray tinge, a nervous response of their chosen form.

"Yes. Any further details?" I asked, turning back to our visitors.

They clicked at me, their many feet scuttling in small circles. I wasn't familiar enough with Claxrion body language to know what that meant. "PRISONER. DANGEROUS. YOU HELP."

Excellent. Now I had a perfect understanding of the situation.

The Claxrions did not accompany us across the gangway to their vessel.

As I stepped into the airlock, I caught a glimpse of my reflection in the shiny metal exterior of the Claxrions' ship. My chosen form was based off a creature I'd seen on the third planet of the thirty-second star in the IL-290 sector. The creature had stalked across a plain, its iridescent purple fur camouflaging its powerful body in the tall grasses. I'd gone to the BioLab immediately, and it had been my chosen shape since. It wasn't quite the right fit for a starship, but then again, neither was I.

When the airlock opened, I couldn't stop the shudder that rippled down my spine. Usually my form's strong olfactory organ was a positive feature.

"Life forms?" I asked Security Thirteen. Their nose flaps, designed to prevent fluid from entering when submerged, snapped shut.

Security Thirteen stepped around a pile of refuse to interact with one of the ship's consoles. They tapped the screen, then pulled their webbed digits back.

"Why is it sticky?" Their thought slipped out. Security Thirteen apologized for the lack of professionalism before returning to the task, cross-referencing the panel's data with a handheld scanner.

"Three life forms in the main chamber beyond this one," they thought.

Well. We wouldn't discover anything unless we went forward.

Engineer Six activated the door.

Two Claxrions crouched behind a heap of material. Some of the items I recognized—textiles, technical devices, an upturned table. Other items were completely foreign. How did they travel through space in such a mess? Did they secure anything when pulling maneuvers or just let the items fly through the air as hazards?

A laser bolt exploded against the bulkhead near my head, singeing the tips of my whiskers and the hair on my right distal ear. I leapt back behind the door, cautiously peeking in this time.

In a corner, half behind a pillar, a creature held a laser firearm.

"Why do you even have a weapon like this on your ship!?!?" I thought-yelled at the Claxrions. "The fire risk alone, much less potential hull breaches...there are safer options."

The two looked at me, then at each other. Their hands moved, communicating in their native sign language. Eventually one responded to me. "SAVE US. DANGEROUS PRISONER."

It was difficult to get a good view of the creature in their hiding spot, but one thing was very clear. The prisoner was not a Claxrion. Long strands of hair flowed from their head, ratty and tangled. The laser firearm hadn't been designed for their slender, pale digits, and their whole body shook .

"Engineer Six," I thought. My crewmate was already moving. "Find out where this vessel has been."

"Envoy," Engineer Six thought only to me, stretching out a gelatinous appendage to interface with the control system. They then gestured to the filthy makeshift holding area in the corner of the room.

Piss in the distilled water, was that where they'd been keeping the "prisoner?"

I wasn't completely sure what the Claxrions had done, but one thing was positive—this was neither ethical, moral, nor legal.

"What did you *collect* this time?" I asked the Claxrions. Anger seeped into the tone of my thoughts and pinned back my ears. Everyone, even the unknown creature, flinched.

The Claxrions bickered behind their refuse barricade, before one repeated: "SAVE US. DANGEROUS PRISONER."

I could tell these two were going to be helpful.

Before I could argue further, the prisoner released a piercing noise that sliced through the air. It reverberated in the small space, shaking the walls of my world. It dissipated, only to be replaced by a low thrum in my eardrums. The vibration built, higher and higher, blocking out the rest of the world. I brought my tails forward to try and block my ears, but with four ears and only three tails, the basic anatomy of my form betrayed me.

It wouldn't have helped anyway. The sound wasn't real. It was only in my head. The Claxrions must have designed some sort of new weapon. Yet, my crewmates and the Claxrions stared at me, unaffected and unharmed. Why was I the only one experiencing this?

Except I wasn't.

The alien prisoner rolled on the filthy floor, clutching their head.

No. No. This couldn't be happening. Not to me.

Yet the universe didn't care about my feelings. The not-sound slid into synchronicity with my mind, pushing my thoughts around. My very molecules vibrated. I locked them down, refusing to let this change me.

I was the Envoy of the third ship in the Fourth Golden Age's twelfth fleet. I was the eighth offspring of the thirty-sixth brood spawned in the Third Golden Age. I was immutable.

No. I wasn't a freakin' alien. I was Abigail Wilson from Des Moines, Iowa. No one, no one, would change that. It didn't matter what was happening, I wasn't going back in that godforsaken cage.

Our thoughts twined together like spaghetti. No. That was their word. The Abigail's word. What even was spaghetti?

An Italian pasta dish. A picture popped in my head, a memory of tastes that I had never experienced before, yet knew was butter and garlic. These weren't my thoughts or my memories.

You asked.

I absolutely had not!

Eventually, the wave abated, and I was able to find the edges of myself. I detangled our minds, pushing theirs away. Still, they pressed in...or I pressed out? I couldn't tell. Hastily, I constructed the strongest mental wall I could. It felt as thin and weak as a sheet of graphite. I could feel The Abigail's thoughts pounding against me, but the wall held.

For now.

"Envoy?" Security Thirteen asked.

I picked myself up. (When had I fallen?) My legs wobbled.

"I am fine." My thought came out as a growl and my crewmates flinched away. Which irritated me further. Turning my head, I focused my attention on the Claxrions. This was all their fault.

They gestured at each other, then at the ground. At some point, the weapon had fallen. It lay on the floor between the two opposing sides. The Abigail lay on the ground, stirring but not yet aware of the changed circumstances.

One of the Claxrions broke from their cover, darting for the weapon.

I leapt in front of them, blocking their path. A primitive growl escaped my throat as one of my tails knocked the firearm away. I prowled the space, forcing the Claxrion to retreat.

"SECURE PRISONER," they said, gesturing behind me. Their little feet scuttled. Claxrions weren't built to walk backwards.

"DANGEROUS. PROMISED TO HELP."

"We are not fools." It took all my restraint not to strike the criminal with my claws. "It's obvious what happened here. You abducted a sentient creature! Were you planning on selling them in an auction or did a patron fund this endeavor?"

The Claxrion's eyes darted around, but it received no help. "FALSEHOOD. FAKE." But its thoughts sputtered out once it was clear no one was convinced.

"Security Thirteen," I thought. "Secure the prisoners."

***

"Our engineers are scouring the Claxrions' ship and records," I thought to the Captain. They had been taken into custody, and I'd found temporary accommodations for The Abigail on our ship.

A set of the Captain's eyes met mine for a moment, before focusing on one of my ears.

"There have always been rumors of the Claxrions selling creatures, but..." Their stalks waved through the air, as if catching errant thoughts.

"It is deplorable," their Resonance thought, completely still for once. "It will be stopped. They will be judged and found guilty."

I agreed, but we weren't law authorities or enforcement or prosecution. We were explorers. The Claxrions and their trafficking, however deep it might go, would have to be someone else's mission.

"I recommend commendation for Engineer Six," I thought. "They have already integrated The Abigail's language from the Claxrions' computer and into our database, which greatly assisted in de-escalating the situation on the ship."

"The Abigail?" The Captain missed nothing.

My inner thoughts rolled around, as I tried to figure out what to share. Even now, with The Abigail across the ship, their thoughts brushed against my mind. Impressions leaked through—they were hungry and tired and grateful to be clean.

"They are my Resonance." I'd meant for the thought to come out casual, unimportant. I failed.

"Envoy," The Captain's Resonance thought, shocked. "Are you—"

The Captain waved a limb, cutting their partner's thought off.

"How would you like to proceed?"

There was no hesitation in my response.

"Get rid of them."

Hell To The Holler
by
Brian James Lewis

After she brought on Pop's final heart attack, I knew it was time for me to do something about the witch's curse on our holler. Somebody had to stop that miserable old bitch, Ms. Jackson, and her domineering ways! I figured that person might as well be me. Because without Pop to look after my welfare, my chances of staying alive were slim to none. I thought about crime, but how the hell would I spend the money with this horrible face? That was Ms. Jackson's work, too. She nailed me with that black magic, evil eye, whammy shit of hers on the day I tried to protect Pop. Totally ruined my face. I look like a fucking monster now! No woman's ever gonna take up with me, and our neighbors, who've known us forever, keep their distance. They won't even return a simple wave from me since Pop died. He used to say you could find out more about a man through his actions than by listening to his words. Going with that, our neighbors are a bunch of snobby shitbirds who aren't even worth the powder it'd take to blow 'em away. The lousy Turncoats!

You would think that growing up in the mountains, tucked into some of the real outback hollers, everyone would share that kinship. From the few people that had made the trip, I'd heard that the rest of the world was like getting onto a crazy spaceship. People carrying around their own little TVs right in their jeans pocket! There were cupboards you put your food in, and it came out all cooked up in just five minutes! No fire needed, no hunting game for supper, or having to keep a garden for vegetables. Damn! Sounds crazy.

But here I went to the same school as everybody else until I was sixteen. I got the same shitty grades, crushed on Betty Perkins with the rest of the boys, and knew I had a job waiting for me at the same Kentucky coalmine every other male resident of our holler did. The K & L Mines motto was, "If You're Willing To Work, We've Got A Job For You!" I'd shared my lunch with others who had none and talked fishing down at Rogers' Creek. Was it really so hard to see me as a human being? I never got to work in the mines, but that was Ms. Jackson's fault, not mine. At least I tried.

We never had a lot and that was okay with me. Give me some pork 'n' beans and a sleeve of Saltines with a cup of coffee, and you're looking at a happy guy! Like Pop always said, "Simple is best." But once he was gone, it didn't take long for the food to run out, even with me doing a little hunting. Plus, you want some cornmeal to roll your squirrel meat in before you cook it up in bacon fat and sweet tea to wash it down. Pop handled all the face-to-face stuff with folks. He was the one who went to Reed's Deli Mart, gassed up the truck, and traded work for stuff like eggs and bread. Without him, I had a choice of trying to buy my own supplies or slowly starving to death.

But trouble started the minute I walked through the doors of Reed's Deli Mart just like I often had before the incident with Ms. Jackson. Mr. Reed shoved me out the door with a shotgun under my chin, saying, "You ain't coming in here looking like that! The place for weirdos like you is the city." I tried to plead my case with him until he clicked the safety off on his weapon. Then I made a run for it, the tires of Pop's old truck spewing gravel as I pulled out of there with a face redder than a stop sign, and I headed to the Walmart on the edge of town.

When I made it to Walmart, it looked like I might be able to blend in after all. For one thing, there was a ton of people, and what a crazy mix! There were farm folk with shit on their boots and worn-out clothes, like me. But son, those city folks had them all beat! Many of the women strutted around damn near naked, while their men flopped around in pants big enough to sail a boat. Some of 'em had pants so big that their underwear was showing, but they seemed happy enough. And language! Them folks made more racket than a yard full of mine workers at dinner time. Still, I played it safe by keeping the hood of my jacket up over my head until one of the blue vests made me put it down. It didn't take long for people to notice me after that.

Luckily, I was already at the checkout when a woman with two kids started screaming her fool head off and pointing while the rug monkeys made faces at me. Then a guy with a lot of muscles and not much clothing started calling *me* a freak as some parents covered their kids' faces and zoomed out of my vicinity. Things were bordering on riot mode as the kid at the register stopped ringing up my order and leered at me.

"Why don't you go back to where you came from, freako?"

It didn't take a rocket scientist to see that I wasn't going to get any carry-out service. In fact, I'd be lucky to walk out of there at all. So I dragged the big talker over the counter by his shirt and jammed my face right up to his. "Take a good look at me, buddy. Does it look like I'm having fun? Do you think I WANT to be this way?" His eyes went wide when he realized that my face wasn't a mask. Then he cowered behind the counter as I grabbed what I could and left right quick. Ain't been back, either. I'm hungry and need food, but there's no way I'd make it home from a second trip. How did things get this bad? Let me take you back a few years and explain...

I was only a month shy of heading down to the K & L Mines with Pop's old metal lunchbox and a new pair of boots when Ms. Jackson started in on her ruckus.

"Junior!" She hollered at me, as I stacked the wood the way Pop had told me.

"Yes Ma'am?" I asked her, real polite.

"I don't want my wood stacked that way," she said, pointing at it with one of her fingernails. Dang, those things were terrible long and twice as dangerous looking. Looked like she could pluck your eyeballs right quick like a pair of olives if she wanted.

"No disrespect Ma'am, but Pop says..."

"I don't much care what Pop says!" She glowered at me. "My wood is to be stacked directly against the wall of my home!"

About that time, I heard Pop's apologetic chuckle behind me as he climbed out of our old Dodge.

"Well, hey there, Masie!" Pop always tried to take the tension out of things by making a joke out of it. That worked okay on most folks. Especially if we were dickering about prices and such. But Ms. Jackson wasn't having none of it.

"Carl! I told your boy here to stack the wood against the house, and he won't do it!"

"Aw, you don't want that! You'll get all kinds of critters living in there. Besides, it's a fire hazard up against your trailer like that and... Ugghhh!" I looked back and saw Pop bent over like somebody just kicked him in the stomach. His face was white.

"I KNOW what I want! Now tell him!"

Pop teetered around with his eyes shut tight. Finally, he looked at me and groaned out, "Stack it against the house, son."

Ms. Jackson glowered at me, and I got right on the job because I didn't want her to hurt Pop any more than she already had. Oh, she thought she was real smart and that I didn't notice her waving her fingers around when I glanced back to see if Pop was all right. But my eyes caught her. She was poking and pointing her fingers at him like she was working a puppet. After a minute, Pop straightened up, turned around, and got back in the truck. His eyes were wide and his muscles straining, but he couldn't break the spell.

Before Ms. Jackson caught me watching, I laid into stacking that wood like I was training for the damn Olympics. But I couldn't escape her meddling fingers. Soon it got to where I wasn't even sure how much of my body I was controlling. Never worked so fast in my life!

Ms. Jackson grinned at me with her snuff-stained teeth as she gave me the money, but the smile never touched her eyes. I wanted to say something to her right then, though I knew that would be a mistake.

When I got in the truck, Pop didn't say a word. He just kept staring out the windshield at something I couldn't see. I tried putting the money in his hand, but his fingers were ice cold and stiff. For just a minute I thought he might be gone. Then he jammed the cash into his shirt pocket without checking it, and we drove away. That wasn't Pop. He always counted the money twice and cracked a smile before we left a place. Usually, he'd shake the customer's hand and wish God's blessing on them in thanks. Not this time, though. It scared me to see him that way, and I hoped it was the last time Ms. Jackson pulled that trick. But life doesn't often go the way you wish it would.

A month later, we were back at Ms. Jackson's place delivering wood again. She had a few odd jobs for us to do as well. That wasn't anything unusual because Pop was the handyman in our neck of the woods. He'd lost his job at the mines due to a heart defect. The valves didn't always work right, and that would lead to Pop getting kind of wifty. If he didn't sit down and rest, he'd start stumbling around and drop things. Since he made his own hours and did a lot of the repair work at home, this wasn't a huge problem. But after Ms. Jackson got her hooks into him, she used that weakness like a bridle on a horse.

I remember working extra hard that day to keep the heat off Pop, but Ms. Jackson wasn't easy to satisfy. Plus, she enjoyed torturing him and making us miserable. Before long, she began poking her fingers at Pop again. Soon he was kneeling on the ground and clutching at his chest, his breath coming out in gasps. I knew Ms. Jackson was leaning on him too hard and that, if she didn't let up some, he would die. To take her attention off him, I ran up and yelled real loud into that evil face, "Knock it off, you creepy bitch! What the hell you trying to do? Kill him?"

That got her attention, alright! I remember smiling for a second at the fury on Ms. Jackson's face until the burning pain started in my cheeks. That woman literally tore my smile apart. Pop yelled as I wailed like a banshee and tried to hold my face together. It felt like my entire head was on fire, so I dunked it in the rain barrel to put it out. But it was too late. My mouth was turned sideways and ran from my hairline to the tip of my chin. There was an eye on either side of it, and my nose was on top of my head. I ran my hands all around my skull in disbelief, surprised that there wasn't any blood. But the pain—the pain! It hung on like a bulldog and was worse than the time I fell into a hornets' nest. Pop was screaming and begging Ms. Jackson to change me back, but she just laughed at us like we were Laurel & Hardy. But nothing was funny. Finally, we left, knowing that we would be her servants forever. Where else was I going to show a mug that opened like a book whenever I talked or tried to eat?

Nowhere, I found out real quick, when I tried reporting for work at K & L Mines. The receptionist screamed when I walked in the door and kept going until she passed out. An old guy, who was probably Mr. K or Mr. L, came out of his office to see what happened. He pulled a snub-nosed pistol from inside his jacket and yelled at me to leave. I froze up, so he fired a warning shot over my head to get me moving. I raced home in the truck with tears running down my face and apologized to Pop.

"Ah, don't worry about it, Junior." He smiled at me. "We'll be fine." Then he apologized for ever taking me to Ms. Jackson's and getting us bound to a witch. I wasn't mad at him, either. He never did anything except try to keep our cupboards stocked and smoke a home-rolled cigarette now and then. It was all Ms. Jackson's fault for using her magic to hurt rather than heal.

As Pop got older, Ms. Jackson liked causing him pain in order to make me work harder. Everywhere else we worked had to either be a place that the owners wouldn't see me or where I had to stay in the truck while Pop sweated. One thing that did was give me lots of time to think. I know I'm not super bright, but I only really thought about one thing: giving Ms. Jackson what she deserved for her cruelty. It wasn't going to be easy with that weird sixth sense she had. It had already saved her ass a few times. Once, I nearly got her with an axe, but she hurt Pop terrible bad after that. So I decided it was better to bide my time. Meanwhile, I watched and learned.

She thought she was real smart, nearly killing Pop at her place, only to have him die in our crappy little shack. When I tried pointing the finger at her, she just laughed. "Who are they going to believe? A nice little old lady or some strange monster from a nightmare? Hmm?"

But in my free time, cleaning up the place after burying Pop in the back yard, I found something that I was pretty sure would do the job on Ms. Jackson.

See, Pop used to tell me stories at night when it was bedtime. But they weren't the usual fairytales a lot of kids got. No, these were stories about a real faraway place called Vietnam. In this place, Pop and the other guys had to burn down acres and acres of jungle searching for the enemy. A lot of really weird stuff happened there that sounded downright awful, but there was other stuff that sounded kind of cool. I remember Pop laughing while he told me about this party some of the guys in the motor pool pulled together. They used fire extinguishers to chill the beer, drag-raced tanks, and even managed to smuggle in some women! Pop fell asleep that night with a smile on his face, which was rare.

Sometimes when I felt low, I thought about that story and nearly always dreamed about it. Having sex with exotic women in a strange place that you hated but loved at the same time. Becoming a man and forging a new life at the expense of others. Dealing with the consequences while fighting battles in your head as the flames were swirling, burning, and taking down everything in their path. What was right? What was wrong? The government was the boss, so Pop did as he was told to avoid serving jail time.

Mom, while she was still living with us, said that Pop was different after going to that place. She claimed that he was scary and mean, but I never saw that side of him, just the broken, sad man who made sure that I never went hungry. I'm not saying he wasn't that way, I just didn't have that life with him. He took time to teach me things. Mom never did. Then one day she took off with some truck driver who delivered diesel to K & L Mines once a month. We got one letter from her that Pop burned after he read. He never told me what it said, but I got a pretty good idea.

Anyway, what I found stashed in the tool shed was Pop's old flamethrower. The whole rig was there, with the tanks and everything! You had to wear all the fuel on your back and run the nozzle with both hands. It was tricky to use, but when I figured out how to make that bad boy shoot fire, I knew it was the tool I needed to clean up all the old business with Ms. Jackson. One weakness that she tried hard not to show was her fear of fire. I remembered that the few times Pop lit up a smoke at her place back in the early days, she'd always shrink away from it.

So when ten-foot flames shot out of Pop's old war buddy, I smiled real wide. Besides clearing the back lot in fifteen minutes, I also managed to roast a squirrel, which made a good dinner.

So tonight, I've got everything packed in the truck and our alarm clock set for two a.m. When it rings, that'll be the signal to take my fiery new friend over to Ms. Jackson's place and burn it to the ground. After that, I'll keep on turning homes into balls of flame until I run out of fuel. This holler needs a cleansing of all the filth and those who just don't give a fuck. When trouble came to me and Pop, you'd have thought our neighbors would be kind enough to at least offer a hand or a prayer. And yet, despite our kindness to others, nobody did. They just shunned us like we were lepers. Abandoned us to our fate. The jobs dried up until all we were good for was delivering cheap firewood.

But maybe that's for the best. I know where everybody's woodpile is, and I've got a flamethrower, so we'll see who gets the last laugh! Even though it was a source of misery, I'm glad that Ms. Jackson always went against Pop on where to stack her firewood. Having it up against the house *can* be a real fire hazard, and I can't wait to see how fast it turns into a wall of Hellfire that gobbles up this poisoned place! Maybe death will destroy the witch's curse and give me my face back. If it does, I'll drive that old Dodge away from here and try to start a new life. But if it doesn't, then I'll just roll right into the middle of those raging flames and let them consume me. Either way, it's time to bring some Hell to the holler.

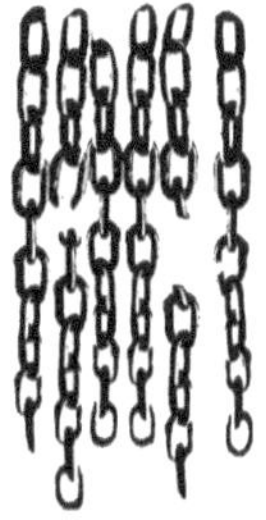

Unconditional Love
by
Diane Arrelle

"You found it in our cellar?" Janet asked, fighting off a shudder.

"Yeah, Mom," Buddy said in a breathless rush. "You know...where the cellar stops and that dirt shelf goes the rest of the way under the house!"

Janet frowned, "I've told you not to go into the crawlspace. It could be full of rats or something."

"Ah Mom, come on, rats? I haven't seen a rat since we moved. Anyway, nothing happened except I found this locked crate down there. Can we open it?"

"I...don't...know," Janet said, hesitating. As much as she loved this ramshackle old row house, the cellar just gave her the creeps. Jim said he'd fix it up so she'd never have to be afraid again. He even promised to cover over the crawlspace with drywall.

She smiled at the thought of Jim. After she got that huge insurance settlement from the accident, she knew things were finally going to be alright. She had always said that if it weren't for bad luck, she'd have no luck at all, but that money proved her wrong. Her luck was finally turning.

She glanced at Buddy and felt a twinge of guilt. That child was the cause of all her bad luck. His loser of a dad had knocked her up. Sure, they married, but he'd been abusive and, when he finally left, he took what little money they had, as well as the TV, stereo, and truck. He also left her to deal with unpaid back rent on their public housing apartment and, even worse, with a ten-year-old boy labeled emotionally disturbed and neurologically impaired thanks to a few bad beatings when he'd been a toddler.

Then…then…the insurance settlement came and turned her life around. She was still smiling as she remembered purchasing this place. It had been a wreck but, like a knight on a white steed, Jim showed up on her door looking for work the day after she moved in.

"Mom, quit daydreaming and answer me. Can we open it?"

Janet stopped smiling. "Why don't we wait for Jim to get home?" she said, and realized her mistake immediately.

"I don't need to wait for him," Buddy snapped. "I don't need his permission to do anything."

Janet opened her mouth to protest as Buddy grabbed the hammer Jim had left out that morning and smashed the lock on the wooden box.

"NO!" she screamed, as the lock held but the wood around it splintered. She had no idea why she was breaking out in a cold sweat and panicking, but she felt a sick churning in the pit of her stomach as she stared at the box. She was suddenly terribly afraid of what was inside. She just knew it had to be something beyond awful. "Please stop!" she cried, and grabbed at Buddy's hands, but he was faster and threw open the lid.

"Oh God," she moaned, as the churning turned to pain. She thought maybe she was having a heart attack, her breath freezing in her throat.

What horrors had her son impulsively unleashed, she wondered, as she doubled up in agony. She wanted to cry out and beg Buddy to slam the lid, but instead she fell to the floor, and the world drifted away out of her grasp.

***

Janet opened her eyes. She was confused. Why was she on the floor? Then she remembered. Buddy was sitting next to her. He was holding a piece of silky, shiny black cloth, and he was crying.

"Buddy."

Buddy stopped sobbing. "Mom!" he shouted. "You're alive! I thought you were dead."

Janet managed a weak smile. She sat up and was surprised to discover she felt fine. No weakness, no nausea. She reached over and patted her son's head. "I guess I fainted," she said, red with embarrassment. How typically and melodramatically weak to faint at a climactic moment. She remembered her terror, the fear that paralyzed her.

"Buddy...Honey, what was in the box?" she forced herself to ask.

"This!" Buddy exclaimed with total, childish excitement as he held up his hand.

Janet stared at a small black and white tuxedo partially covered with a shimmering black cape. After a second's hesitation she realized she was looking at a hand puppet. Her eyes focused on the wooden face, and she smiled. It looked like a handsome classic movie star. It even had a tiny top hat.

She started to laugh. A puppet, an old-fashioned child's toy. She'd fainted over a puppet! Suddenly the laughter froze in her throat. Why was it in a locked box? "Buddy, take that filthy thing off your hand. You don't know where it's been," she shouted.

Buddy looked down at the puppet and then up at his mother. "Ah, Mom, it's fine."

"Put it down!"

"No!" Buddy shouted back. "I'm keeping it, and you can't stop me!"

Janet stopped yelling. She could tell by Buddy's tone he was about to go over the edge, and then he'd be out of control. *God, I hate my life,* she thought. *I hate Al for doing this to Buddy.* "Ok, Honey, keep the puppet for now."

It didn't work. "For now? He's mine for always. I hate you, you bitch. I hate you. I love my puppet. He's the only friend I've got, and you aren't going to take him away."

Janet watched with resignation as he headed for a full tantrum, kicking the television stand and knocking over the end table. She didn't say a word as he ran from the house; she just hoped he wouldn't hurt anyone's pet or property.

"It is alright, and I love him," she reminded herself. "He's my son, and I love him. Yes, I love him." She hated the fact her litany was getting more and more difficult to repeat. She hated she was so tired of being on the losing end of life. She wondered why she always seemed to make the wrong choice, why she was always stuck with all the problems others created, why she had to be the caregiver when all she really wanted was for someone to take care of her, to give her unconditional love.

She glanced out the window at the sidewalk and street and didn't see her son anywhere.

"I'll throw that nasty thing out after he goes to sleep," she muttered, looking at the broken crate. She walked over to it and gasped. It was full of dolls—very old, fragile dolls—and even to her untrained eye, she instinctively knew they were worth a small fortune.

When Jim came home that night, he looked at the dolls as she stood by. "What do you think?" she asked.

"I think that maybe they are worth something, just don't get your hopes up. I'll take them to a dealer tomorrow."

She nodded and started to make dinner. As she was cooking, she felt a soft caress on the back of her neck. She smiled and turned around to kiss Jim.

She jerked back as Buddy lowered his arm. The disgusting puppet was still on his hand.

"Hi Mom," Buddy said, and rubbed the puppet tenderly across her cheek. "The puppet wanted to say hi. What's for dinner?"

Janet shuddered. "Don't touch me with that thing!" She immediately felt guilty. Buddy couldn't help the way he acted. She knew he needed more help than she could give him and worried he was eventually going to have to be locked away if his outbursts got worse and he became a menace to others. So far he'd only hurt himself, which was bad enough, but at least she'd been able to get him medication for that, when she could afford it. Maybe, if the dolls worked out, she would have enough to get insurance. All she needed was a little more money and some good luck, and she could get this house fixed up and pay off all the debt Al had left her. The insurance settlement was a good start, but it wouldn't last forever.

Buddy didn't even blink, "Come on, Mom, the puppet is great. He says he likes you a whole lot. He says he loves you. So can I keep him? I really want to keep him."

She could tell by the tone of his voice she better not argue or else he'd lose it again. "I guess if you really like that dirty old thing that much, we can wash it."

"Thanks, Mom!"

After Buddy went to bed that night, Janet went into his room to get the puppet. It was still on his hand, and she had to struggle with it to get it off. She tugged, and finally it came off in her hands. She was surprised it wasn't dirty at all. In fact, it felt nice in her hand, still warm from Buddy. She studied the puppet in the yellow laundry room light and actually smiled. It was such a handsome face: dark eyes, smiling lips, a pencil-thin mustache under a perfect nose. So handsome, and yet the smile was just the smallest bit cruel, turning up slightly at the corners. The painted flat eyes looked—she groped for the word—looked…sort of sinister. She laughed at herself. "Too much imagination, Janet. Get a grip," she muttered. She dropped it next to the washing machine and went up to her bedroom to watch TV with Jim.

***

The next morning, when she went to wake Buddy, the puppet was back on his hand. She frowned. The kid was definitely being difficult.

"Come on, Buddy, give me the puppet so I can clean it."

Buddy opened his eyes, "Morning Mom. I'll give it to you later. It wants to stay with me right now."

Janet sighed and left the room; she just didn't have the energy this morning. Buddy played all day with the puppet on his hand. Every time Janet tried to get it, he insisted the puppet didn't want to leave him.

When Jim came home, he held up five one-hundred dollar bills. "Look what the dolls brought in!" he shouted and hugged her. "A windfall!"

She looked at the money and felt a letdown. She had hoped the dolls were worth more, she had been sure of it, but once again her luck wasn't really good. $500 was nice, but it wasn't going to solve any of her problems.

Janet hugged him back, though she couldn't shake off the hollow feeling in her gut that things weren't right.

After dinner, she went to bed early and woke with a start. Someone was in bed with her, touching her thighs, caressing them. It wasn't Jim. He'd gone out for a few drinks with the guys, and besides, it wasn't his touch. He didn't know about gentle. She lay perfectly still and held her breath. The soft warm touch moved a little higher. As the hand moved up even more, the paralysis left her. She sat up, reaching for the light.

"Who's there?" she screamed.

She felt lightheaded, feared she'd faint again, as the room lit up and she saw her son on the bed next to her. The puppet was on his hand, and he looked startled.

"Buddy!" she screamed. "Buddy, what are you doing?"

"Huh?" Buddy mumbled, looking around the room. "What am I doing here? Why'd you wake me?"

Janet felt like throwing up. Buddy was sleepwalking and acting out his fantasies. What was she going to do? Her little boy had almost molested her in his sleep.

She jumped out of the bed and took a few steps away from him.

"Buddy, don't you ever, ever do that again!"

Buddy looked confused and hurt. "Do what, Mom?"

She didn't know how to answer. "Don't...don't touch me."

"I didn't."

"Yes, you did!" she shrieked, starting to lose control. "Don't ever touch me again. Now get out of here and go back to bed."

Watching him get up, Janet felt the tears on her cheeks. He was only a little boy, her little boy, and she could tell by the look on his face she had hurt him. Suddenly, she moved around the bed and hugged him.

"I'm sorry, Honey. Mommy loves you. I'm sorry. I just had a bad dream."

"I love you too, Mom," Buddy said, and hugged her back. She felt the puppet gently rub her hair, a soft, lingering touch, and Buddy added, "And the puppet says he loves you too."

Janet avoided being too close to Buddy for the next couple days. She was ashamed about the way she was acting, but she just didn't know what to do. He hadn't touched her since, but still, what was a mother to do when her young son makes sexual advances? She had no one to ask for advice. It was times like this she felt the loneliest, when she realized no one really loved her the way she needed to be loved. No one was there to take care of her, to ask nothing of her at all, but instead to give.

After lunch, she watched him talk to the puppet. He was sitting on the dirt in the tiny fenced-in backyard, having a one-sided conversation and getting upset.. His voice grew louder and louder. Soon he was shouting. "I can't...I won't!"

She watched from the window, fascinated. Without warning, he slapped himself across the face with the puppet. Hard. She heard the smack through the glass. Then he smacked himself again. She started for the door as he picked up a flowerpot and cracked it over his head. She saw the blood and ran to him.

He sprawled on the ground and cried.

"Why'd he do it, Mommy?" he wept, as she wrapped a towel around his head. "I thought he was my friend. I thought he liked me. But he likes you better."

"Shhh," Janet crooned, rocking him in her arms. She wondered what he was talking about. She was pretty sure she knew the answer, her son was hearing voices in his head. He was insane!

She washed him up, took him on the bus over to the emergency room, explained he had fallen while playing, and let them bandage him up. After she got them home, she gave him a sleeping pill and put him to bed. She'd have to talk to Jim later. In the meantime, she wanted that puppet gone. During the entire ordeal, the thing never left Buddy's hand. He had even insisted on bathing with it earlier. And now he was convinced it was talking to him, telling him to hurt himself.

She tiptoed into Buddy's room and tried to remove the puppet. It didn't budge. She struggled, pulled, tugged, and ripped at it, but Buddy's hand must have been balled into a death grip fist.

Wiping the sweat from her forehead, she stopped struggling and gave up. Jim would have to get it from him when he got back from wherever it was Jim went.

Three hours later, when Jim came in, she rushed to him.

"Jim. Buddy got hurt today. I had to take him to the emergency room."

Jim frowned. "You did? How much did it cost?"

She ignored the question and the implications that he never asked how Buddy was or whether he was badly hurt. "I need you to help me get the puppet off his hand."

Jim's expression changed. "The puppet? What on earth are you talking about?"

She heard the desperate edge to her voice. "Don't ask me anything. Just help me!"

Jim walked into Buddy's room, Janet right behind him. Buddy was out cold. Jim went over and grasped the puppet. He pulled but only succeeded in jerking the boy to one side of the bed.

"Tough," he grunted, and gave it a yank.

The puppet...the hand...the arm suddenly lashed out. It grabbed at Jim's throat, throwing him off balance. Buddy had Jim, a full-grown man, down on the floor. And he was trying to choke him.

"Don't you ever touch it!" Buddy screamed. "Don't you ever bother it. Die! Die! Die!"

Jim rolled over and tried to pry the puppet-covered hand off him.

Janet stared, not knowing what to do. She felt like a deer caught in headlights. Mesmerized. She watched as his strong fingers worked at the puppet's tiny arms, clawing at it. She gasped as he punched Buddy full in the face.

The boy fell backwards, blood gushing from his nose and mouth.

"Stop it!" she screamed, running to her son. She was cradling him in her arms when she heard grunts behind her. She turned and saw the puppet was still attached to Jim's throat.

She gasped and started pulling at the puppet. Suddenly it popped off. She fleetingly wondered what had held it in place since it was free of Buddy's hand.

She started crying. Buddy really needed help.

Jim got up cursing and went to the phone. "That boy needs to be put away," he said in a raspy tone. He rubbed his reddened throat. "I'm calling an ambulance."

***

Janet spent the rest of that night and the next day and night at the hospital. She nodded dumbly as the doctors explained about mental illness and the treatments available. They were going to lock her baby up in a charity ward at a mental institution, but at least he'd finally get the help he needed.

Janet was numb by the time she got home. She went into Buddy's room to clean up the blood and get rid of that horrible puppet. To her surprise, it wasn't there. She shrugged and washed the stains off the floor. Struggling against exhaustion, she put up a load of laundry and went to find Jim. She figured he'd be asleep; the sun was just coming up.

Janet stumbled into her bedroom and stopped, the exhaustion forgotten. Her eyes were riveted to Jim.

He was standing with his back pressed to the wall, his face distorted with terror. The puppet was on Jim's right hand, and gripped in both its tiny hands was a large serrated kitchen knife.

Janet watched in fascinated silence as the blood glinted off the shiny blade. She saw the bloodstains on Jim's pant leg and T-shirt. He looked at her, and their eyes met. He pushed at the puppet with his free hand, trying to keep it away from his body. His muscles quivered as he struggled with himself. "Make it stop!" he screamed. "Get it off me!"

Janet jumped into action. She grabbed at the puppet-clad arm and pulled with all her might. The arm seemed to move away from Jim. She relaxed a little and, before she could react, the puppet ripped from her hands and plunged the knife into Jim's stomach. She grabbed and pulled it back, then ripped the knife from its grasp as Jim's shrill scream echoed in her ears.

Throwing the knife to the side, she helped Jim slide to the floor. He held the wound with his free hand and said, "I'm...I'm sorry. The... mon...money is in the garage, I'm sorry...just get it off my hand and make it stop..."

His head bowed forward, and Janet watched his ragged breathing to make sure he wasn't dead. Blood leaked from his gut, and he groaned. She took his hand and removed the puppet. She was still carrying it when she called the police, and was still carrying it when they loaded Jim onto the ambulance. She absently rubbed the smooth, satiny fabric against her face as the police officer repeated, "Lady, you are so lucky you stopped him. Jim Owens is wanted. He killed three women in two states. There's even a huge reward posted for his apprehension. Consider yourself very, very lucky."

She nodded and showed them to the door. Let the police think what they liked, she decided. Let them think she'd done this to Jim in self-defense. She had too much to wonder about to worry about the police.

When the house was quiet, she went out to the tiny garage and found Jim's toolbox. There was a check for $55,000 from a rare antique collection house made out to cash. *That bastard,* she thought, finally beginning to feel emotion again. *This has to be the money from the dolls!*

Janet looked at her hand and was shocked to discover the puppet on it. A surge of fear began to work its way from the tip of her head down to her toes. About halfway down, the icy horror turned into a rush of warmth. "I love you," echoed in her head and she nodded, realizing that it did.

She went back into the house and climbed into her bed, exhaustion returning and slamming her like a physical force. She had known all along the puppet was something evil, that it was more than a puppet. She knew it from the start.

"I have to get rid of it," she mumbled. But...she...was...just...too...tired. "I'll take care of it when I wake up."

***

She slept and dreamed and, when she woke, she was smiling. She was rich. Between the dolls and the reward, she was really, really rich. As the puppet on her hand lovingly caressed her breasts, her smile widened.

She was finally and unconditionally loved.

The Crawling Skin
by
Shaun Avery

I find the crawling skin in my back garden, laid there in the shape of a face right next to the hole it must have come out of, and I reach towards it gently, tenderly, with grace...

Mark heard the door open behind him, quickly closed the web page as Ellen entered the room.

But not quick enough to outfox her—he never was. So it came as little surprise when she walked up behind him and said, "Morning, honey. What was that you were reading?"

He looked over his shoulder at her, smiled. "Oh, nothing."

But it seemed she wasn't buying it, as she replied with, "Don't *nothing* me, mister. You've got that look all over your face."

Mark was never quite sure what "that face" was. But according to Ellen, he showed it often.

"What was it?" she went on, her own face hardening, letting him know he'd better answer truthfully.

"Oh, all right," he said. Then, thinking fast on his feet, using the first thing that came to mind, he told her, "It was another short story rejection, that's all."

Her face softened. "Oh, Mark..."

"That's okay, babe." He spun the computer chair round to face her. "I wasn't really bothered about this one, anyway."

"You always say that," she commented.

"I know." He reached for her. "But I *mean* it this time."

He drew her down to kiss her, but his hands wandered a little too much as their lips met. It was like they had a mind of their own sometimes.

"Hey, enough of that," she said, pulling away from him, smoothing down the edges of her skirt where his hands had pushed it up. "I'll be late for work."

"Right," he replied, spinning back to face the computer, mood changing in an instant. *That* had been happening more often lately, too. And unlike his amorous hands, the mood transformations were not such a good thing. "Wouldn't want that now, would we?"

"Mark..." she said. Her tone pleading, so much said with just that one word. He suddenly felt like an ass for the way he'd spoken to her.

"I'm sorry," he said, meaning it. But he didn't turn the chair back round to face her as he spoke the words.

"Don't worry," she said. "It'll be all right." She placed her hands on his shoulders. "Something will come up."

"I know." He kissed her fingers, feeling that everything was all right between them once again. "Now go to work."

She obeyed, giving him a quick peck on the cheek before heading for the living room door.

He turned to watch her go. Taking in the long legs, the high heels. Basically, all of her. He'd always thought he was punching well above his weight with Ellen, and that was *before* he'd lost his job and she was forced to essentially support him.

Mark knew how lucky he was to have her. Would never do anything to jeopardise the love she felt for him.

So how come he had just lied to her about what was on the computer screen?

***

I hide the skin under my bed, not sure what to do with it. But no matter what I do, no matter where in the house I'm at, I can hear it calling me...

***

Ellen left at about eight-thirty in the morning and normally got back home around six o'clock. Which left Mark with a lot of day to fill.

Once upon a time he would have filled that void by writing short stories, most of them pretty dark in nature. Throughout the years, he'd been quite successful on a small scale, winning money in competitions and appearing in a few magazines and anthologies. But after the year he'd had—the year he was still *having*, in fact, so full of rejections, so long since any of his work had been accepted and released—it was hard to drum up the motivation for such creative endeavours. So instead, he spent most of his day on a horror-based Internet forum.

That was where the strange message had popped up this morning, the one he'd lied to Ellen about. Now he sat and looked at another one.

According to the screen, the person he was talking to was called Mystery Twenty-Seven. But who in the name of God *were* they?

Mark now asked that very question.

He sat back and waited as the computer told him his mysterious correspondent was typing out another message.

But when the reply came, it took him no further forward:

I took the skin out from my bed, and now it's talking to me. It tells me it was buried there in my garden, but it got out when it sensed me, and then—

Enough with the skin bullshit! Mark wrote back, quicker to anger than he had been before the last twelve months took their toll on him. *Who are you? Why are you private messaging me?*

He leant back from the keyboard, breathing hard, trying to calm himself down. Watching the three dots that indicated an incoming message and assuming more skin-based nonsense.

But he was wrong this time.

Instead, they wrote back, *nobody you know.*

Mark was ready to write this person off as a loon. Just another waste of his time when he should have been writing or looking for another job.

Until they typed out another comment:

But I can tell you I know you, Mark.

***

Whoever they were, they logged out after that. Leaving Mark to try and comprehend whatever had just happened. And when that didn't work, when he could make no sense of the situation, to just try and forget about it.

This got a little easier to do so when Ellen came home. Seeing her smile as she opened the front door, hearing her sigh in relief as she pulled off her high-heeled shoes, it always made him forget the things that worried him. Only briefly, of course…but that was enough.

She padded over to the computer chair in her bare feet, bent down to kiss him.

"Hi, honey," she said. "How was your day?"

"Good," he said, though he was not quite sure if that was true. "Yours?"

"The usual," she said. She drew herself back to her full height. "I'll tell you all about it later."

And she would and she did, and by unspoken agreement the computer always went off when she got home and they headed into the kitchen and ate tea together; something quick, a pair of curries from the microwave, neither of them in much of a need to make anything fancy.

They took these things to the table, where, as promised, she filled him in on her day, told him all about the happenings in the PR office where she worked. A year or so ago he would have been jealous and resentful over this, over the continued employment that meant she had these tales to tell, but now he enjoyed it, now he *liked* he hear about her experiences out there in the working world that was currently denied to him. So he listened and laughed as he ate and increasingly began to feel better about things, to put the strangeness of the day so far behind him.

When they were done with the curries and the stories, they threw their used cutlery in the sink for him to wash tomorrow, then they sat down on the couch to watch a little mindless TV, sometimes a precursor to sex and sometimes not. But when she looked at him with that special glint in her eye, he knew this was going to be one of those former times. So he nodded and switched off the TV and they kissed and touched a little, teasing each other, before they stood and headed up the stairs and took a bath together before making love on the bed, licking each other's skin clean, and finally she was snuggled in his arms and they were together and all was well in the world and Mark ended this strange day asleep and happy.

Until suddenly he wasn't.

***

Asleep, that was.

He was awake just a few hours later. But he was still very happy. For he was back at the computer. Writing.

Once, this would have been nothing out of the ordinary for him. Once, he was used to waking up in the midnight hour with a short story idea he just *had* to write down. But that was before last year, before the avalanche of rejections that had come his way, and thinking back, it was funny. All of that had started about the same time he was let go from his job, the day that Mr. McGee called him into the office and told him the company was "downsizing," and it was hard not to think that the two things were connected, his creative life and his working life bonded in some way Mark could not quite see.

Now, though...

He felt like he was onto a winner with *this* story. Felt like it would turn the tide, bring some money his way once again.

It was about a stalker slowly going crazy. Told entirely from their point of view.

He'd got the idea from the strange messages he'd received earlier.

Thank you, Mr. Skin Man, he thought.

And started pounding at the keyboard.

***

So much so that he woke Ellen up, and she came down at about four a.m. in the nude to tell him to keep it quiet. She could have shouted the same thing from the bedroom, of course, but then Mark would have missed out on that fine view and been more inclined to ignore her. He guessed she knew him well enough to realise this would be the case.

She was still surly as she got dressed up in the bedroom a few hours later—he could hear her slamming doors and drawers up there. But by the time she came down to grab her breakfast, she seemed to have noticed how long he had been at the computer and had taken heart from it, saying, "You seem full of energy this morning, young man."

She often called him this, though there was only a year between them. Mark didn't mind, though. No girlfriend had ever given him a pet name before Ellen, and he had found that he rather liked it.

"I am," he told her, turning from the computer screen. "I got this great idea last night, and...um, sorry about all the noise."

"Don't be." She came over, kissed the top of his head. "It's good to see you busy."

He nodded, feeling and thinking the same as she headed into the kitchen to grab some cereal.

Moments later she came back, bowl in hand, crunching away, talking with her mouth full as she asked him, "So when will I get to read this one?"

"Probably tonight."

"Oh?" She raised an eyebrow—and God how he loved the way she looked when she did that, though he had no idea why. "So soon?"

This was a legitimate question. Mark had become rather precious with his work, taking multiple drafts and many weeks before he let her see a finished short story. But this idea seemed different, and already he was thinking that all those edits were what had been stifling his output this last year, making his stories unsalable.

"Yeah," he eventually said.

"Good. Look forward to it."

Then she headed back into the kitchen to finish her breakfast.

Mark watched her for a second before spinning back to face the screen.

Where he saw he had another message.

***

A few weeks later they sat in a restaurant facing each other.

Mark wouldn't go so far as to say it had been a roller coaster ride… but it *had* been an interesting time of late. All of it starting with the story he had written.

He'd thought it was a cool idea, that of a person being stalked online—so cool, in fact, that he wondered why he hadn't thought of it before. Better late than never, though, he reasoned, editing the story when Ellen was at work and having it ready for her to proofread when she got back from work. She'd said it was "great, but different," though he'd only heard the first part of that statement. Then he'd sent it off, choosing a new horror magazine he liked the look of called *Cutting Glass*. And thus had begun the waiting game.

He kept busy while he waited, though.

He had more stories to write.

And more messages to read.

Yes, his strange message-mate was still active, always lurking on the forum whenever Mark logged on. Which was perhaps the most unsettling thing of all, making him wonder if the guy really *was* stalking him, if he somehow knew whenever Mark was about to come online.

He'd tried to find out the guy's identity.

But much like before, all he got were skin comments:

I love to take the skin out and dance with it.

The skin makes me happy, gives me someone to talk to at last. But it tells me it needs something in return...

Which led, disturbingly, to:

The skin demands a sacrifice...

That was where Mark got out, stopped logging on altogether. Sensing that the guy was obviously deranged.

Still, he had gotten a story out of it. And in homage to his unknown inspiration, he had called the tale, "The Skin Stalker." Now all that was needed was for *Cutting Glass* to buy the thing.

***

It did.

That was how they were out tonight, and Mark felt good about being able to pay for once, using the money he had received for the story. Said money had been paid in dollars, of course. He lived in hope of selling a story to a UK-based magazine or anthology, but his writing style seemed to resonate with editors across the pond a lot more than it did with people over here...the influence of reading too many trashy American horror novels when he was a teenager, Mark supposed. Still, the exchange rate was good right now, so he was splurging while he could.

It was a nice place they'd come to, one he'd often passed on his way to work back in the old days. *La Buccia,* it was called, an Italian restaurant, and the smell of the food had almost been enough to make him drool when he'd come in.

Doing similar things to him, but for very different reasons, was Ellen. She'd bought an expensive green dress when it was on offer from a designer website ages ago, and had been looking for an occasion, a special event, to wear it. When he'd told her how much he been paid for his story and then said where he wanted to take her with the money, she had squealed with delight and went and pulled the dress out of her wardrobe, hung it up ready. Now she sat wearing it, looking across at him and smiling.

"What are you getting to eat?" she asked.

He didn't know. But nor did Mark care. The food itself was unimportant. All that mattered what that he could get whatever he wanted, no matter the price. And he could add champagne on top, too. The expensive stuff.

He did so, and this was probably why he got a little drunk, the pizza and dessert he ate not doing much to soak up all the alcohol he consumed alongside it. Why, too, Ellen had to support him as they weaved their way out of the taxi and through their front door.

He tried to kiss her then, went straight in with the tongue. But she pushed him away, saying, "Later. Let me shower first. I want this to be special."

Mark took a step back from her. Wanted to tell Ellen that every day with her was special, that he would never have made it through this slog—the unemployment, the constant rejection of stories he'd thought were good—without her. But even whilst sober, he had no way of telling her this in words, instead letting his hands and penis do the talking for him. So drunk, he had no chance whatsoever.

Instead, he just smiled, told her, "Okay."

She kicked off her shoes—heels higher than the ones she took off after work, sexier, too—and walked slowly up the stairs. Teasing him, Mark knew, wiggling her bottom, that green dress so great on her. But even better, he suspected, when it was back on the hanger, leaving her gloriously naked once more.

Oh yeah? Said a voice inside. *What about her bra and underwear, dummy?*

But he shushed the voice.

He'd had quite enough of reality for one year, thank you very much.

The thought made him look to the computer, as he heard the shower start upstairs. Maybe he should start another story. Tonight had given him a taste for spending money and, now that he had found he could earn cash from his writing, he was keen to do so again.

So he sat down at the screen. Booted the computer up, tried to do the same thing with his mind. Which was tricky—he'd never operated very well when drunk, and that was undoubtedly what he was now.

He clicked onto the usual forum when he was waiting for inspiration to strike.

Saw Mystery Twenty-Seven was waiting for him. Like usual.

But now there was something extra.

The mystery man requested a video chat with him.

Mark looked back around, heard the shower still going. Ellen liked to spend a while getting washed at the best of times, and since tonight she was in full-on "tease" mode, he knew he had a while to spare.

He accepted the request.

Then sunk back in his chair, gasping.

It was like he was seeing something from one of his stories.

The man on the screen before him was fat—almost grotesquely so. His hair was dirty and matted, unwashed, sticking to his oily, greasy skin. One hand was out of shot, the other waving at Mark. But he did not pay much attention to the hand. No, his attention was on the man's face.

At the large, dough-like sheath of skin that was crawling all around it.

"The skin," the man said, his hand coming to rest on the keyboard before him. "The skin that I've been telling you about."

The skin paused. Seemed to look towards the Webcam, though it had no eyes. Seemed to stare straight at Mark.

"I found it in the garden, like I told you," the man said. "I talked to it. And it made my life so much better, took away my loneliness."

Mark had heard all of this before, felt the urge to click off this forum, never log back on again. But he was still curious about why this guy had targeted him. And what was supposed to happen next.

"But remember what I told you?" the man went on. "It said it needed something in return. I had to sacrifice the thing I loved the most." He paused, looked away from the screen for a second. "And that was *you,* Mark."

"What are you talking about?" Mark replied. "I've never even met you before."

"I know," the man replied. "But I've met *you,* Mark."

Then his other hand came into view, holding something: a horror fiction anthology called *Beyond the Dark Shade.*

Mark recognized it well.

He was one of the authors in it. Had sold a story to it back before the dry spell.

"It's great," the man continued. "*Your* story, I mean." He said this quickly, like he was making up for some vocal *faux pas,* almost like he was apologizing. "I mean, I didn't read any of the others in there. I never do." Then smiled. "I've read *all* your published stuff, you know. I can always relate to the way you tell your characters." Paused. "That's when I knew from your art that you got me, you understood me." A tear ran down his face. "And you're the only one that ever did."

Mark said nothing. Was too flabbergasted to do so. *All this,* he thought, *from a deranged fan, some guy who thinks my stories make us* bonded *somehow?* He shook his head, disbelieving. *But I'm not even a* professional *writer!* His thoughts went on, spinning with a mind of their own now. *How can this be happening to me?*

He didn't know. But it was. And he had to deal with it.

"I found your profile on social media," the man said. "You always posted links to this forum. I just went there and waited. Then, when you appeared, I knew it was you—you use the same picture on both profiles." The man looked almost sheepish saying this, as if embarrassed on Mark's behalf. "So I started showing you the truth. Doing it the way you would do it, you know? In one of your stories, I mean. Bit by bit. Getting you hooked."

The skin started to crawl again as the man spoke. Squirming down over his chins towards the camera.

"The skin told me we would make your life better before we...before. Has it?"

Mark thought of his recent writing success, the night he'd just had and how it had improved his life, how it made him feel human once again. But he said nothing, not trusting his own words.

"Well," the man said, seemingly seeing the answer in him somehow, sounding pleased, "I'm glad. But like I said, you've got to sacrifice the thing you love most when you wear the skin. So that means…"

That was when something started rumbling inside the computer. Something that needed to get out.

Mark leapt out of the seat, stepped back. Looked to the screen. Saw the skin had gone. Saw that the man was simultaneously laughing and crying, waving the book around, screaming, "I'm sorry, Mark, I'm so sorry!"

He took another step back, eyes fixed on the computer, the machine rattling like crazy now. And suddenly he knew what was inside it, what was about to come out, to be released.

He ran for the door, hearing an immense explosion behind him. Mere seconds later, he felt it land on his back. Slimy and rough. But somehow soothing, too, and he no longer knew why he was running, a sudden voice saying, *Stop, relax. Let me take over things for you. Let us connect.*

Mark tried to fight it, but found that he could not. Fell to the floor and found he did not really *want* to fight, the voice inside his head smooth and soothing as the skin draped itself around his face, sealing up his eyes and mouth, taking charge of things. Feeling it. *Understanding* it. Seeing that its previous host had forced it to take things slowly, make it *wait* for its sacrifice. But now he knew that it was hungry. Ravenous. Needing to be fed. Unable to wait.

Then it stood him up. Led him towards the kitchen. Toward the knives. That one line still ringing in what was left of Mark's mind: *you've got to sacrifice the thing you love most.* That had meant him and his stories, for the other man. *But for him…*

There was a sudden silence upstairs as the shower finally stopped running.

"Mark!" Ellen called out. "I'm ready!"

And the thing that had once been Mark smiled.

He was ready for her, too.

Also by

No Bad Books Press, LLC

The Animal Court
By S. Faxon

Foreign & Domestic Affairs
By S. Faxon

The Gulch Jumpers
By Catherine Pomeroy

Lost Aboard
By S. Faxon and Theresa Halvorsen

River City Widows
By Theresa Halvorsen

Tiny Dreadfuls
By S. Faxon

Warehouse Dreams
By Theresa Halvorsen

www.ingramcontent.com/pod-product-compliance
Lightning Source LLC
Chambersburg PA
CBHW050851190726
48286CB00007B/2323